PARANORMAL ROMANCE NOVELLAS

Court of the Yuletide Fae
The Yule Cat
The White Stag
The Krampus

Court of the Springtime Fae
Jack Frost
Prince Charming
The Oak King

—

URBAN FANTASY

The Blades of Janus
PACK
PROGENITOR
PERIHELION

PARANORMAL - HORROR ROMANCE

The Summer Park Psychics
WANDERING SOUL
WHISPERING HEARTS
LINGERING TOUCH

—

COLLECTIONS

The Department of Homeworld Security
THE DEPARTMENT OF HOMEWORLD SECURITY OMNIBUS 1
THE DEPARTMENT OF HOMEWORLD SECURITY OMNIBUS 2

Courts of the Fae - Duets
WINTER AND SPRING

Perihelion

The Blades of Janus
Book Three

Cassandra Chandler

Copyright Page

Perihelion
The Blades of Janus, Book Three
Copyright © 2025 by Cassandra Chandler
Print ISBN: 978-1-945702-05-1
Digital ISBN: 978-1-945702-04-4

First eBook edition: June 2025
First print edition: June 2025
10 9 8 7 6 5 4 3 2 1

cassandra-chandler.com
P.O. Box 91
Mission, Kansas 66201

Dedication

For Megan (in RL) and her curiosity.

Don't miss out on any of the dark alien action. Subscribe to Cassandra Chandler's newsletter at https://sendfox.com/CassandraChandler

Chapter One

"Huh." Damien glanced at the high-tech display on the van's main console for the seventh time. Another red blip had appeared on the screen, but vanished so quickly he wondered if he'd imagined it.

It was probably nothing. He didn't know how the scanners in the vehicle worked, but doubted they could analyze every animal he passed and check them for characteristics that might mark them as something unnatural—especially with how fast he was driving down the dark highway.

Most people labeled the creatures they couldn't understand as fairies or monsters. Blades called them dwellers. Damien wasn't sure why, but went along with it. He'd been going along with a lot of things, all while not knowing his bosses—his friends—were lying to him. No, not really lying. But they were keeping important truths hidden.

Bringing his mind back to his current situation, he had to consider the possibility that he might be hallucinating. Being awake for forty-eight hours was a lot, even for him. He hadn't reached the most dangerous part of his journey

—the Providence base for the Blades of Janus, otherwise known as the ranch. It wasn't the place that was the threat but the people living there. If they even *were* people.

A blue light flashed on the dashboard, letting him know someone was trying to contact him.

Speak of the dweller, Damien thought.

Damien only paused a moment before activating the comm link. There was no sense putting off the inevitable.

"Yeah," he said.

"Hey, Damien." Vaughn's cheery voice filled the van. "How's it going?"

A frisson rocketed down his spine at the sound of her voice. It always did.

"Fine," he said.

"Cool." There was a brief pause before she continued. "It looks like you're about half an hour out."

Damien didn't bother responding. He'd thought he was farther away, but she knew the area better. And the tech. And more about everything in general. She was an absolute genius.

Vaughn had designed the sleek van that Damien was driving, along with all of its high-tech components—some of which Damien hadn't even figured out how to use. He'd been a member of the Blades of Janus for five years and was still learning what all the buttons did.

"I just wondered if you have any questions I can answer before you get here," she said.

Damien looked at the rear view mirror. Soft blue and white lights blinked along the sides of the two stasis pods that took up the sizable space. In the dim light that illuminated the back of the van, his gaze lingered on the pod behind the driver's seat. The pod that was empty.

Damien only had one question that really mattered. Too bad he didn't have the guts to ask it.

"You still there?" Vaughn asked.

"Yeah."

"Cool. Comms have been a little glitchy."

Damien focused on what he could see of the road ahead, occasionally glancing at the overland display that fed him data about his route and its surroundings. He hadn't been surprised by a single curve while driving into the mountainous region around the ranch, even with only his headlights to see by.

"I've been meaning to ask…" Vaughn said. "Are you one of those people who doesn't talk much, or is it that you like silence? Because if it's the first, we'll get along great when we finally meet in person. And if it's the second, you're going to hate me."

Damien let out a little snort before he could stop himself. He heard an answering chuckle from her. The only good part of all this mess was that he was finally getting a chance to meet her in person and put a face with that sultry voice.

"There's hope for us yet." She cleared her throat, then

said, "And by that I mean—"

The red blip appeared on the display again. It lingered this time, letting Damien know it wasn't his imagination.

"Are you seeing that?" he asked.

"Seeing what?"

"Red blip. Northwest quadrant."

Vaughn was silent for a few moments. "Okay, that's weird."

"What is?"

"My data feeds aren't picking it up, but I can see it in the sensor logs from the van," she said. "It looks like a kind of sensory echo. I don't know how else to describe it. The scanners are detecting something, but they're... I don't know. Reflecting off of it. They can't get any data."

That didn't sound good.

"The anomalous readings only started a few minutes ago," she continued. "But there are a lot of them. It could be a glitch in the van's sensors. We've been seeing a lot of those the last few days. I'm going to dispatch a team to meet up with you and escort you to the ranch just in case."

Damien's skin prickled into goose flesh. He did not want an escort. Not from the ranch.

From his days as a hunter, Damien was used to going into situations where he wasn't sure who to trust. He *wasn't* used to not knowing who was human.

"They're en route," Vaughn said. "Should intercept you in three minutes."

"I thought I was thirty minutes out."

"We have… alternate transportation here."

Damien stifled another snort. With Vaughn being at the Providence base, these Blades probably used teleportation devices to get around. Or maybe some kind of portable wormhole generators. The vans, cars, and motorcycles—not to mention the weapons and holding systems—she designed for all the Blades bases had always seemed so far ahead of what everybody else was using, it was like they were straight out of a sci-fi movie. And if that was the stuff she shared, he had to wonder what kind of tech she was keeping to herself.

That wasn't the most immediate question on his mind, though.

"Who?" Damien asked.

"Dexter, Tessa, and Marcus," Vaughn said.

The only unknown on the list was Tessa. Marcus had a good reputation among the Blades. He was one of the most effective Guards when it came to taking out dangerous dwellers. Dexter… Dexter was a fucking legend. The Blades received training on how to put dwellers at ease if there wasn't a kill order on their species. They only took out dwellers who were too dangerous to coexist with humans—the ones that were using humans as breeding material or a food source or just for sick entertainment.

Damien's stomach clenched at his memories of dwellers who used humans for all three. He shoved away the thoughts. Now was not the time for a trip down memory lane. He couldn't lose focus.

Dexter was one of Damien's heroes, and Damien was about to meet him. Dwellers feared Dexter so much, there was a special sub-unit just on how to handle it if Dexter's name came up while in the field. Dwellers were terrified of him. Damien had always used Marcus and Dexter as inspiration. Train harder, fight better, and maybe he'd come close to hitting their numbers. With what had happened to Carey, Damien wondered if there had ever been a chance he could approach the other men's skill.

After all, Damien was only human.

His grip tightened on the steering wheel as thoughts of his past failures threatened to push their way into his mind. He couldn't afford the distraction. Not with Zach helpless in that stasis pod. Not with the chance of getting Carey back.

"Um, apparently the roster's been changed." Vaughn's voice was tight. "Dexter's benched."

Who the fuck could bench Dexter?

She let out a sigh that had become familiar. She'd made similar sounds a lot while talking Damien through the process of getting Zach into his stasis pod.

"Brock and Megan are with Tessa and Marcus instead," Vaughn said.

Damien had never heard of either of them. He didn't bother asking who they were. It was more important to know *what* he'd be dealing with.

"Classification?" Damien said.

There was a pause before Vaughn asked, "What do you mean?"

"You gave me the 'who,'" he said. "Tell me the 'what.'"

When Vaughn spoke, her voice was colder than he had ever heard it. "The four of them are a fully stable... pack."

That little pause in her response set his stomach to churning again. A pack. All four of them were dwellers then. Was anyone at the Providence base human?

"Lots of dwellers run in packs," Damien said, praying they weren't what he feared they were.

The next pause was even longer before she spoke again. "Werewolves."

Bile rose in the back of his throat. The prickling in his skin intensified painfully and his heart rate picked up.

Werewolves? Motherfucking werewolves?

"I know what you're thinking," she said.

He seriously doubted that.

"I've..." she cleared her throat. "I've read your file."

His jaw clenched painfully.

So she got to know all of his secrets, but he barely knew anything about her? Hell, he didn't even know her first name. Damien hated the power disparity. If she knew about his past, then she knew... She knew that when it mattered most, he had failed. Just like with Carey.

Damien's head swirled as a mix of terror and rage swept through him. His heart was pounding so fast that his chest hurt. He felt like his skull was in a vise that was quickly tightening, threatening to make him black out. He took a deep breath and let it out slow and quiet.

Vaughn wasn't the enemy. She was an ally. And if she knew about Damien's background, she also knew that he would never stop trying to be better. Never stop trying to make the world safer for everyone. For the past few years, that meant working with the Blades. After checking out what was really going on at the ranch... Damien wasn't sure what his future held.

"Damien?" Vaughn said. "Are you still with me?"

Her voice brought him back from the edge, like it had in countless battles. He still couldn't form words to reply. All he managed was a grunt. That must have been good enough for her. She went on, her tone more subdued.

"The pack is made up of two mated pairs," she said. "And they're *Blades*. Marcus was one of the first Guards ever. He's been fighting for peace between humans and dwellers for twelve years—ever since he was colonized."

No wonder Marcus was so effective as a Guard. He had parasites living in his body that made him into a killing machine—and something out of a storybook nightmare. Damien wasn't entirely sure how it all worked, but he knew that much.

"Brock is the guy who founded the Blades of Janus,"

Vaughn said.

Damien was still trying to wrap his head around *werewolves* on the way to *help* him. He couldn't even look at 'founder' and 'werewolf' in the same sentence. What the fuck kind of organization had he signed up with?

The Blades had one order for dealing with werewolves. *Run.*

They weren't even supposed to try to engage with them. They were too dangerous and powerful. Werewolves were deadly, insane, and violent. Damien's time as a hunter backed up the Blades' 'run and report' policy as the only way to survive an encounter. And he had only become a hunter originally because...

His chest constricted painfully—almost like his heart was trying to eject itself through his mouth. More bile rose as those memories threatened to surface. Memories that would lead to him running over any fucking werewolves that tried to 'escort him safely' to the ranch.

Carey. Think of Carey.

Repeating the mantra helped him shove the memories back down. Carey might have been a dweller—a surprise Damien was still working to process—but he was also Damien's mentor and best friend. And it was Damien's fault that Carey was dead. Or gone. Or... whatever the hell he was. Still, things at the ranch were worse than Damien feared. Much worse.

"Our founder..." Damien swallowed hard, almost

choking on the words, "is a werewolf."

"Kind of," Vaughn said.

Damien ran one hand down his face. He wanted to blow out a breath, but knew she would hear. He didn't want to let any of them know how bad this was getting under his skin—even if Vaughn had read his fucking file.

"Care to elaborate?" he clipped.

"He only became a werewolf recently, and before that..." she let out a deep sigh. "It's a long story, and one that's better told in person."

A soft *whump-whump-whump* noise broke into the conversation. Damien leaned over the steering wheel so he could look up at the source of the sound. A dark silhouette hovered above him, two blue circles glowing brightly on each side of it. The... whatever the hell it was... flew in front of the van. In the headlights, he could see that it was a motorcycle. Four circular lights spun around it parallel to the ground, two on each side near where the wheels must be.

Holy shit.

Two figures were riding the bike. The person on the back—a woman—looked over her shoulder at him, her dark hair whipping behind her wildly. He hadn't had a chance to fully digest the idea of flying motorcycles when his headlights caught in the woman's eyes, gleaming back at him. Gleaming gold.

Werewolves...

She had long black hair that fanned out around her head from the buffeting wind. Her features were oddly familiar. He could see in the light that she had olive-hued skin—just like his. Just like Tammie's.

Shove it down. Shove it down.

Seconds before the bike hit the ground, the blue lights on either side folded along the midline, snapping onto the wheels. It didn't slow—barely even bounced—as it touched down on the pavement.

"Keeping the best toys in Providence?" he forced out.

"Cutting down on unauthorized air traffic," Vaughn replied.

Damien couldn't believe he had to suppress a chuckle. He looked at the screen that showed him the road behind the van. Another bike just like the first was tailing him. There were no headlights to catch those wolves' eyes, but it didn't matter. They were glowing gold on their own. Just like that, the lightness Vaughn had introduced into the moment vanished.

What the hell am I driving into?

"I'm gonna need more than that," Damien said.

"Let's just say I have access to certain technology that has proven very enlightening to reverse-engineer."

He snorted, desperate to distract himself with the most outlandish thing he could think of. "You have a spaceship in the basement or something?"

She laughed, but it sounded forced. "Not in the

basement." She cleared her throat. "It's in a cavern beneath the sublevels."

Damien's mind just kind of… stopped at that.

"A spaceship." He said it out loud more to process it than anything else.

"In the sublevels," she said.

"So, what? You guys are aliens or something?"

Vaughn laughed again. It started out more natural than her previous one, but faded oddly.

"Not me," she said. "I don't think so, anyway. But dwellers are."

"Dwellers… are aliens," Damien said.

Yeah, that sounded as crazy out loud as it did in his head.

"This whole conversation would go over better in person," she said. "I probably should have waited… But I'll answer all your questions when you get to the ranch. I haven't seen a blip in a bit. That doesn't mean we should let down our—"

The sound of screaming metal cut off her transmission as something rammed into the side of the van. The vehicle fishtailed, the whole thing rocking back and forth ominously. Damien cut the wheel to the right, trying not to tumble down the mountainside. He managed to stay on the road, but the van tilted over. Somehow, the glass of his window didn't shatter as the side of the vehicle hit the pavement. It skidded a hundred feet to a stop. The seatbelt kept him mostly against his chair, but cut into his chest and side painfully as he dangled from it.

As soon as the van stopped moving, Damien hit the release for the belt. Nothing happened. He drew the short knife he kept in his right boot and sliced through the thick fabric, catching himself on his elbow as he landed against the door. The lights were on in the van, dim as they were. The stasis chambers were still attached to the walls, but Damien didn't know how long they'd stay that way—or if Zach had been jostled in the crash.

Zach's chamber had been on the side that was hit. If it fell, he could be injured. Damien wouldn't let that happen. Not after what had happened to Carey. Not after what Damien had done.

Climbing over the seat, Damien made it into the back section of the van just as something pulled off the doors. He held up his pathetic knife, ready to defend Zach from whatever the fuck this was.

Gold eyes stared at him from a pale face surrounded by dark red hair. Her features were delicate, gorgeous even, but there was something unhinged about her eyes that went beyond their unnatural color.

Gold eyes means werewolf.

Damien's heart was pounding in his chest. He tried to calm himself to seem less like prey. Again, fury and terror battled within him in equal measures. Part of him *wanted* her to attack.

The woman held the crumpled remains of the door with a chrome hand that was streaked with glowing blue light. The metal continued up her arm to just below her elbow, fading into her flesh.

'What the hell?' Damien thought for the hundredth time.

She stepped aside so that the man next to her could jump into the back of the van. He had black hair that brushed his shoulders and matched the all-black ensembles that the Blades wore. The tight T-shirt and cargo pants outlined his muscular form. Lines of white scar tissue criss-crossed his arms—rows of claw marks, jagged bites. Damien had only seen scars like that on the toughest, craziest werewolves in Vaughn's Dwellers Database.

For some reason, the guy was wearing thick-framed glasses. Werewolves wouldn't need the help. Becoming infected should have fixed any vision issues he had. The lenses obscured his eyes, but Damien didn't need to see their color to know this guy was a wolf, too.

"You okay?" the wolf said.

Damien wasn't sure how to respond. He felt something sticky and wet trickling down the side of his head. If it was blood, it could set them off.

The wolf sighed, then said, "You need to leave."

Damien bit back the obscenity on the tip of his tongue. He widened his stance and shifted the knife in his grip.

The werewolf held up his hands. "We're here to help.

I'm Marcus."

Marcus? This *is Marcus?*

"The red-head is my mate, Tessa," Marcus said.

Tessa peered around the side of the opening and waved with her non-metal hand. "I'm staying put till the testosterone thins out in there. But you might want to hurry, with an unknown nasty running around. Oh, and here." She messed with her ear for a moment, then threw something to Marcus.

He caught it easily, then opened his palm so that Damien could see what he held. An earpiece.

"Vaughn wants to talk to you," Marcus said.

Damien held his ground. Every instinct he had told him to prepare to fight. But fighting these two was a death sentence.

"Maybe Damien's worried about werewolf cooties," Tessa said.

Marcus closed his eyes and let out a sigh that sounded a lot like Vaughn's when she was frustrated. When Marcus opened his eyes again, he tilted his head back toward Tessa.

"Damien is one of our top Guards," Marcus said. "He knows there's no such thing as werewolf cooties."

"Does he also know he needs to get his ass out of the van before Brock and Meg tip it back over?" Tessa said.

"What about Zach?" Damien straightened a bit, glancing at the stasis chamber.

He could see Zach's still form through the clear window built into the top of the chamber. However Zach was strapped in, he didn't seem to have moved at all during the crash. Vaughn had said the stasis chamber actually made a zero-G environment. Damien hadn't said anything, but part of him didn't really believe her at the time, even with how Zach's hair was floating around his face. After what she had just told him, it didn't seem so far-fetched.

"We aren't going to let anything happen to him," Marcus said. "But we need room to work—and that means we need you out of the van. Please."

A polite werewolf. If Damien hadn't witnessed it himself, he never would have believed it. He held out his hand, focusing all his energy on keeping it from shaking. Marcus dropped the earpiece onto Damien's palm.

Now for the hard part. Walking past a werewolf in the cramped space.

Damien put the earpiece into place as he carefully headed toward the back of the van, skirting the empty stasis chamber by walking on the van's wall. His heart was pounding against his chest in a punishing beat. He breathed a little easier when he heard Vaughn's voice in his ear.

"Damien? Damien, can you hear me?" she said.

"Yeah, I can hear you." He glared at Tessa as he reached the opening where the back door had been and jumped down onto the pavement.

She stepped in front of him, blocking his way. Her eyes brightened.

Maybe there was a reason Tessa hadn't been mentioned before. She didn't seem as 'polite' as Marcus.

"We have a problem?" Damien asked.

Showing weakness didn't seem like a good idea, so he held his ground. Tessa's lips pulled back from her teeth. Her canines were growing longer. Sharper.

Shit.

Yeah. They had a problem. Well, *he* did, anyway.

The light cast from the inside of the van dimmed briefly Something blurred next to her, then Marcus was at her side.

"Tessa, calm down." Marcus grabbed her arm and pulled her away from Damien, but not before her fingers had lengthened into claws—even the metal ones.

"What's going on?" Vaughn asked.

Damien ignored the voice in his ear. He needed his full attention on the werewolf who was glaring at him like she wanted to rip out his throat with her teeth. Maybe he'd get that fight after all. And finally a release from living in this world of blood and chaos.

"What's taking you guys so long?"

Damien jumped at the new voice right next to him. He backed away from the people surrounding the van. The pack of werewolves and...

"Holy shit." The words slipped out before he could stop them.

Vaughn had said that Brock was 'kind of' a werewolf. Damien was pretty sure that's who he was looking at. Brock had black hair with streaks of stark white running through it. He was thick with muscle—almost as big as Damien, and Damien always got crap from the other Blades about being the biggest Guard.

Four jagged lines ran down Brock's face, starting at his hairline above his left eye, crossing his nose, and running down to his chin. It looked like something had practically ripped off his face. The wounds hadn't healed right and the scars were still dark red, even though the wounds seemed to be sealed.

His right eye glowed gold, like the other three werewolves surrounding Damien. But his left eye was entirely white—except for a gleaming blue pupil that sparked and crackled like a live wire. Tiny motes of energy continuously emerged from it, fizzing out when they were a few inches from his face with quiet 'pops.'

Brock just stared at Damien for a few moments, then turned back to the van.

"Everybody in position," Brock said. "Let's get my brothers home."

"Wait, 'brothers?'" Damien started forward, but balked when Brock leaned down and wedged his hands under the van. The dark-haired woman joined him, sliding her slender hands beneath the vehicle. She must be Meg. Inside, Tessa and Marcus had braced themselves against the stasis chambers. Damien hadn't even seen them move, they were so fast.

"I'll explain when you get to the ranch," Vaughn said. "Right now, we have to get all of you out of there. We still don't know what attacked or if it's coming back."

"On three." Brock nodded to the woman crouched next to him. "One, two, three."

The two wolves lifted the enormous van as if it was made of balsa wood. It crashed onto its wheels and rocked on its suspension a few times before settling. Brock headed for the opening in the back of the van while the woman Damien assumed was Brock's mate walked up to him. Her hands were held in front of her, fingers interlaced.

Damien's heart felt like it stilled for a moment before starting that punishing beat again. The big eyes, high cheekbones, the shape of her chin and lips... She looked just like he imagined Tammie would have—if she'd lived long enough to grow up.

If something like *this* hadn't killed her.

The *wolf* said, "Hi, I'm Meg. Or Megan, if you'd like. That's what Vaughn calls me. It's nice to meet you."

Her build was slight, but muscled. He didn't dare underestimate her.

"I'd offer to shake your hand, but I don't think you'd

like that very much." She cast a warm smile at him. If he didn't know what she was, he might almost be starting to like her.

"I do have some unsolicited advice, but it's really important." She took a step closer.

He jerked back, wanting to keep at least some distance between them. As if that would make a difference if she went for him. She actually winced, like it hurt her feelings that he didn't trust her. What the hell kind of pack was this?

"Nobody's going to hurt you," she said. "We're here to help. But it would maybe be a good idea to not make so much eye contact with the others." She cast a chagrined smile at him and half-shrugged. "It's you know... a werewolf thing."

He *didn't* know. Because he wasn't a fucking werewolf.

"Damien, you have to chill." Vaughn's voice sounded in his ear. He was surprised at how much it reassured him.

"I've opened a private channel for us," she said. "Eventually, I'll teach you how to subvocalize so you can talk to me without the others hearing."

Of course she would.

"Listen, we've all been through a lot in the last couple of days," Vaughn said. "And Tessa is still recovering from... a lot of things."

Damien's gaze flicked to that metal arm of hers. Had she lost the original before, after, or during her being turned into a werewolf? Any of those scenarios was a nightmare.

"Just ease up on the eye contact," Vaughn said. "And try to give them a break. We could all use one right about now."

Damien snorted. Tessa glanced over at him, and this time, he stared at her chin. He'd still be able to track what she was doing, and maybe this way he'd avoid a fight there was no way he'd survive.

Two people had now given Damien hope that Carey could somehow be restored. Damien had no idea how that would work, but he hung onto the possibility as tight as he could. There was so much blood on his hands already. If there was any chance he could wipe this stain away, he had to do everything in his power to make it happen.

"The stasis pod is intact." Marcus hopped down from the back of the van. He pulled off the glasses and tossed them to Damien. "Vaughn wants you to wear these, just in case I have to change."

The idea of Marcus transforming made Damien's heart pick up again. His skin joined the party, electric gooseflesh of the most unpleasant kind skittering over his body.

Damien wasn't surprised Marcus's eyes were gold. He *was* surprised they weren't glowing like Tessa's. She was shifting her weight from one foot to the other, eyeing the trees around them, obviously spooked. She cast a meaningful look at Marcus, and he shook his head.

"Use your words, Tessa," Brock said.

"How about these words—fuck you." She flipped Brock off for good measure.

Who the hell was the alpha here? From what Damien knew about dwellers, the alpha of a werewolf pack would skin any member who showed such disrespect. There was something familiar in the way Tessa was ripping on Brock, though. A dynamic Damien could almost remember.

Brock's boots crunched on loose gravel as he jumped down from inside the van. He shook his head and laughed.

"You'll have to excuse Tessa's manners," Brock said. "Little sisters can be a pain in the ass."

"Sister?" Damien said.

Brock shrugged. "Foster sister. We grew up together."

Damien's stomach lurched.

Yeah, that was the dynamic he was picking up on. The way Tessa was picking at Brock was just like—

Damien shook his head sharply. He couldn't let himself think about his past, especially with Tammie's werewolf-doppelgänger standing nearby. It was done. Dead and buried, like his entire fucking family. He had to stay in the moment, remember the fight. It was the only thing that kept him going.

"Nobody subvocalizes or uses the mental link while Damien's with us," Brock said. "It's rude."

Brock smirked at Damien. Damn, those freaky eyes…

Megan picked up the door Tessa had ripped off the van

and walked past Damien with it, shifting it in her grip as she passed.

"Sorry," she said, smiling at him.

A pack of considerate werewolves. As if Damien's life wasn't bizarre enough already.

"Let's load up and get the van moving again before our uninvited guest decides to come back," Brock said.

Damien wasn't sure which he should be more afraid of —whatever had attacked the van, or the group who claimed to be protecting him. He glanced into the gaping hole in the back of the vehicle, catching sight of the stasis pods.

None of it mattered. He had to get Zach to Vaughn. Get Zach to Vaughn and somehow they might be able to get Carey back. That was Damien's mission. If he had to work with a pack of werewolves to do it... He would get it done.

Chapter Two

"What the hell is out there?" Vaughn muttered the question after turning off the connection with the teams' earpieces. Her fingers flew over the surface of her desk, tapping in commands that would modify the algorithms she'd developed to detect and identify dwellers.

Whatever this was, it had to have a lot of mass and strength to knock over the van. But how had it managed to get so close without showing up on her scanners? Okay, it *had* shown up for a few seconds right before impact, but knowing that wasn't enough to keep everyone safe.

One of her monitors fizzed into static. That sure as hell wasn't going to help.

"Dammit."

The explosion that had taken out sublevel 2 had messed up so much more. Vaughn hadn't had a chance to track down all the damage yet, and weird anomalies kept cropping up—like her feeds going out. She reconnected the feed through an alternate router, holding her breath until she saw a clear image appear.

"Well, that's one less thing," she muttered.

She turned her attention to the satellite monitor that

was displaying thermal signatures of the area. Four bright red dots and one orange dot surrounded the cooling yellow engine of the van. Vaughn could barely see anything. She switched her focus to the monitor feeding her images from the glasses Marcus was supposed to be wearing. All Vaughn could see was Damien's huge thigh. Not that she minded the view. Damn, that guy was huge. But she really did need to see more of what was going on. She opened the private channel between them.

"Hey, Damien," she said. "Would you mind putting those glasses on?"

In the monitor, he tilted the glasses toward his face. She did her best to ignore the warmth that spread in her belly whenever she saw him. The guy was gorgeous, in what Tessa would call a 'man-wall' kind of way. His amber brown eyes narrowed, the furrow that was permanently etched between his eyebrows deepening. His hair would be black, if he ever let it grow out to more than stubble, and his skin was a rich olive hue.

He scowled—but then, Damien always scowled—and dropped his hand back to his side. "Not my style."

"Wait a minute." Vaughn sat up straighter. "Could you point the glasses at your face, please?"

The view once again changed as he held the glasses up, this time holding them higher. A deep gash marred his forehead, blood trickling down the side of his cheek and into his collar. She blew out a breath, then hit the command that opened the comm channel for everyone.

"Why did you all neglect to tell me that Damien has been injured?" she snapped.

"It's barely a scratch," Tessa said.

"Oh no." Megan's voice grew louder as she approached Damien. "I'm still not used to being around humans. I just assumed it would heal."

Vaughn caught sight of Damien's scowl deepening before he once again dropped the glasses to his side. She could see him stepping back, away from Megan.

"There's a first aid kit in the van," Megan said. "I can help you with that cut in the back while Tessa drives us to the ranch."

Opening the private channel again, Vaughn said, "It's okay. You can trust Megan."

"No thanks," Damien said. Vaughn was pretty sure he was talking to her and not Megan.

"Look, would you put the glasses on, please?" Vaughn said. "I need to be able to see what's going on up-close. They'll feed you more data, too."

She wasn't sure which argument worked, but he lifted the glasses and finally put them on. It took a moment for the data feed to start up again. After a few seconds, the monitor she had linked to the glasses started scrolling with data. It was displayed over the road where he stood. The nightvision function engaged, helping her make out more details of the area. He didn't say anything about his new view, even though he was seeing the same thing that she was on the monitor. He kept staring at Megan and the others as if nothing had changed.

"I just want to help," Megan said.

He had to be able to see the concern etched on Megan's face. Vaughn tried not to be irked that he didn't seem to be moved by it.

"Do me a favor and scan the trees." Vaughn could help Damien make friends later. The data feeds said the wound wasn't that deep, and they had other problems.

"I'd rather not," Damien said.

Damn, was he doing that on purpose? All of his responses could be for Megan *or* Vaughn.

"Come on, Damien," Vaughn said. "Whatever else these guys are, they're Blades. You can trust them."

Damien snorted.

Vaughn's stomach twisted a little. "Can you at least trust me?"

Megan's lips were pressed in a thin line and her knuckles had turned white, she was clasping her hands together so tight. Vaughn hated seeing her like that— falling back into the Omega behaviors she'd learned from the abuse of her previous pack.

"How many times have I saved your ass in a fight?" Vaughn said.

Damien stayed silent.

She went on, letting her anger seep into her voice.

"Megan is the sweetest person you will ever meet in your life. She might be a werewolf, but she's only ever been in two fights, and… she was pretty bad at it. But both times she was trying to help us and she was risking her life. If you don't want her to treat your wound, fine, but you need to stop staring at her like she's a monster."

"You need someone to look at that," Megan said.

"It's fine," Damien said.

"It isn't." Megan reached toward Damien's forehead.

He grabbed her wrist and held it, cocking his head to the side as he looked away from her. With his free hand, he drew a knife.

"Damien, stop," Vaughn yelled.

Brock suddenly filled the monitor. For a moment, Vaughn almost regretted being able to see what Damien saw. Her skin crawled as both blue and gold lights flickered from Brock's eyes, bright enough to cast a greenish tinge to the feed.

"Let. Her. Go," Brock said.

Damien tilted his head further to the side, ignoring the implicit threat in Brock's tone. From the camera feed in Damien's glasses, Vaughn could see that he was staring into the forest that covered the side of the mountain and encroached on the road. What the hell was he looking at? All she could see were gray-black silhouettes of trees.

"It's okay," Megan said.

The lights from Brock's eyes flared. "It is not okay. If

that knife had silver in it, I'd have gutted him already."

"Silver or not, if he doesn't let Meg go, I'm going to tear off his head." Tessa joined the group. Blue light pulsed over her body. Fur started to sprout from her skin.

If she changed, she'd be less in control. The situation was enough of a mess as it was.

Vaughn opened the communication line between all of them and said, "Marcus, do not let Tessa change. Damien, let go of Megan."

"Shh," Damien hissed.

Vaughn felt her eyebrows rise. "Did you just *shush* me?"

"Listen," Damien said.

Tessa started growling.

"Shut up and listen," Damien shouted, glancing briefly at the shifting werewolf.

Vaughn had never heard Damien shout outside of combat. That and the fact that he'd already turned back to the woods when there was a werewolf in mid-transformation right next to him... A deep, sick feeling started in her stomach. She didn't know which monitor to focus on. The camera mounted in the back of the van? The front of Marcus's hoverbike? The satellite feed of the area? Her gaze darted between them all.

There hadn't been any red blips in minutes. Whatever had knocked the van over was probably gone. Her sensors would pick up any threats. They were how she kept the

Blades safe while she was stuck at Ops. It was the *only* way she could keep them safe, aside from her gadgets. She had to be able to rely on her tech.

Everyone on the monitors paused. Even Tessa seemed to calm, the blue lights fading as she managed to get herself back under control.

"I don't hear anything," Megan whispered.

Vaughn didn't either. No night owls. No insects, even though it was the middle of summer.

Nothing.

Damien straightened a bit and backed away from the forest. He pulled on Megan's arm, shifting her behind him.

"Megan, get in the van," he said.

Tessa let out another growl. "You don't give orders."

"Vaughn said she can't fight," Damien said.

Megan stammered a bit. "What? I've started training…"

Marcus was staring at the trees, his head cocked to the side as if he was listening intently. "Maybe you should do what he says, Meg."

"Nothing's stupid enough to take on an entire pack of werewolves." Tessa nodded toward Damien. "Except maybe this guy."

"Megan, get in the van." Damien's voice was low and remarkably calm. He let go of her wrist and gently nudged her toward the van. "Now."

"Okay." Megan hesitantly stepped away and leapt up

into the van, one hand braced against the side of the opening Tessa had made by ripping off the door.

Vaughn felt dizzy. She realized she was holding her breath. Her mind was spinning as it went through scenario after scenario, trying to make sense of the data and figure out what would happen next. Dammit, if she couldn't figure this out—

Red blips appeared on her satellite feed at various places near the van. They didn't give off heat signatures, just that weird sensory echo.

"Shit!" Vaughn yelled. "Multiple incoming…"

She didn't know what they were. She wasn't even sure what she was seeing. The dots on her monitor were appearing and disappearing so quickly, she could barely track them. There never seemed to be more than one on the screen at a time. Could it be another glitch? Or was it a single dweller that could teleport? Something using interphasic energy to shift in and out of corporeal existence? But if so, how would it have knocked over the van?

Nothing they'd encountered before could do what this dweller was doing. Her stomach started to hurt. She had no idea what they were dealing with. All she could hear was her own labored breath. The others had gone completely still, waiting.

Please… Please let them come home safe.

Something burst out of the forest—a shadow darker

than the inky blackness around it. The feed from Damien's glasses showed streaks of green light skittering across Vaughn's monitor, the afterimage of multiple sets of eyes. The glasses' camera started shorting in and out, blue lines glitching across the screen intermittently. The speakers connecting her to their earpieces fizzed and popped in time with the static. The feeds from the hoverbikes and the external van cameras started scrambling as well.

"Shit," Vaughn said again, typing furiously as she tried to get her tech back online.

Only one screen seemed to be functioning normally—the one linked to the camera *inside* the van, and Megan was partially blocking that. Vaughn could see Damien slashing at something, but couldn't make out a shape. The satellite feed showed red dots appearing and disappearing. They all converged on a single spot—Damien's location.

"Protect Zachary," Brock ordered.

"Get Damien to the van." Megan's voice was shrill, spiked with panic.

"Damien, you're the only human," Vaughn said. "It'll target you."

Dwellers didn't usually go after each other, especially if there was a human available. Vaughn could see Damien fighting—tortuous glimpses that never let her get a good look at what was actually attacking.

"Get in the van!" she yelled.

"I'm not leading it to Zach." Damien sounded

breathless. He let out a pained grunt.

"What's going on?" Vaughn said. "I can't see."

"Let me help," Megan screamed.

"Stay in the van." Brock's voice was raspy and about an octave lower than normal. He must have transformed.

Vaughn checked the data Tessa's cybernetic arm fed her. The schematic she pulled up flickered briefly on the human-looking form, then settled onto a larger version with wickedly curved claws. Tessa had transformed, too. Which meant they probably all had, except Megan, who was still learning how.

Indirect data was all Vaughn had. It was still data. She switched the input for that monitor to draw from Marcus's hoverbike instead of Tessa's arm. It was sitting dormant near the van. The camera feed was just as garbled as the rest, but all the other systems seemed okay.

Maybe the dweller was putting off a localized disruption feed. That would fit with it being an interphasic entity. And it would mean her tech was still working as it should be. It just needed to get outside of the dweller's field of effect.

Vaughn turned on the engine remotely and engaged the hover function. When the bike was about thirty feet off the ground, the feed from its camera cleared, as did the audio. The moment of relief she felt was short-lived.

"No…" she said.

Damien was on his knees, one hand on the pavement

and the other clutching his abdomen. The light filtering out from the back of the van caught and reflected off of a growing pool of darkness beneath him.

Please, don't let that be blood.

The three transformed werewolves were gathered around Damien in a circle, their backs to each other as they clawed and snapped at... nothing. Vaughn still couldn't see what was attacking them. From the way the pack's heads darted from side to side, she wasn't sure they could see it, either.

She activated the communications feed within the ranch, letting everyone hear at once rather than trying to track them down individually. "Dexter, I need you in Ops. Eli and Porter, prep the OR."

She didn't need to tell them who it would be for. Damien was the only one who wouldn't heal—except maybe Zach. No one was sure how Brock being colonized by the werewolf parasite would affect Brock's replicants.

The door to Ops opened and Dexter ran in. "What's going on?" he said.

"Damien's hurt." Her heart was beating so hard it hurt. Saying the words made it more real. She had to focus. Everyone was counting on her. "I have multiple hostiles. Or maybe one."

Dexter came up behind her chair. "How can you not know?"

"I've never seen anything like it," she said. "I need

your take."

"I can't…" He let out a frustrated grunt. "There's just me now. I can't draw on the power of the others' minds, even if they weren't in stasis."

Shit.

She hadn't thought of that. She was so used to calling on them for help.

Dexter and Porter had been the first people Vaughn had ever met who had seemed like they could keep up with her mentally. She'd only recently found out that they actually had access to nine different brains that could work together as a kind of biological supercomputer.

That supercomputer had been linked through Brock, though—the progenitor who created Dexter, Porter, and all his other replicants. When Megan had introduced the werewolf parasite to transform Brock and save his life, the link with his replicants had been broken. Vaughn was still adjusting to the change. She couldn't imagine what Dexter and Porter were going through, having their mental links severed so abruptly.

"That doesn't mean I don't need your expertise." She brought up a feed of the data she'd collected so far and started playing it on the monitor closest to Dexter.

"We don't have any clear visuals," she said. "Just streaks of green light and a shadowy form that the others can't seem to see. Whatever it is, it's interfering with our audio and visual feeds. I think it might be some sort of interphasic entity."

"Ghosts don't knock over vans," Dexter said.

"I know that, but—" She broke off when she saw his expression change.

Dexter's eyes hardened as he stared at the monitor feed from Marcus's bike. Vaughn followed his gaze. The hairs on her arms stood on end and her stomach cramped, threatening to dislodge her dinner.

Damien was on the ground. He wasn't moving.

"Shit," Vaughn said. "Shit, shit, shit."

She slammed her fist down on the communications control, half-rising from her chair.

"You're supposed to protect Damien," she shouted. "What the hell are you doing?"

"We can't even see what we're fighting," Tessa shouted. "If we didn't heal so fast, we'd *all* be dead."

This couldn't be happening. Vaughn pressed her hands to the top of her head, trying to think of what to do— anything she could do. They had never lost a Blade before. Not permanently.

She had to do something. But she was stuck at Ops thanks to her agoraphobia. She couldn't even step outside without having a fucking panic attack.

Dexter headed toward the door. Vaughn quickly muted their side of the communications channel.

"Where are you going?" she shouted.

"Where I should have gone in the first place."

"You'll never get there in time."

"Maybe not for Damien, but I can protect Zach."

Vaughn's heart stuttered at the thought of Damien dead.

"You can't fight the way you used to," she said. "Not now that you're cut off from the others."

"I can't just sit here!"

"Like I do every goddammed battle?" she yelled. "Watch the screens and *think*. You still have one brain left."

"The others can't get to us," he said. "They're too busy engaging whatever the fuck that thing is. We have to get to them."

Vaughn turned to the monitor with the best feed—the one on Marcus's bike. She sat back down and worked the remote controls, steering the vehicle around to give her a better view of the battle. She would engage its weapons system, but couldn't target anything without risking hurting the others. The infrared scanner didn't show anything except bright red werewolves lashing out in seemingly random patterns, surrounding the orangey-yellow of Damien's still form.

Vaughn switched off the infrared and turned up the bike's full-spectrum lights as slowly as she could stand so she didn't blind the werewolves. The sun-replicating bulbs were meant to be used against vampires, but she would try anything at this point.

The scene was even worse than in her imagination.

Damien was face down on the pavement in a pool of crimson. For a brief moment, his body was obscured by a cloud of black smoke. Marcus whirled around and slashed at it, his claws passing through the substance as it dissipated. Another wound had appeared on Damien's back.

A sick wave of relief hit Vaughn. If it was still attacking Damien, that mean he was alive, right? Her thoughts spun until she was dizzy, trying to come up with a plan that would keep him that way.

"We have to do something," Dexter said.

Vaughn couldn't speak. She nodded, even though she had no idea what to do. The pack was snapping and clawing at nothing. Their motions looked as desperate as she felt.

"What if we use the weapons built into the bikes?" Dexter said.

"What would we even target?"

The creature seemed insubstantial, but had to be manifesting in some physical form to create those wounds. They had to find a way to get Damien to safety.

"Wait…" Vaughn opened the communications channel with the group engaged in battle. "Somebody get Damien to Marcus's bike."

Vaughn couldn't believe she hadn't thought of it sooner. If Damien died because of it, she would never forgive herself.

"Tessa," Brock snapped.

"I don't know how to fly it," Tessa said.

"I can pilot it remotely." Vaughn programmed in an autopilot sequence, just in case whatever was scrambling the AV feeds started to affect her connection. "Just someone get him on the bike now!"

"Protect Tessa so she can disengage the opponent," Brock said.

"I've been…" Marcus grunted as a deep wound opened on his side, "trying to protect her this whole time."

Megan bounded into the fray, still in her human form. Smoke appeared near her and a huge gash opened on her face. She barely seemed to register it as she picked up Damien, then immediately leapt at least thirty feet into the air. Straight up into the air.

"Vaughn?" Megan squeaked.

"Oh shit." Vaughn quickly piloted the bike beneath Megan, catching her as she fell.

The bike lurched as something hit it from below. Megan screamed, but Vaughn was able to maneuver the bike so it stayed beneath Megan. Vaughn couldn't get it to rise. The monitor glitched and the speakers crackled with painful feedback. The readings the bike was managing to send didn't make sense.

"Vaughn," Dexter said.

"I know, I know!" She furiously typed in commands, trying to get the bike to respond.

"Oh my god," Marcus said.

Vaughn could hear the signal from the others clearly now, but the only video she could see was from the back of the van. She glanced at the monitor to see a long, scaled tail whipping back and forth. Whatever had been attacking them must have grabbed onto the bike and was hanging from it. The bike should still be able to rise, but the data feed said whatever was hanging onto it was somehow becoming heavier by the second. Even its tail seemed to be getting bigger. The bike started to lower, engines straining.

"What the fuck is that thing?" Tessa said.

Vaughn would love to analyze what she was seeing, but that would have to wait. Megan and Damien needed help now.

"It's something that's still attacking your pack," Vaughn shouted.

Brock crouched briefly, then lunged, leaping up and grabbing onto the creature. Marcus and Tessa quickly joined him. A loud pop sounded and another screech of feedback stabbed through Vaughn's ears. All three wolves fell to the ground. Megan screamed as the hoverbike shot up into the air, the weight holding it down suddenly gone.

"Shit, shit, shit," Vaughn hissed, scrambling to reduce power and stop the bike's climb slowly enough to not throw them off of it. She set a course that would bring it straight to the ranch as it descended.

"Dexter, I need you in the garage." Vaughn's gaze was

locked on the monitors. "Help Megan get Damien to surgery."

Finally, she had solid data. Maybe she could figure out how to predict where and when that thing would appear next. If it went after Zach, she wasn't sure how she'd stop it. She couldn't remote drive the van back to the ranch without risking the creature interfering with her ability to see the terrain around it. The curvy mountain road was treacherous enough with someone physically at the wheel.

All of the monitors were staying clear. Vaughn tapped into the nearest satellite so she could watch the team on one of the monitors in her periphery. They had put Brock's bike on the roof of the van. One of them was crouching next to it—probably Brock, based on the size of the wolf form. Tessa was inside the back of the van. Her arm was still feeding Vaughn data. It had been the most reliable source through everything. Vaughn should ask Tessa about installing a camera and communications relay in it, but… she probably wouldn't want that on one of her appendages.

Marcus's heat signature flared, then dimmed as he shrank. He got into the driver's seat, then the van's engine started to warm. It's comm system activated.

"There's no sign of the thing at the moment," Marcus said. "We're hauling ass back to the ranch while we can."

A joke popped into Vaughn's head about them running back with their tails between their legs. In other circumstances, she might have shared it to try to lighten the tension, but not after this. They really were running away.

Other Blades retreated all the time. But the Providence team? It had never happened before.

Her stomach roiled again as she realized they had never lost a Blade. Ever. Not permanently. Dammit, they weren't going to lose a Blade today.

Megan had already reached the ranch. Vaughn quickly modified one of her algorithms so that any sign of that thing on her monitors would send her an alert. She could control the whole facility from her watch if she needed to. As soon as the new protocols kicked in, she ran to the door to Ops and opened it.

She balked at the threshold, staring at a line of red trailing across the otherwise pristine white floor. The wall was smeared with it, too.

Damien…

Vaughn stepped into the corridor and looked toward the entrance to the emergency operating room. Megan and Dexter were standing in front of the door. He was holding her against his chest as her body shook with muffled sobs. A wave of dizziness hit Vaughn. They couldn't have been too late.

"Dexter?" Vaughn said.

Dexter glanced up, his face pale, making his pitch black eyes seem even darker. His lips were pressed into a thin line.

She moved toward them, keeping one hand on the wall to keep her balance—the wall that didn't have bloody handprints on it. Megan turned and pulled away from Dexter a bit. She pushed a lock of black hair behind her ear, smearing her cheek with red and not seeming to notice. The wound on her cheek had already healed.

Everything about a dweller vaporized in some kind of blue energy field when they died or when any part of them was removed. That included blood. All of this—the trail on the floor, the blood on the walls and covering Megan—it was all Damien's.

"I'm so sorry," Megan said. "I got him here as quickly as I could."

"Where are Porter and Eli?" Vaughn asked.

Dexter cleared his throat before he spoke. "They're still trying, but Porter... He's like me. Diminished."

A week ago, Porter could have worked miracles on the operating table. With the link he shared with the other replicants through Brock, Porter could have drawn on the mental power of nearly a dozen minds and all their experience and expertise to help him—even their muscle-memory. Now it was just Porter and Eli.

Vaughn slammed her hand down on the access panel across from the OR. The door to Porter's lab slid open. She stalked inside. Dexter and Megan didn't follow. The door slid shut.

She sat on one of the stools along the counter that ran

the length of one wall in Porter's lab. She knew she shouldn't, but she brought up a view of the OR on one of the monitors. Porter and Eli were bent over a metal table. Damien's clothes had been cut away and lay in a pile on the floor. From the bloodstains on the wall above, they'd just tossed them there. Bags of fluids hung above the table, tubes dangling down and trying to feed life into Damien. He was naked, not even covered with a sheet. Goddammit, it didn't seem right, but they had more important things to

—

Vaughn retched as Porter shifted to one side, revealing Damien's abdomen. What was left of it, anyway. She turned away, clamping a hand over her mouth and willing her body back under control.

"You're doing fine," Eli said.

For a moment, Vaughn thought Eli was talking to her. Then she realized she'd turned on the audio as well as the video feed.

"He's bleeding out faster than we can get blood back into him," Porter said. "There's too much damage. There's not even enough to stitch back together. I can't stop the internal hemorrhaging. Maybe I could have before, but…"

"You can only do your best, son," Eli said. "Damien would understand that."

Damien *would* understand that. He wouldn't blame any of them for this, even though he had to have had serious reservations about coming to the ranch.

There had to be something Vaughn could do. For fuck's sake, she had *built a new arm* for Tessa after she'd cut off her original one to try to save them all from the dweller who had infected her with parasites she had kept contained in her right forearm. The new cybernetic arm Vaughn created had fused with Tessa's body. It even transformed with her.

That was just the beginning of what it could do. It was still surprising Vaughn by doing things she hadn't programmed into it, thanks to the ingenuity of the nanites she'd designed for the procedure. The nanites had really taken the programming that enabled them to improvise and run with it.

But she'd had *time* for all of that. Time to plan and gather data and run through scenarios and create contingency plans and multiple prototypes for each... case...

Vaughn turned toward the canisters that held the prototype nanites she hadn't used with Tessa. One model had been specifically designed to fuse the tissue of her arm with that of the cybernetic prosthetic.

Vaughn glanced back at the monitor showing the OR. Porter and Eli were talking in hushed tones. From the slump of Porter's shoulders, she didn't need to hear them to know what they were saying. How hopeless it was—for them. Not for her.

She leapt off the stool, inputting modified commands

through her watch as she ran toward the canister.

We aren't losing a Blade today.

Chapter Three

The first thing that registered was the smell of antiseptic and... ozone. Damien kept his eyes closed, feigning sleep. It seemed like a good idea until he could figure out where he was.

Soft whirring. Some kind of equipment. A steady beep like heartbeat monitors next to a hospital bed.

Hospital...

That explained the antiseptic smell, but not the ozone. Where was he?

The beeping intensified as Damien remembered where he *had been*. Fighting for his life next to a pack of werewolf Blades. Werewolves who had done their best to protect him. And one of them looked so much like Tammie, Damien's heart ached just from thinking of her.

Someone touched his arm. He sucked in a fast breath, waiting for pain or fatigue or *something* to hit him. But he felt... good. Great, actually.

So did the hand resting on his arm. Soft and warm.

"Damien?"

A wave of sensation swept over his skin at the sound of Vaughn's voice so close. He could feel her breath on his cheek. His skin rose in goosebumps.

So much for pretending to be asleep.

"It's okay," she said. "You're safe."

'Safe' was a relative term.

Damien was at the ranch. He'd been unconscious. The last thing he remembered was being practically disemboweled by a creature he couldn't even see. He'd kept his hands to his guts just to hold them in, and relied on *werewolves* to finish the fight for him.

The bed dipped slightly next to him as Vaughn must have sat down. She squeezed Damien's bicep gently.

"Damien, can you hear me?"

Another wave of… something flooded him. He'd never actually seen her before, but that voice had helped him through countless battles. Now, feeling her touch… It was setting him off in ways he hadn't anticipated.

Vaughn always made sure Damien and the Blades on his team—the people Damien was responsible for—made it home, no matter what they walked into out in the field. Looked like this fight was no exception.

He expected a struggle, but when he tried to open his eyes, it was effortless. The ceiling above his bed was stark white, illuminated by soft lights in his periphery. How did he go from death's door to this? Feeling fine, like he was waking up from a nice nap?

His gaze flicked to Vaughn leaning over him, their faces close. The heartbeat monitor picked up again.

Holy shit.

She was unearthly beautiful.

Damien had never seen such blue eyes. His first thought was of the ocean waters over white sands on tropical beaches that he'd seen in commercials. But Vaughn's eyes were even brighter than that. He tried to take in more details while he could. He doubted they'd ever be this close again.

Thick, dark lashes around large, expressive eyes. Soft features, full lips. Light brown hair pulled back in a ponytail, but with tons of wayward strands framing her face. Perfect skin with olive undertones. Pale as fuck, but then, rumor was that she never left her Ops room.

Except she was here with Damien now.

A huge smile spread across her face. She bowed her head and laughed.

"Thank god," she said. "I wasn't sure…"

He let a few moments pass, waiting for the ever-chatty Blade to go on. When she remained silent, he prompted her.

"Wasn't sure about what?" he asked.

She looked back up at him, locking gazes with those blue eyes. She still had her hand on his arm. His chest felt tight. Like he couldn't breathe—or didn't want to. He didn't want to do anything that might make her move away.

What the fuck is wrong with me?

"I wasn't sure you'd wake up," she said.

That was just part of the job. Being a Blade was safer by far than being a freelance hunter, but he had no illusions about his future. He was a human fighting storybook monsters come to life. He wasn't making it out of this alive.

"Is Megan okay?" He should probably ask about the others in the pack, but Megan was the only one who didn't know how to fight. Plus, Vaughn was right. Megan did seem sweet.

Vaughn's eyebrows rose and she smiled a little. "Megan is fine. Just a little shaken. She was really worried about you. We all were."

That shouldn't make warmth fill Damien's chest. But it did.

"How do you feel?" Vaughn asked, giving his arm a gentle squeeze. Damn, her hand was soft. And strong.

He shouldn't be surprised, knowing how many of their tools she'd made. She'd spoken to him before about working on the equipment at the ranch and how much she had to do manually. For some reason, the idea of this beautiful woman working on the vehicles in the garage was mesmerizing.

Warmth started to fill… other regions.

"I feel great." He forced himself to take a deep breath. He closed his eyes, hoping that would help him calm his body.

Vaughn shifted closer.

Not helping.

He counted to ten. Thought about baseball. He willed the blood in his body to pool anywhere but his groin.

"You don't have to do that," she said.

"Do what?" He glanced back at her, genuinely confused.

Lines of strain appeared around her eyes. She was frowning, too.

"You don't have to pretend to be fine," she said.

"I'm not pretending. What did you do to me, anyway?"

She opened her mouth, then snapped it shut again. The lines at the corners of her eyes deepened.

Oh shit.

"What did you do?" Damien sat up.

Instead of retreating, she grabbed both of his arms and tried to push him back down. He didn't budge, which left them nose-to-nose and chest to chest on the small bed. Her mouth opened slightly, her breath warm on his lips.

"You need to take it easy," she said.

"I need to know what you did."

Scenarios filled his head. There was a whole pack of werewolves here. Being colonized by the dweller that created werewolves would have healed his wounds. But he didn't feel any different. He just felt... better. Better even than he had before the fight.

"Whatever that creature was, it... It tore you up really

bad," she said. "You were bleeding out and surgery wasn't going to fix it."

Damien knew his wounds were bad. He remembered.

"You were dying," she continued. "We had to make a decision quickly. I'm sorry if it was the wrong one."

That was not reassuring. The heart monitor was almost a single, continuous beep.

"What did you do?" He bit out each word.

"We— *I* injected you with nanites programmed to repair the damage," she said.

That... had not been one of the scenarios he was considering. It should have been, though. Vaughn and her tech.

Compared to the other options, this didn't seem so bad. He didn't get why she was acting guilty about it. She looked wrecked.

"You were so messed up," she said. "Porter and Eli did their best, but conventional surgery couldn't save you. Then I remembered the nanites I used to fuse Tessa's cybernetic prosthetic to her arm."

"You put something in me that's been in a werewolf?"

"No, of course not," Vaughn said.

Damien didn't know exactly how werewolf colonization worked, but the idea of something getting that intimate with his body after being in a dweller freaked him out again. The heart monitor picked up, beeping faster. He turned and glared at it, then grabbed the wires taped to his chest and pulled them off, ignoring the stings as some of his chest hair came with them. That just made the thing start to wail.

"Ouch." She winced. "I could have helped with that."

The thought of her fingers carefully exploring his chest as she peeled away the wires set him off again. He was glad he was sitting up and could conceal just how much the idea appealed to him.

"Help with that instead." He pointed at the heart monitor.

Some distance would be good. It would help him rein in his reaction. As long as her body wasn't as gorgeous as her face.

"Sure." She leapt up from the bed and rushed to the machine.

Shit.

If anything, her body was even better than her face. Round and lush, with full hips and just the right amount of curves. Her arms were defined, her engineering exploits leaving their mark on her body. He let out a hiss of air as he tore his gaze away to stare at the white wall on the opposite side of the small room. He bent his knees and leaned forward, rumpling the sheets in his lap to hide his erection.

Why the hell were hospital gowns so thin and unrestrictive?

"Are you okay?" She had quieted the noise and sat

back on the bed. She reached toward his head with long, slender fingers.

Dammit, at this rate, if she touched him, it would take forever for him to calm himself down. He grabbed her wrist to stop her, and even that sent a wave of pleasure right to his dick. He hadn't been this out of control since high school. It had to be the stress of nearly dying. He was a little surprised she didn't complain when he didn't let go. Her cheeks flushed, the color spilling down her neck. She shifted a little on the bed. Damien tried really hard not to read anything into that small movement.

"Porter said…" her voice had a rasp to it. She cleared her throat. "He said your organs were like confetti. No amount of stitches would have saved you. You flatlined five times before I was able to get the nanites into you."

"And then?"

"The nanites repaired you."

Did Vaughn see everything and everyone as a piece of equipment? Damien knew she cared about all the Blades, but it was weird to hear her talking about his body that way.

"Are those nanites a result of the 'reverse engineering' you mentioned earlier?" he asked.

"I'm surprised you remembered that after everything you've been through," she said.

He held her gaze, waiting for her answer. She didn't look away. This woman was steel.

"Yes, they are," she said.

"So, what's the problem?"

"I couldn't get them out of you," she said. "They're still in there."

His skin felt electrified. He wondered for a moment if it was an adrenaline response or something else. Tiny machines were in his body. Machines derived from a *spaceship*.

"I know you didn't volunteer for this," she said. "But there was no other way to save you. I thought... I really did think it was what you would want."

"So, what are they doing in there now?" he asked, forcing his voice to be calm and measured.

"I don't know."

"Will you ever be able to get them out?"

She opened her mouth, closed it, opened it again, then said, "I don't know. But I can try."

"These things... They're your design."

"Yeah."

"And their job is to patch me up when I get... damaged."

She let out a little laugh. The sound reassured him more than anything.

"Yeah, that's their job," she said.

"Will they keep doing that for as long as they're in there?"

"Theoretically."

Vaughn's tech had never let him down before. All the Blades relied on it, and from the looks of things, she hadn't even rolled out the good stuff to the other bases.

"Leave them," he said.

Her eyes widened. "I don't know if that's a good idea. I'm not saying we can't get them out ever. It just didn't seem right for you to not know they were there."

"Leave them. We have other priorities."

Like waking up Zach and trying to get Carey back.

"The longer we wait, the more accustomed to your system they become," she said. "And the harder it will be to coax them out of you."

She made it sound like they were a bunch of feral cats. The image didn't sit well with Damien, but he tried to guard his expression. He looked at the IV that trailed into his arm. He took a breath and held it, then tore out the needle, deliberately gouging himself in the process.

"Jesus, Damien!" Vaughn leapt up, grabbing the bleeding spot and trying to apply pressure.

"Leave it," he said. This time, he actually grabbed her hand and held on to it as he pulled it away from the injury.

Her cheeks pinked again and she became uncharacteristically quiet. They both watched his arm. The bleeding stopped. Reluctantly, he let go of her hand. He carefully wiped a finger over the spot where the IV had been.

Smooth skin. No bruise. No hole. Nothing.

Vaughn let out another laugh. She grabbed his arm and bent over it, pushing gently against his skin and looking at it from different angles.

"That's awesome," she said.

"Isn't that what they're supposed to do?"

"Well, yeah, but I couldn't bring myself to watch before... Seeing it in my head and watching it this close in reality are very different."

She looked up and smiled at him, though there was still tension around her eyes. The tightness returned to his chest. He was glad he'd ripped off the monitoring devices, or his heart rate would surely give away just how much he liked seeing her smile. A muscle in his jaw started to ache as he ground his teeth together to keep from smiling back.

Yes, he and Vaughn had worked together in the past during battles, but that didn't mean she was a friendly.

Even the ache in Damien's jaw quickly vanished. The nanites at work, probably. He knew there had to be a catch —there always was. But damn, he could get used to this.

"I want to know everything," he said.

She nodded. "Where do you want to start?"

There were so many questions lining up in his head. About the werewolves who had helped save him, the nanites, the guy who had founded the Blades.

Most of all, he wanted to know about Carey.

Vaughn had said there was a chance they could get Carey back. Damien had seen a lot of impossible things while working with the Blades and even more before, when he'd been hunting. He'd never seen a dweller come back to life after vaporizing.

And that's what Carey was. What he'd always been. A dweller.

Damien tried not to remember the moment when his sword had pierced Carey's chest during their sparring practice. Or the look of surprise that Damien swore had crossed Carey's features *before* the blade had run him through.

The biggest surprise had come after, as Damien held Carey's limp form, screaming for help, and then watched the blue light consume Carey's body, leaving nothing behind. The same blue light that ate up every dweller when they died.

All that time Carey and Zach had been preaching peace between humans and dwellers to the Blades at the castle— their nickname for the base in Europa, just outside of Chicago—they'd been hiding the truth. They weren't human themselves.

If Carey had told them he was a dweller, it wouldn't have been so bad. At least everyone would have known he had an ulterior motive in wanting peace. But instead, he'd hidden that from everyone. Even Damien, his best friend. Damien hadn't made it to the Providence base before seeing that they were keeping secrets at the ranch, too.

He wanted to ask Vaughn straight-up how to get Carey

back. And was his brother, Zach, the same kind of... whatever Carey was? Damien doubted they were 'twins' in the human sense of the word, though the men were absolutely identical. Damien wanted to ask a thousand questions, but he knew he wasn't ready for the answers.

"Pants," he said.

Vaughn's eyebrows hiked up her forehead. "Pants?"

"I want pants."

She laughed—a big, genuine laugh, that showed her straight, white teeth and had Damien tightening his grip on the sheets. He had to get this under control. Getting back into his gear would help.

"I can do that," she said. "But Porter and Eli are going to want to look you over first."

Eli was well liked by all the Blades—including Damien. He was their main doctor and had visited the castle shortly after Damien joined up.

"Who's Porter?" Damien asked.

"That's... complicated," she said.

He stared at her, again waiting for her to go on. It didn't take long this time.

"Porter is Dexter's twin," she said.

Nothing too complicated about that. Except... Carey and Zach were twins, too. Supposedly.

"But not really," Damien said.

Vaughn did that thing where she opened her mouth to speak, shut it, then opened it again. Damn, her lips looked soft.

She let out a breath and shook her head. "Yeah. 'Not really.' They're dwellers, like Zachary."

"You mean Zach?" Damien had never heard Zach called anything else.

"No, I mean Zachary. They're... Do you know what a hydra is?"

Do you know what a non sequitur is?

Damien opted for a simple, "No," in response instead of voicing his thought.

"In Greek mythology, it was a dragon with a bunch of heads," she said. "When Heracles fought it, every time he cut off one head, two more would sprout from the spot."

"Sounds rough."

She chuckled. "Yeah. Heracles finally figured out he had to burn the stump with a torch right after severing each head to keep them from growing back."

How the hell did this tie in with Carey and Zach? And Dexter and Porter, for that matter?

"When people encounter a dweller, they usually don't know how to process it," Vaughn said. "They come up with a story that makes them feel better—their own interpretation of what they experienced."

This was basic training for every Blade. Guards, Techs, Medics—everyone. The one thing the training had left out was that dwellers were aliens. At least Damien had learned that much from coming to the ranch.

"Myths and folklore have grown around these beings, evolving over thousands of years." She continued the standard lecture. "But they're myths, not facts."

"What *is* a hydra, then?"

The door slid open and Eli stepped through, followed by a dark-haired man who Damien assumed was Porter. He was staring down at one of the high tech, paper-thin tablet computers Zach was always using.

"That would be me," Porter said. He stopped at the foot of Damien's bed and smiled.

The room started to spin. Damien realized he was holding his breath—had been since this guy walked into the room. Everyone was silent, as if they were giving Damien a minute to process what he was seeing. Trouble was, it would take more than a minute.

Looking at Porter was like looking at a ghost. Or a funhouse mirror, only Damien was seeing someone else's reflection. This guy was a dead ringer for Carey—and Zach.

Without the scar that ran along Carey's left cheek, Damien wouldn't have been able to tell Carey and Zach apart. They dressed the same, wore their hair the same.

This guy, though...

The hair was different. Darker. Short on the sides, and sticking up in spikes on top. Carey and Zach had longer bangs, and their hair almost reached their shoulders. Other than that, Porter could be another identical brother. Same straight nose. Same black as pitch eyes. Hell, he even had the same smirk.

Carey had never mentioned being part of triplets. But Vaughn had said Porter was *Dexter's* twin. Which meant there were four of them.

Beneath his white coat, Porter wore the standard Blade uniform. Black T-shirt, black cargo pants, black boots. A thin line of scar-tissue ran across his neck as far as Damien could see. It looked like something had tried to decapitate him and failed. Maybe used a garrote on him.

Slowly, Damien blew out the breath he'd been holding, trying not to be too obvious about it. He glanced over at Vaughn, looking for answers.

"Damien, this is Porter," she said.

"You can call me Dr. Rhodes, if you'd rather." Porter smiled, but it didn't reach his eyes. They were flat black, not even reflecting the lights in the room. Again, just like Zach's and Carey's.

"Come on, now." Eli stepped forward, placing the earpieces of his stethoscope into his ears. "No need to be so formal. All the Blades are family."

Eli smiled, too, the gray and white streaks in his beard shifting. Unlike Porter, Eli's blue eyes crinkled around the edges as he smiled. They also reflected the light.

"May I?" Eli held up the listening piece of the stethoscope.

Damien nodded, leaning back slightly. He tried not to

flinch when Eli placed a hand on his shoulder. Eli listened to Damien's chest in several places, his eyes getting that unfocused look doctors had when giving examinations.

"Deep breath." Eli nodded as Damien did as he asked, listening to another spot. "Good." He pulled the stethoscope down around his neck and smiled again, squeezing Damien's shoulder. "I'm glad you're still with us. How do you feel?"

"Fine," Damien said.

Eli squeezed his shoulder again. "How do you feel, really?"

Confused as fuck?

Damien glanced over at Porter, then retreated into silence.

"You must have a lot of questions," Porter said.

"He wants pants." Vaughn was standing on the opposite side of the bed, close to the wall with her arms crossed. When everyone turned to stare at her, she shrugged. "What? It's a reasonable request."

"I'll have Dexter bring some clothing." Porter smirked, then his eyes grew unfocused and almost confused. He winced and shook his head.

Eli stepped away from the bed and rested his hand on Porter's shoulder.

"I'll tell him," Eli said. He looked at Vaughn and Damien, and added, "I trust you all to behave in my absence."

Vaughn snorted, but Porter remained quiet. His expression had taken on a haunted quality. A few moments after Eli left, Porter seemed to shake himself out of whatever funk had fallen over him.

"Vaughn should have been able to explain several things by now," Porter said.

"I told him about the nanites." Her lips thinned to a line and she looked away. "And I mentioned the ship earlier and that dwellers are aliens."

"Very good." Porter turned to Damien and said, "I'm sure I can answer any further questions that you have."

Vaughn stepped closer to the bed. "I thought I was reading him in."

"We need you analyzing data from the fight," Porter said.

She shook her head. "This takes priority."

"Over an unknown dweller that nearly killed Damien and handed our entire pet pack of werewolves their asses?"

"I can multitask," she said. "And don't call them 'pets.'"

"If you need to go, go." Although, Damien really wanted Vaughn to stay. On many levels.

She glared at him. "*I can multitask.* I have algorithms chewing through everything to help analyze the fight, and I've already checked and rechecked all of my security systems and reviewed every bit of the data we have available. We don't have to worry about that thing attacking here. The ranch is the safest place on the planet."

The door slid open again and a guy strode in carrying a pile of clothing. He paused right next to Porter. Damien had to stop himself from running his hand over his face.

Dexter. Has to be.

And Damien had thought telling Carey and his brother apart was bad. Dexter and Porter went beyond being identical. It was more like double-vision, except for Porter's white lab coat. Their expressions, their movements, everything was the same. Dexter even had the same scar around his neck—and without the coat, Damien could see that it really did go all the way around.

At least the uncanny experience of looking at the pair was keeping Damien grounded. He'd wanted to meet Dexter for longer than he'd been a Blade. It was part of the reason Damien joined up. Now that they were in the same room together, Damien was too messed up about the whole twin-triplet-quadruplet thing to be properly in awe.

"Somebody wanted pants?" Dexter said, placing the stack of clothing on the foot of Damien's bed.

Pants were no longer the priority.

"What is a hydra?" Damien said. "And I don't mean the myth."

Dexter and Porter tilted their heads toward Damien in the exact same motion. Same speed, same everything. Damien almost expected them both to speak at the same time, but it was Porter who talked.

"We are," Porter said. "Dexter, myself, Zachary, and some others."

Damien shook his head. "You mean Zach?"

"I mean Zachary," Porter said. "He is… was… a single being housed in two bodies."

Dexter's hands clenched into fists at his sides. He was staring at the wall behind Damien as if he was trying to burn a hole through it.

Sore subject?

Damien turned toward Vaughn. "Is that why you think you can get Carey back? Something with that… growing two heads?"

She nodded. "Yeah. With a hydra, if you kill one of their bodies, the other one usually—" She stammered a bit, her face draining of blood. "They grow a new one."

Damien looked back at Porter and Dexter. "How the hell does that work?"

Porter smirked. "Unpleasantly."

"Very unpleasantly." Vaughn shuddered.

"You wouldn't have witnessed it if you hadn't decapitated Porter." Dexter's smile was cold.

They had to be joking. But Vaughn didn't look amused.

Damien's gaze fell to that line of scar tissue around both Dexter and Porter's necks. The hair on his arms stood on end as he imagined the connotations.

"Can we stay focused here," Vaughn said. "The point

is, after we get Zach out of stasis, he might… grow a new Carey."

Carey. Zach. Zachary.

Damien felt a laugh building in his chest. If it came out, he knew it wouldn't sound sane. He wasn't sure he'd *be* sane. So he stuffed it down, as deep as he could. He buried his hope and his fear in that dark place where he kept all of his brightest memories and darkest horrors. He swung his legs over the side of the bed and stood, pleased when he didn't waver. A little zing shot through him, despite himself, when he caught how Vaughn's eyes widened as her gaze travelled up and down Damien's body.

No distractions.

He was here for a reason. This was his mission, on behalf of every human Blade who had placed their faith in the Blades of Janus. Damien would determine if these people—dwellers and humans alike—truly were allies, or if they were the enemy.

"The ship," Damien said. "I want to see it."

Chapter Four

"Are you sure you're up for it?" Vaughn still didn't know how her nanites were affecting Damien's body. Having him wandering around the ranch seemed ill-advised.

Damien crossed his arms over his chest, the thin fabric of his hospital gown pulling tight across his shoulders.

Damn, why did we put him in a standard hospital gown?

They had nice, thick, bulky robes for people who were staying in the infirmary. Damien was wearing a flimsy little gown that barely closed in the back, letting Vaughn see just how thick and bulky he was. She could curl up on his back and take a nap without worrying about falling off. She didn't know if she could wrap her arms around him, but could imagine how it would feel to have those arms around herself.

"What does the doc think?" Damien nodded toward Porter.

"All our tests show you being in perfect health," Porter said. "A little exercise might do you some good."

Damien grabbed the neck of his gown and started to

pull it off. He stopped as a small choking sound garbled up from Vaughn's throat.

Way to play it cool.

Hunters fought and died together. Most lived in cramped quarters that didn't give much privacy. Even after being with the Blades for years, Damien was still a hunter at heart. Vaughn quickly turned away, but from the corner of her eye, she could see that he was pulling his boxer-briefs on underneath his gown.

She let out a little breath of relief. It was hard enough to control her reactions to him when he was covered. The idea of being in a room with him naked was more than she could handle. Well, as long as Porter and Dexter were there. If they decided to give her and Damien some time alone... She was sure she could find plenty of ways to handle that scenario.

"Let me know if you experience any new symptoms," Porter said. "Shortness of breath. Dizziness. I wouldn't worry about it, though. Vaughn's tech has never let us down before—which is why we need her working on repairs to the ranch. We're still tracking down all the systems that need her attention."

"Did that thing attack again while I was out?" Damien asked.

"No, the ranch sustained damage in a previous attack," Vaughn said.

"An attack we suffered only a few days ago." Porter

leveled his cold gaze at Vaughn.

"Look, if this is about me decapitating you, I said I was sorry like a hundred times already," she said. "I didn't have a choice."

"You really decapitated him?" Damien asked.

Porter jumped in before Vaughn could reply.

"She did," Porter said. "And then she burned my body with a flamethrower. Luckily, Brock hadn't split yet, and Dexter was able to grow a new body for me."

Vaughn turned to glare at Porter, no longer caring about Damien's state of dress. "Again, no choice. You were infected with a hostile dweller that would have killed us all."

Porter gripped Vaughn's shoulder firmly.

"I never said you did the wrong thing." He squeezed her shoulder harder, then released it. "I just like giving you a hard time about it." Porter's smirk deepened as he turned toward the door. "Enjoy your tour. I'm sure it will be extremely informative, since Vaughn seems to be dead set on conducting it."

Dexter followed Porter from the room silently. The door slid shut behind them, leaving Vaughn and Damien alone. She did her best not to think about the scenarios— more like fantasies—that had been running through her head for just such an event.

"That guy's an asshole," Damien said.

Vaughn snorted. "Wait till you spend a little quality

time with Dexter."

They stood in silence for a moment, then Damien said, "None of this is what I expected."

She nodded. "I get that. Life seldom is. But you're not alone in this."

His gaze intensified, his eyes locked with hers. She stammered, her cheeks burning.

"I mean, none of the Blades are," she managed.

Finally, he turned away, grabbing the standard issue black cargo pants from the pile and starting to pull them on. It took her a second to realize what was happening before she quickly spun around to face the wall. There was no way she'd watch him get dressed. Instead, she listened to it.

She pinched her eyes shut as she heard the soft sounds of clothing moving across his skin. The crisp rustle of his cargo pants was followed by a zipping sound. She let out a shaky breath.

Think about data sets. Think about data sets.

"You sure you have time for this?" His voice was pretty close. She decided to risk turning around.

Big mistake. Really big. Massive, even.

Damien was standing with his legs braced in a stance of casual readiness, staring at one of the walls as if deep in thought. He had on the black cargos that all the Blades wore—thank the Internet—but that was it. Seeing his bare feet against the cold metal of the infirmary's floor made more of that warmth bloom in her chest. It quickly spread lower as she took in his massive arms and stocky build. He was holding his hospital gown in both hands, low enough that she could see every bit of his torso.

He was thick with muscle—not too defined, but it was obvious the muscle was there. A substantial dusting of dark hair covered his chest and trailed down his stomach, disappearing beneath his waistband. Her mouth went dry. She licked her lips just as Damien looked back at her.

Oh great. Great timing.

Vaughn didn't think she'd ever seen someone stare at her so intensely. Damien's amber eyes darkened, a muscle along his jaw started to flex. It brought her attention back to his face. His nose was stronger than most people would find attractive, and bent in the middle from a break that hadn't set right, but it worked with the rest of him. His lips were full, his dark eyebrows drawn down over his eyes, watching her… staring at him.

He held the eye contact as he dropped the gown on his bed. He picked up his T-shirt and pulled it over his head, then down across his stomach. It almost seemed deliberately provocative, but that had to be her projecting. It didn't help that he seemed to give off an incredibly sexy vibe naturally. She swallowed hard as he tucked in his shirt, trying to will herself to look away—and failing. Probably because all of her willpower was going into not reaching out and untucking that shirt again so she could let her fingers follow that trail of dark hair.

"I, um…" Vaughn shifted her weight and finally looked down at the floor. She'd never reacted so strongly to someone before. It was almost electric in its intensity. For a moment, gravity felt like it shifted around her. The lights became brighter and everything blurred.

Oh, great. Here we go.

At least she was about to get a great distraction. Chemistry this time… And something explosive.

"Hold on a second," she said, tapping on her watch to bring up a holo-display. When inspiration hit, she knew she didn't have much time to catch it. And this one was vital to the security of the ranch.

Damien stepped closer to the wall as lines of blue light filled the space in front of her. She slid her fingers against the chemical structures in the image, changing molecular bonds and adding in circuitry that would activate what she needed it to at exactly the right time.

She opened the communications channel and said, "Porter, I'm sending you an update on the composite material we'll be using to seal and fill the troll tunnels."

"That's great," Porter said. "Could you go to sublevel 2 and repair enough fabricators for us to get this done by next year? I'd like to avoid another invasion if possible, especially with an uncategorized dweller running around."

She ignored the thick sarcasm in Porter's voice. "With this new molecular structure plus the integrated detonators, we'll be able to use the fabricator on sublevel 1 and get all the materials we need in an hour."

"One hour?" Porter's surprise was harder to ignore.

Vaughn didn't let herself smile at the coup. Instead, she sent the new models to Porter and dismissed the hologram. The projectors in the room blinked off, the sensors that read her movements powering down with a soft hum.

"We should stop fabricating materials to repair the infirmary and give this priority for the moment," she said. "We have what we need medically speaking, especially with so many stasis pods available in case of emergencies."

"Sounds good to me." Porter ended the transmission.

"Okay, where were we?" She looked over at Damien, whose eyes were wide.

"What the hell was that?" he asked.

"It's a project Porter and I are working on. The ranch was breached by a horde of trolls in that recent attack, and they left all these tunnels that lead from the surface right to the cavern that holds the ship. We need a way to fill the tunnels that doesn't involve shovels and us spending the rest of our lives…"

Her voice trailed off as Damien's eyebrows rose higher on his forehead. He angled his head at her, giving her an incredulous look.

"That's…" she said, "not what you were talking about, was it?"

"No. The lights. The hands." He swirled his hands as if he was messing with an invisible holo-display.

"I guess the castle and the loft aren't quite as high-tech as the ranch," she said. "That was a holographic interface that allowed me to input—"

This time, she stopped when Damien ran his hand down his face and let out a big sigh.

"What?" she said.

He took a few steps closer. Her heart quickened and her breath caught in her throat. She wanted him closer. Which was... unusual.

"Who the hell thinks that fast?" he said. "I mean, I've seen the tech you create, but never how you create it. That was..."

A freak show. Frightening.

Inhuman.

She pinched her lips together, keeping her unhelpful suggestions to herself. She'd heard them so many times. That and worse. Ever since she was a child and would build intricate contraptions with nothing more than her toys and anything in reach that she could manage to disassemble for parts.

Damien let out another huge burst of breath and shook his head, then actually smiled at her. The sight felt like a sledgehammer hitting her in the chest.

"That was incredible," Damien said.

"I... Uh..." That was not what she had expected. It was

so outside the realm of her experience, she couldn't think of how to respond. So, she just said, "Thanks?"

"How's that going to fill the tunnels?" he asked.

She felt her own eyebrows hitch up. The Blades loved to use her tech, but they rarely asked about projects they weren't directly involved in. It felt good to be asked to explain things. She took a moment to remind herself that professional curiosity was not the same as personal interest.

"We can spray the chemical I was tweaking into the openings in the cavern and it will expand into foam that spreads through the tunnels, sealing them," she said.

"Kind of like the foam insulation you spray into the walls of houses?"

She smiled. "Exactly. This stuff hardens when it hits sunlight, with a chain reaction that will solidify all of it. I've scanned the tunnels to make sure they all lead to the surface eventually and aren't connected to anything we don't want buried. We'll send out a pulse that will scare off any animals that might be investigating them and do a thorough scan so we don't catch any bunnies or anything in it."

"Wow." Damien's smile had faded. She wished she could get it back.

"I can show you the fabricator, if you'd like," she said.

He shook his head. "Actually, I'd like to see Zach."

That made sense. Damien and Carey had been so close.

She couldn't imagine what Damien must be feeling after what had happened. How Carey had... died.

"The stasis chamber room is in the ship," she said, keeping her voice gentle. "That's where we moved Zach when you arrived."

Damien nodded, then sat in one of the chairs near his bed and pulled on his socks and boots. He laced them up with the efficiency of someone who was experienced with getting dressed quickly and under urgent circumstances. Most of the Blades had started out as hunters. She needed to remember that if she was going to have a chance at convincing him that the Blades were the good guys. Damien was well respected by the others. The probability that they would accept his appraisal of the group and not disband when they found out their leaders were actually dwellers was high—but only if he thought the Blades of Janus was worth saving.

As soon as Damien was ready, Vaughn led the way into the corridor outside of the infirmary. Thank the Internet the operating room hadn't been destroyed during Brock's temper tantrum when he'd first awakened as a werewolf. As it was, she had only needed to repair a bed for Damien to recover in. It looked a little weird to her, having the one bed in the huge room, but he didn't say anything about it.

The recent attack on the Providence base had held a few blessings in disguise, one of which being that they now had access to much more of the ship. Vaughn couldn't wait to explore it—but knew she had to. There were dozens of tasks on her list that were much more urgent, including working with Damien. Plus, the cavern had been expanded enough to set off her agoraphobia. Or maybe it was all the stress. Either way, she needed to build herself a corridor or something that led to the ship. A very narrow corridor. With no windows.

"We can take the elevator down," she said. At least that was working—for the moment. She pressed her palm against the biometric scanner, then entered the small space when the door slid open.

Once they were inside, Damien said, "Tell me more about Zach and Carey being hydras."

"They're actually *a* hydra. Parts of one being. Sort of." She ran her fingers over her hair, as if she could smooth her thoughts as much as the wayward strands. "I don't know how to explain this in a way that makes sense."

"Start at the beginning," he said.

That might just work. Grateful for the help, she smiled and nodded. She pressed the button that paused the elevator, then leaned back against the plain white wall behind her.

"You haven't by chance read the newest entry in the Dwellers Database regarding Hive Fathers and Mothers, have you?" she asked.

"I read every update," he said. "They're apex ghouls, made up of thousands of smaller organisms that can fuse together to make themselves appear human or break into their individual components to infect humans and make the ghoul thralls we're more familiar with."

"Wow." Warmth again spread through her chest. Damien hadn't just read the update, he'd practically memorized it. "Yeah, that's right."

"How the hell do you even kill one of those?" he asked. "The entry said you have to get all the separate parts at once."

"Marcus and Tessa took out a pair a couple of months ago by electrocuting them," Vaughn said. "But that was after Tessa cut off her arm to stop the spread of a Hive infection in her own body and Marcus turned her to keep her from bleeding out."

"Damn," Damien said.

"The Hive Father had this warped idea of starting a family with a human woman."

Damien cast Vaughn a sharp look, his brows drawing down in a menacing arc.

"Right there with you," she said. "From what I know, he actually courted his target and married her. Katey had no idea her husband wasn't human until her pregnancy started progressing way too quickly."

Damien hissed in a breath and crossed his arms over his chest. The muscle in his jaw started to twitch again. She could practically hear his teeth cracking as he ground them together.

"She ran away and crossed paths with a hunter," Vaughn went on. "He gave his life to help Katey get to Tessa's mom. She and Eli were already working together on dweller issues. They helped the woman deliver, but..."

"The woman died," Damien offered.

"She turned. They had to destroy her shortly after."

"Shit." He started to pace in the small space. "And the child?"

"They decided to raise him," Vaughn said. "And named him after the hunter who died trying to help Katey. They named him Brock."

Damien stopped his pacing. Slowly, he turned to face her.

"You're telling me that our leader, the man who founded the Blades, is the son of a Hive Father?" he said.

She nodded. "Yeah. He's a hydra. *Was* a hydra. Honestly, none of us are sure what he is anymore."

Damien shook his head, resuming his pacing. His long strides kept bringing him close to her, and every time, her mental stream rippled with an awareness that derailed her train of thought.

"Keep going," Damien said.

She reached toward the controls to start the elevator again, but Damien grabbed her wrist. They stood so close, she could feel his body heat. She swallowed hard, staring up into his amber-brown eyes. He stepped even closer, and for a stupid, ridiculous moment, she thought maybe he was going to kiss her.

"More data," he said.

"What? Oh, sure."

Another little zing of warmth shot through her. Vaughn had a feeling Damien was choosing his words with her in mind. That plus the proximity and… She was just grateful to have something to divert her thoughts to—other than the growing warmth spreading through her belly.

"Brock seemed totally normal," she said. "All the tests we've ever run on him showed him as one-hundred percent human."

Same as me, not that I can trust them anymore.

She shook off the thought. At least it helped rein in her physical reaction to Damien.

"Eli and the hunter married and had another child," she went on.

"Tessa," Damien said.

"Yeah."

"Did this hunter Eli married have a name?"

Vaughn sighed. "Janice."

Damien's eyebrows arched.

"Janice," he repeated.

"Yup." The 'p' came out with a popping sound.

"There's a whole training segment devoted to pronouncing 'Janus' as 'yah-noos' so we get it right, and you're telling me the guy who started the team is actually a dweller who has a mom that was a hunter… and her name is Janice."

"Yup." Vaughn really couldn't think of more to say. Rather, nothing she *should* say. "And that is all the data I have on that topic. Everything else is speculation."

Damien shook his head. "It's obvious Brock had something to prove."

She shrugged. "Maybe. That doesn't change the fact that he was right to found the Blades of Janus."

She pronounced the word with the proper pronunciation. Apparently, Damien wasn't having it.

"Blades of Janice," he corrected.

Vaughn snorted. She swore she saw a hint of a smile at the corner of his lips.

"Not all dwellers are evil." Her voice had grown softer, and even she could hear the rasp to it. "We can coexist peacefully."

"With the ones that don't try to eat us," he said.

And, again, mood destroyed.

"The Blades exist to protect everyone," she said. "Dwellers *and* humans. We find threats, we resolve them. But the answer isn't always violence or death."

Damien let go of her wrist, then paced back to the other side of the elevator. He nodded toward the controls.

"Moving on, then," she murmured, under her breath. She pressed the control to resume their descent.

Only seconds later, the elevator stopped, the doors opening on sublevel 2. The scent of charred wiring and melted plastics rolled in, along with the sound of voices calling to each other in the ruined space.

"What the hell, guys," Vaughn said.

No one was there, though. Maybe it was another glitch in the systems from the explosion. One more thing for her to track down. She tried to close the doors again, but before they could shut, two pairs of hands grabbed their edges and pushed them open again. Her stomach sank.

I was really hoping we could put off this introduction.

Jon and Nathan stood on either side of the opening, staring down at her with matching blank expressions. Their hair was stark-white and they had the same scars running over their faces that Brock had—among many others. The eye beneath their scars was also completely white, even over the pupil. Their right eyes were the same light-consuming flat black as Dexter and Porter's. Unlike the other replicants, Jon and Nathan were huge. Thick with muscle, even bigger than Damien.

Damien sucked in a breath, and whispered, "Shit."

Nathan looked over at Damien and smiled. A chill swept over Vaughn at the off-ness of it.

"Vaughn!" Megan's cheery voice rang out, getting closer. "I was hoping to see you."

Jon and Nathan parted for her, but kept their hands on the elevator doors.

"Brock found this in the wreckage from my collar's explosion," she said. "It looks like it might almost be intact." She was beaming with pride as she held up a twisted piece of metal that was covered in scorch marks.

"That's great, Megan," Vaughn said. "Where is Brock, by the way?"

"He's over in the boom room." Megan shifted her weight uneasily. "What's left of it."

Vaughn glanced at Brock's newest replicants, cautious of every move she made near Megan. Vaughn reached out and gently touched the other woman's arm.

"None of this is your fault," Vaughn said.

"I, um…" Megan looked down and cleared her throat. Her eyes glistened a bit when she met Vaughn's gaze again. "I appreciate that, but, it really kind of is."

Damien stepped forward a bit, peering through the open doors at the gnarled metal and dangling wires that was all that remained of sublevel 2.

"What the hell happened here?" he said.

"Damien!" Megan's eyes widened, along with her smile. "I didn't notice you there." She stepped into the elevator, bringing an even stronger stench of burned… everything.

Jon and Nathan closed ranks, glaring at Damien intensely enough that the hair on the back of Vaughn's neck stood on end.

"My nose is so messed up from working in the bomb site, I can't smell a thing." Megan beamed at him.

"Bomb site?" Damien said.

Her smile faded. "Vaughn didn't tell you?"

"I'm still working my way through 'dwellers are aliens' and 'we have a spaceship in the basement,'" Vaughn said. "You remember how it was."

"I do." Megan turned to Damien. "Having Brock to help me through it was incredibly helpful. I'm so glad you have Vaughn."

Vaughn sucked in a breath to say... something, but ended up aspirating some saliva. All she could manage were stifled coughs. She swore Damien smirked.

"We have plenty of time to catch up now that you're okay," Megan said. "You are okay, right?"

She stepped even closer. Damien backed against the wall. Megan's smile faltered again.

"Sorry, I forgot." She shrugged and feigned a laugh. "Werewolf."

Damien shook his head. "Honestly, I'm more concerned about the hydra at the moment."

Jon and Nathan had ratcheted up their glare. Both men stood in the opening to the elevator, completely filling the space.

"These guys?" She playfully swatted Jon's shoulder. "They're teddy bears."

Vaughn felt her eyebrows rise. Damien's did the same.

"Obviously," Vaughn said, nodding toward Damien and hoping he'd play along.

"Yeah." Damien stood straighter, slowly bringing

himself a little closer to Megan. "It's good to have friends."

Her smile returned. "I know it's weird, but… I really hope *we* can be friends."

Damien's lips twitched briefly. His features relaxed, as he said, "Me, too."

"I guess you can check this out later." Megan lifted the metal scrap in her hands briefly. "The boys just heard me saying how excited I was to show this to you. They must have noticed the elevator and decided to check to see who it was."

She turned back toward the sublevel. Jon and Nathan parted for her again, their attention eerily focused on her.

"You guys spoil me," she said.

So creepy.

The replicants followed her from the elevator, casting one last glare at Damien over their shoulders.

As soon as the doors closed, Damien said, "What the fuck was that?"

"I…" Vaughn raised her arms, then dropped them to her sides. "I honestly don't know. Jon and Nathan are the most recent set of replicants Brock created. They didn't turn out quite right."

"You think?" Damien's brow furrowed and his lips pulled into a frown. "Wait, Brock made these things? How?"

"We're still trying to figure that out. The leading theory

is that he builds up quantum energy and once he has enough stored, a replicant emerges from him. Then that replicant splits into the binary beings we know as Zachary and Jonathan and Dexter-slash-Porter and the others."

"Wait... They *emerge* from Brock?"

"Oh, no. It's not what you think," Vaughn said. She thought back to when she'd had to assist when a new version of Porter emerged from Dexter and shuddered. "Okay, it's awful in its own way, but not like that."

Damien leaned heavily against the wall of the elevator. "Vaughn..."

Goosebumps rose over her skin, hearing her name in his husky voice. She dared to reach out and rest her hands on his shoulders, though she kept herself at arm's length.

"I know this is a lot," she said. "But I swear to you, we're the good guys."

Damien let out a mirthless laugh. "So Dexter, Porter, Zach and..."

"And Carey." She put as much strength into her voice as she could.

"Now these Jon and Nathan guys. 'Jonathan,' right?"

She nodded. "They're all part of the same hydra. They call Brock their progenitor, since he's the original life form they came from and linked them all together."

"How many parts are there to this hydra?" Damien asked. "How many versions of Brock are running around?"

"Including Carey, there are eleven."

Chapter Five

"Eleven?" Damien repeated, his mind spinning. "There are eleven of those things running around the ranch?"

"Okay, first, they aren't 'things.'"

Vaughn glared up at him. He didn't back down. Didn't so much as flinch. It wasn't just that he wanted to hold his ground. He liked her being close. More than he wanted to admit.

"And second?" he prompted.

"Only seven of them are at the ranch," she said. "Counting Carey."

"Where the hell are the others?"

"Two in Paris, two at the loft."

The loft? That was what they called the Blades base in Cayman Beach.

"Let me guess," Damien said. "They run the place."

"Yeah, Bradley does. And to excellent effect. They may be dwellers, but they have always used their special abilities to keep us all safe. To keep *everyone* safe—dwellers, humans, and Blades. Brock and his replicants used to be linked up mentally. They were like a giant supercomputer."

"'Used to be.'"

"The mental load was physically killing Brock. Megan turned him into a werewolf to save his life. But when she did, it severed his connection to the others, as well as the link between each set of replicants. They all became trapped in their individual bodies."

"But you called them replicants. Are any of them their own person, or are they all just versions of Brock?"

"Usually, they start out as copies of Brock as he was when they emerged. It started when he was eighteen— that's when Dexter and Porter were... created, I guess. And it's happened every three years on Brock's birthday. One replicant body emerges from Brock, then that replicant splits into two. That's when it gets weird."

Damien's guts felt like they were twisting. He appreciated Vaughn trying to explain everything, but he didn't know how much more of this 'mental load' he could take.

"*That's* when it gets weird?" he said.

"The replicants start off as a snapshot of Brock at whatever age he was when they emerged. Even their personality. But after that moment, they evolve along their own paths."

She kept going, no longer even looking at Damien, though they stood close. Her hands were still on his shoulders. It was so tempting to reach out and rest his hands on her hips.

"Dexter and Porter never really lost that kind of cocky arrogance of youth," she said. "Bradley was the next pair, and he's the most fun-loving of them all. That makes sense, with Brock still doing well when they emerged. By the time Zachary came around, Brock's health was starting to decline. Zachary's always been more... reflective, I guess."

That fit what Damien knew of Zach and Carey. *Zachary.*

The elevator beeped softly. As the doors opened, Vaughn tightened her grip on Damien's shoulders and shifted closer, staring at the space beyond with wide eyes.

"You okay?" Damien asked, even though his own head was spinning.

"Yeah." She let out a little forced laugh. She seemed to finally realize she was practically leaning against him and stepped back. He tried to ignore the way his chest tightened at the increased space between them.

"Let's go," she said.

They exited into the biggest cavern Damien had ever seen. Lights were embedded in the walls and ceiling—which had to be seven stories high. Lamps stood on the ground in front of them. Every inch of the place was brightly lit. Damien would bet those were full-spectrum lights, Blades style. They would take out or repel any number of dwellers species. Vampires, specters, shades, and ghosts. Definitely Vaughn's design.

A trail had been cleared through hills of rubble. It wound in a curving path, not giving them a clear view of the cavern's far side. From what he could see of the ceiling, though, the cavern could hold several buildings in it. Vaughn wrapped her arms around her middle as they walked forward, her shoulders hunched and her eyes locked on her feet.

"Does your stomach hurt?" he asked, growing genuinely concerned.

"What?" She dropped her arms to her sides, but they remained clamped against her body. "No, I'm fine. The ship is on the far side of the cavern." She started off in a determined stride, but it wasn't long before she was hunching over again, her arms back around her waist and her gaze fixed downward.

"Hey." He reached out to touch her shoulder.

She yelped and lurched forward, crouching close to the ground. Somehow, she was even paler than before. Her lips were practically bloodless.

"It's all good." Damien held up his hands and backed up a step.

Vaughn let out a tense laugh, the whites visible all around her irises. He had seen that look before, but only during hunts that had gone way south.

"Yeah, right," she said. "Nothing to see here. Perfectly safe." She glanced around, her gaze locking on the ceiling. Her mouth opened and closed repeatedly, even though no sound came out.

"Vaughn." Damien stepped closer, not sure what the hell was going on.

"I'm going to fall," she murmured the words, as if she was speaking to herself, but her panic seemed to grow as she went on. "I'm going to fall. I'm going to fall. Nothing to stop me but gravity. What if it stops working? The ceiling's too high. I'll be killed."

"Vaughn!" Damien barked, hoping to snap her out of it.

She jerked at the loud tone, her gaze finally dropping to him, even though her eyes still held that somewhat crazed look. She shook her head, pinching her eyes shut and curling up with her head near the ground. Damien crouched next to her.

"What the hell is going on?" he asked, as gently as he could.

"Sorry." Her voice was thready. "The stress is... It must be worse than I thought."

"What stress?"

She let out a laugh that was sharp with sarcasm. Even still, his chest felt a little lighter at the sound.

"I mean, things seem pretty messed up here," he said. "You're going to have to narrow it down for me."

She started rocking back and forth. "I'm agoraphobic."

"What?"

"I'm afraid of large open spaces."

"I know what agoraphobic means," he said. "But...

we're in a cave."

She laughed again, softer this time. More authentic. "Tell that to my amygdalae." She curled into a tighter ball. "There's too much space. The trolls made the cavern so much bigger."

"Why would they do that?"

She shook her head. "They were being controlled. Ordered to dig out the ship. We don't know why."

That was scary as fuck.

"Did you get the person behind it?" he asked.

"The others think so."

"But not you."

"I want to know…" Her voice was shaky, her body trembling. Talking was costing her. "…who made the tech."

Damien looked around for anything or anyone that could help. All he saw were the mounds of rock surrounding them, three times as high as he was tall. The path between them was clear and wide enough to avoid risking being buried in an avalanche, but that very spaciousness was probably making Vaughn's reaction worse.

Help wasn't coming. He didn't even know how to call anyone. He only had himself. Hopefully, that would be enough. Damien leaned forward, pressing his chest to Vaughn's back and wrapping one arm around her.

She stiffened. "What are you doing?"

"You said the ceiling's too far and there's too much open space. I'm pretty solid."

"No kidding," she mumbled.

"What do you need me to do?"

"I don't know. The cavern's only been this big for a couple of days."

"Do you think you can make it?"

"If I keep my eyes shut, maybe." She snorted and shook her head. "The first time this happened, Dexter threw me over his shoulder and carried me to the ship."

"Sounds like a dick move," Damien said.

"That's pretty on-brand for Dexter."

People said, 'never meet your heroes.' Damien tried to quell his disappointment.

"Hang on a second." He put his hand on her back and stood. He pulled his shirt free, then tore a strip of fabric off the hem. He tucked his shirt in quickly, then bent over her. "Can you trust me?"

"Of course."

The way she agreed so readily made warmth spread through his chest. Whatever else was going on at the ranch, he was glad he at least had one person he could count on. One person who could count on him. Because that's all this was. Connecting with a person he could trust.

Yeah, right.

Damien gently looped the blindfold over Vaughn's eyes, then tied it snugly, but not too tight in the back, careful not to catch any of her hair. God, it was soft. She reached up and adjusted the blindfold a bit, then let out a breath. She didn't seem to be shaking as much.

"I'm not going to carry you, but I'll lead you to the ship," he said.

"Thanks. Just… Just give me a minute to psych myself up. Maybe ten."

"Here."

Damien knelt again. He took her arm and draped it across his shoulder. Slowly, he helped her stand, holding her wrist tight. He wrapped his other arm around her waist, keeping their sides pressed together.

Different circumstances…

He shook off the thought, angry with himself for even having it. Vaughn needed… He didn't even know what she needed. But she sure as hell didn't need to be hit on right now.

"Tell me about your ops room," Damien said. "Is it just like the one in the castle?"

"Yeah. We copied the design for both of the other bases. Well, except for my computer desk."

"How's that different?"

As she began to talk, he slowly started walking, urging her along.

"I don't really need a raised keyboard or track pad," she said. "My eyesight is pretty epic, as well as my… tactile capabilities."

He glanced over to see her waggling her eyebrows. She even had a little smile. Damn, maybe she did need a little flirting. If only he knew how to flirt.

Her eyebrows furrowed and she shook her head, frowning and angling her head away. "Sorry."

"Crow all you want," Damien said. "I want to know about all your skill sets."

She laughed, though he couldn't tell if it was a general release of tension or that she found his attempt at a flirty joke funny. At least she wasn't trembling anymore.

"Aside from the computer desk design, the ops rooms are all the same," she said. "Mostly monitors, white walls and floors."

"I've been meaning to ask about that. What's the deal with…"

His voice trailed off as they rounded a hill. Before them, the cavern stretched for hundreds of yards away. And a lot of that space was filled with a ship. An enormous ship.

Holy shit…

Damien didn't want to distract Vaughn and maybe have her relapse. But damn, he had even more questions than before. He kept moving them toward the ship, trying to take it all in.

The back of the ship had three huge, triangular panels that looked kind of like thrusters. The ship itself was of oblong design—gray metal dotted with red, blue, green, and white lights. If the rest of the cavern hadn't been flooded with the lamps the Blades had added, Damien was pretty sure he still would have been able to see by what the ship was putting off. There was a gaping hole in the front of the ship, the metal peeled away in jagged edges. Blue light skittered over the surface, like a force field in a sci-fi movie. Only this wasn't a movie. This was real.

"...really did make it a lot easier to see the individual parts of the dweller approaching us. Textures and colors would have made them harder to spot."

Vaughn had been talking the whole time. Damien tried to parse what she was saying, to remember his initial question.

The white walls. Right.

"So, if the white surfaces are to make it easier to spot dwellers, why are the holding areas a darker gray?" Damien asked.

"Ah, good question. It's because of the alloy I use to shield them. I can't get it to turn out white, and I don't want to risk having a double-layer that things can hide between."

What the hell was thin enough to hide between two layers of paneling? Damien held his question. They had reached the back of the ship.

"How do we get into this thing?" he asked.

"We're at the ship already?"

"I said I'd get you there."

"Wow. Thanks." She cleared her throat and nodded toward the cavern wall. "There should be a hatch on the starboard side about twenty yards from the thrusters."

Damien rotated her around to face the direction he assumed she had intended to indicate. There was a rectangular indentation that was roughly door-shaped, though it was probably ten-feet high and six across.

"I see it," he said.

He steered them to the door, regretting that once they reached it, he wouldn't have an excuse to keep her tucked against his side. He was enjoying having his arm wrapped around her waist way too much. When they stopped in front of the door, she reached out with her left hand and ran it over the door till she felt the edge. Damien let her go reluctantly, but kept a hand on her shoulder to let her know he was still close.

She placed her palm on a section of the hull that was a slightly duller gray. It was about twice the size of the hand scanners upstairs. The metal glowed, then the door slid up into the ship. He was about to step into an alien spaceship. Even after everything he'd seen on his own as a hunter and later with the Blades, he was having trouble believing this was real.

Vaughn stumbled inside, Damien close behind her. As soon as the door slid shut again, she tore off the blindfold. She looked around a little wildly, then leaned with her back against the wall and rested her head on it. Closing her eyes, she took several deep breaths. As much as he wanted to help her out, he couldn't keep his attention from the ship.

They were standing in a small room with wires dangling from the ceiling and panels removed from the walls. More wiring spilled out of the revealed sections—some of it spliced together, some tagged with labels he couldn't read from so far away. An open hatch revealed a hallway that led deeper into the ship. Damien could see other openings off the corridor. Even with light spilling out from doorways, the gray metal and dangling wires made everything seem dim and ominous. He'd seen too many sci-fi horror movies to relax even a little bit.

"Sorry for the mess." Vaughn swallowed a few times. "I'm still learning from everything. It's more organized than it looks."

"You sure there's nothing left on the ship?" he asked.

"There's plenty left. Tons. I've found anti-gravity systems, weapons, shield generators, thrusters. But I never found anything like a medical bay or research stations or..." She stopped when she opened her eyes and saw Damien's expression. "That's not what you meant, was it?"

He shook his head.

"Honestly, I don't know," she said.

The hairs on his arms and the back of his neck stood on end. If this ship was the source of the dwellers he'd been fighting most of his life, who knew what could be lurking in the enormous vessel. Damien did not want to be on the receiving end of any nasty surprises.

"But we've put in motion sensors and shielding," she hurriedly said. "If anything tries to get out of the ship or into this section that we're in, we should know about it."

"*Should,*" Damien repeated.

"I'm not perfect." She bit out each word, harsher than he had ever heard her speak.

"Could of fooled me." He hadn't meant to let the words slip out. He hoped she wouldn't hear, but apparently her vision wasn't the only epic sense she possessed.

"Right," she said. "After having to drag my sorry ass across the cavern just to get here."

There's nothing sorry about your ass.

He clenched his teeth to keep his thoughts to himself. He didn't want to slip up again.

"There's nothing wrong with needing help sometimes," he said.

"I have precisely one source of help that I can count on."

She reached into one of the pockets in her black cargo pants and pulled out a long, chrome cylinder. The tip was covered with a small dome of clear blue material. She pressed the side of the device, and it lengthened a few inches, the blue bit at the top lighting up.

Damien did not want to speculate about what that was

for.

"This is David," she said.

Was he supposed to introduce himself? Fuck, was that thing sentient?

"He's one of the first devices I made when I started reverse-engineering the technology from this ship." She frowned as she looked at the tool, her expression becoming wistful. "I still had time for fandoms back then." Her features hardened as she went on. "I don't have time for anything now except keeping people alive."

"That can't all be on you," Damien said. "You have the other Blades. Porter, Dexter, Marcus."

"Right." She let out a short laugh. "What kind of help should I need? I'm just the IT gal. All I do is make the gadgets and fix the toys and watch over the battles to make sure everyone comes home. Oh, and I guess I fix bodies now, what with the nanites and making Tessa's new arm. The only thing I can count on in this world is my tech."

Vaughn stepped away from the wall, her dark brows furrowed over those brilliant blue eyes. She was practically snarling as she went on.

"When Brock showed up *dying*, I was the one who had to keep everything together," she said. "I'm the one who sees the patterns. If he died, the Blades would break apart and *everyone* I care about would have fallen after him or become lost. Every single Blade."

"We would have kept the Blades going. *You* would

have kept us going."

"For how long?"

Damien shrugged. He had a hell of a lot more faith in Vaughn than he did in Brock.

"Dwellers always come after groups of hunters who've banded together," she said. "There's a 99.978 percent probability the only reason they've left the Blades alone is because every base is headed by a dweller. Now that the replicants are all in stasis, what if the hostile dwellers near our bases attack?"

A chill shot through his gut. His team at the castle had been benched until further notice—per Vaughn's orders—but Damien didn't know how long they'd actually listen to him before heading back to the field. What if that set off an attack?

"Yet another thing I have to figure out with the clock ticking away in my head." She tapped her device to her forehead, then waved it in the air as she went on. "'Fix the base, Vaughn.' 'We only have one replicator left, Vaughn.' 'I need something to track Jon and Nathan because they're being creepy, Vaughn.' 'There are a couple thousand holes leading from the surface into the cavern that need plugging, Vaughn.' 'The systems have been a little buggy since the fucking base exploded, Vaughn.'"

She started pacing back and forth in the small hallway. "I have to get everyone safely out of stasis and I barely even know how I figured out a way to get them *in* stasis.

And what if bringing them out kills Brock? What if it kills them?" She was barely taking a breath between words. "Tessa was being mind-controlled by a psycho werewolf from the moment she was turned and only just stopped trying to kill me—*very specifically me*—a couple of days ago. And I have no idea why I was targeted, aside from being a *curator*, whatever the hell that means. But before I could question the psycho werewolf, Jon and Nathan took care of him by ripping him into tiny pieces over several minutes while he was still alive. And since Brock can't see into Jonathan's head, I don't know if any of us can even trust him... them... whatever."

She stalked closer. "Now I have to convince *you* that we're the good guys to try to make sure none of the Blades run off to become hunters again, which will one-hundred percent end in their eventual deaths. Or worse, they might decide to keep fighting together and get killed even quicker. The replicants can't help me strategize or figure anything out now that they're 'diminished' since their links are broken."

She leaned in, getting right in Damien's face. "I have always existed in aphelion—the farthest orbital spot from the sun. Everyone else can go into the field or even just go outside, leaving me here. Leaving me behind at the base, but still somehow expected to be omnipresent during battles while keeping every fucking thing running here, there, and everywhere on the goddammed planet. So I ask you, Damien," Vaughn bit out his name. "Besides David, who is left to help me?"

As gorgeous as she was before, with her this worked up, ready to throw down... Christ, it was the hottest thing Damien had ever seen. He clenched his hands into fists to keep from grabbing her, crushing her to his chest, and kissing every burdensome thought out of her head. It would make him feel better. Hell, it might make her feel better, too. But everything she had unloaded was starting to register, bringing with it a sickening dread that he hadn't felt since he'd been hunting alone. They stood staring at each other, nose-to-nose, for several long moments, breath mingling.

"That's enough weight to crush anybody," Damien said. "Fuck the cavern. I don't know how you walk around anywhere without crumbling."

The lines between her eyebrows lessened. Her lips were still pulled in a frown, though. He tried hard not to stare at them. But that just left him looking into her eyes, like some love-struck kid. It was too hard to look away from them.

He put his hands on her shoulders, gripping them tight.

"I don't know how I can help you," he said. "I'm nowhere near smart enough to keep up. But I'm here and I want to help. And even if I can't, you can talk to me. You can trust me."

Chapter Six

Vaughn's heart pounded against her ribs. Her mouth was dry enough that she couldn't form words. If only she'd had that problem a few seconds ago. She couldn't believe how much she'd unloaded on Damien. Things she hadn't even told Marcus, and they were supposed to be best friends.

Damien leaned forward, pressing their foreheads together. The contact sent deep, thrumming waves of pleasure and reassurance through her body. She closed her eyes and focused on that feeling, trying to push everything away, to lock it back down where it wouldn't keep her from focusing on actually fixing the clusterfuck that was her life.

Finally, she found the strength to step back. Her heart was under control—at least physically. She didn't want to think about the ramifications of spilling her guts in front of Damien… and being accepted. Supported, even. No wonder everyone listened to him, if this was how he made them feel. Including Zachary.

"The stasis room is this way," she said, sliding David back into the pocket where he lived.

If Damien was disappointed that she didn't say more, he didn't show it. She turned and headed down the hall. They'd set up the stasis room as close to the hatch as possible. She entered the complicated series of commands that would unlock the DNA scanner that would then finally open the door—after deactivating her countermeasures. As soon as the ship had read the DNA and biometrics from her palm pressed against the scanner, the door slid open. Damien followed her into the room, glancing all around. He kept his back to the wall, angling his body so he could see the entire space. She couldn't fault his caution. He was a hunter, through-and-through.

The stasis pods were secured against the wall to the right of the door. Directly opposite the entrance, a much larger version was actually built into the ship. Wires and pipes fed into it, giving it power, sensor readings, and the ability to be filled with a bio-slurry that she and Porter had been working on to help with Brock's split. Brock had split earlier than anticipated, and they hadn't been able to use what Vaughn had simply dubbed 'the tank.'

Damien made his way to Zach's stasis pod. It was the only one that was illuminated, casting a soft blue-white light from the window she had built above the faces of whoever would be inside.

He stared intently at Zach for a few moments. "Why is his hair floating around his face?"

"Zero-G," Vaughn said.

Damien's gaze snapped over to her, that intense stare unnerving her a bit. "You weren't kidding about that."

"I want them to be in total stasis," she said. "Not even gravity is affecting them currently."

"You really think we'll get Carey back when Zach comes out of this?"

"I haven't given up on getting Carey back. In fact, I have some ideas for modifying the tank that might help the splitting process." She pointed at the huge stasis pod on the far wall.

Damien walked over to it. "Holy shit. This thing is huge."

"It's built to hold up to three bodies," she said. "We were hoping to use it for Brock's split, but didn't get it finished in time."

"Did you think he'd split even in stasis?"

There Damien went, asking the good questions.

"We were actually envisioning what might happen when he came out of stasis," she said. "The replicants and I worked up a formula for a liquid that holds bio-matter that might have helped Brock create the latest replicant without as much drain on his body—and then help that replicant with their own split."

"So, if you put Zach in here…"

She shrugged. "Hopefully, we can coax him into splitting by providing his body with everything he'd need for it. That's the theory, anyway."

A theory that she would be testing on her own, since Porter and the others had ceased being a biological supercomputer. Maybe she could build her own to help... But that would take time, and she had other priorities at the moment. Too many glitches to track down and fires to put out. She added it to the ever-growing list of projects that could help the Blades.

"We've never lost a Blade," she said. "I don't intend to lose one now."

Damien shook his head. "We have lost Blades. Dozens of them, from what I can tell."

"What do you mean?"

He was quiet for a moment, then said, "Threat level red."

"What?"

"Zach always pulled us back from those. Sent Carey instead. Carey would tell me it was above my pay grade and to let him handle it." Damien lowered his head, his voice barely above a whisper. "You sent in Brock's replicants to die in our place."

Their was no accusation in his words, but they still stung.

Vaughn wanted to defend herself, to let Damien know that it hadn't been long since she was brought in on the whole 'hydra' thing. She'd been just as in the dark as the other Blades about their bosses' dweller natures. But this wasn't about her. It wasn't even about Damien. It was about Brock and Dexter and Porter and Zachary and all the others who put themselves on the line to keep the rest of the Blades safe. If that didn't convince Damien that he was working with the good guys, she didn't know what would.

"It was their choice," she said.

"How many times did he not come back without us even knowing it?"

She knew Damien was asking about Carey. She also knew the number, and since she had been brought in on their secret, she knew all the gruesome details. She really wished she didn't, though.

"I don't have all the answers." She shrugged. "I'm just the IT guy. Gal."

The furrow between Damien's brows deepened. Instead of arguing the point—which was really kind of a relief for her—he said, "What will it take for it to be safe to put Zach in the tank?"

She thought through her list. "Well, we have to finalize the biofluid formula, test out the tank's integrity, and then figure out what sort of energy we should bombard Zach's body with to trigger the split. Brock has a unique quantum signature we'll need to replicate."

Damien nodded. "But we have to make sure the ranch is safe first. Plug those holes and—" he looked around the room, "secure the ship."

"Zach is safe here," she said. "This room is one of the safest places on the ranch. Hell, on the whole planet.

Between the ship's shielding and what I've done to the place, you don't have to worry about him."

"Then let's get to work. What's first?"

The access tunnels leading to the cavern were being addressed and sublevel 2 was getting cleared out. All of the replicants were safe in their stasis pods and the other Blades bases were on lockdown. The glitches were disturbing, but she could iron them out as they finished repairs to all the rest of the systems. That just left the two unidentified bogies actively trying to kill them.

"We still need to figure out what attacked you," Vaughn said. "I think it's safe to assume it has a pretty high threat level to the general populace. And we have to track down the source of the tech that was used to control the trolls and blow up sublevel 2."

"Is that all?" Damien said, his tone dry. "Megan mentioned a collar."

"Yeah, remember that psycho werewolf I mentioned?"

"The one that was mind-controlling Tessa into trying to kill you?"

Wow, he really has been paying attention.

Vaughn nodded. "He sent in Megan wearing a collar that let him see and hear everything going on around her."

"A collar," Damien said. "On a werewolf."

"There's a reason Jon and Nathan killed him the way they did." Vaughn still shuddered at the thought. "The collar was also a bomb. We managed to get it off of her before it blew, but when it did, it took out sublevel 2."

"I can see why you want to know where it came from."

"But the thing that attacked you is active right now," she said. "There's nothing in the Dwellers Database that matches it. I barely know where to start."

One of the lights next to the door flickered green before returning to its usual blue-tinged white. It happened so quickly, she wasn't quite sure she hadn't imagined it. She shook off the feeling of unease. The ship was safe. Her tech was safe. If she lost that anchor point in her life, she had no idea what she'd do.

"How about we ask around?" Damien said.

"Ask who?"

He half-shrugged. "Got any goblins in town? Those guys are always up on the latest gossip."

"True, but... Wow, you really have studied the database."

"It's part of the job."

"Yeah, but most Blades only read up on the threats. Goblins are greenlit. They rarely attack humans."

"Which is why I asked if you have any in town. Or does 'finding a way for dwellers and humans to peacefully coexist' mean we just ignore the ones that aren't threats?"

She shook her head. "We have worked with dwellers before."

Damien cocked an eyebrow.

"Ones that aren't on the team," she added. "And yes,

there's at least one goblin living in Providence. He's made a den in an abandoned apartment building near the pier."

"So, we stop by and ask him if there are any new players around. We can ask about the dweller and the collar."

"The Blades aren't exactly well-received among the dweller community," she said. "I mean, we have Dexter working with us."

"Yeah, but Dexter won't be there. I will."

Vaughn felt as though her stomach filled with ice. "No. No way. We just almost lost you."

"And now you're planning on keeping me benched?"

That's exactly what she was planning. She didn't think he would appreciate that, though.

"Only for a little while," she said.

"Your nanites have fixed me up better than new."

"And we still don't fully understand how they're affecting you."

Damien shook his head. "Look, if you really want to convince me that we're the good guys here, we need to step it up. People are in danger out there."

"I can send Marcus and Tessa."

"Tessa," he repeated, his tone flat.

"Okay, maybe not Tessa."

"The replicants can't do it, even if they were at full strength. Nobody's going to talk to Dexter or someone that looks like him." Damien was quiet for a moment, then said, "You told me you need help. Let me help."

Vaughn jumped as a new voice joined them from the open doorway.

"It's a good plan," Brock said.

"I thought you were working on sublevel 2." She was surprised at the bite to her own tone.

Brock was supposed to be working, not coming down to the ship and interrupting... Well, okay, he wasn't really interrupting anything. But a gal could dream.

"I'm taking a break." Brock walked over to Zach's stasis pod and stared through the window. "I wanted to check on my brother."

He lifted his hand toward the glass. Vaughn quickly moved next to the pod.

"I wouldn't do that if I were you," she said.

"We're not supposed to touch the pod?" Brock scowled. "You should have told us all that."

"Only you shouldn't touch the pod," she said. "You're still putting off quantum energy. It's nothing like the levels before your split, but it's there. I don't know how it will interact with Zach or the pod or the others or—"

Brock cut in. "I get it." He turned back to Damien, and said, "You have a good plan. And you're right. You need to see us in action to decide how you really feel about the Blades."

Was it her imagination, or had Damien's eyes flicked toward her when Brock said that?

"Meg and I will go with you," Brock said. "Goblins don't normally attack humans, but they're still very territorial."

"It'll be too suspicious to have a human running around with a pair of werewolves." Vaughn felt a zing of hope at the thought. It was a good argument.

So was Damien's response.

"You have all this tech lying around and you can't make a pair of colored contacts?" He raised an eyebrow at her, and damn if it didn't feel like a challenge.

"Colored contacts?" she said. "That's your solution?"

Damien nodded. "And grass clippings. The latest report said that messes with most dweller's sense of smell."

"It's a goblin, Vaughn," Brock said, a definite challenge in his tone. "We can handle it."

"If it makes you feel any better, you can trick them out for me," Damien said. "Maybe make them mini versions of those glasses you want us to wear in the field."

Okay, that was a really good idea. Her mind immediately started spinning with designs for a badass set of contacts for him. She could work the full interface into them, projecting a view screen into his field of vision. As more schematics materialized in her brain, she realized these could be incredibly useful in the field for all the Blades' bases. Even more useful than the glasses. For all her issues with her own eccentricities, this was the part she loved. When she came up with something genuinely cool that would keep the people she cared about safe.

All hail the IT gal!

And Brock had a point about them being able to handle a goblin. Hell, Damien could handle a dweller of that level on his own, given the right tech. He must have taken her lack of an immediate response as a concession because he turned back to Brock.

"We need to bring an offering," Damien said. "A goblin won't give us information for nothing."

Brock nodded. "Okay, then. Meg and I will get cleaned up and meet you in the garage."

"Wait, you're going now?" Vaughn gasped.

"Repairs are going well," Brock said. "Jon and Nathan will keep working on sublevel 2. Dexter and Porter are ready to deploy your innovative solution for plugging the tunnels, so that'll be done within the hour. Marcus and Tessa are helping Eli repair the infirmary."

"But…" Vaughn tried to come up with another reason to delay the mission, but Brock had cut off all her excuses. He might not have access to all those other brains, but he was still plenty smart on his own. And Vaughn was tired.

"Do you have a reason we should put it off?" Brock smirked at her as if he knew the answer already.

Because I'm not ready to see Damien head into danger again?

This was happening, whether she liked it or not. She turned her thoughts to ways of protecting Damien in the field.

"I need to get to my lab if I'm going to make those contacts before you go," she said.

"Sounds good." Brock cocked his head toward the door. "I want a minute alone with Zach, if you don't mind."

"Fine," she said. "Just be sure to initiate all the security protocols before you leave."

Brock glared at her.

"Which, of course, you know to do." She sighed. "Sorry. I'm just tired."

"You're stalling," Brock said. "You made it here. You can make it back."

Vaughn considered flipping Brock off, but Damien reached out and gripped her elbow, turning her toward the door.

"Let's go," Damien said.

They didn't say another word until they had reached the hatch. Damien pulled out the blindfold again. Before he could put it on, Vaughn grabbed his wrists. She searched his eyes, looking for answers.

"You don't have to go," she said.

"I know. And you don't have to blame yourself if anything happens to me."

Her stomach felt like it had bottomed out again. Her grip went lax. Damien placed the blindfold over her eyes. It was probably her imagination working overtime again, but it felt like he lingered a bit, the warmth of his body, his breath, seeping into her. He gripped her shoulders gently and turned her toward the hatch. They stepped out together, Damien turning his body to help guide her into the cavern's terrain.

Would it be too obvious if she 'tripped' and fell into him?

Probably.

The hatch let out its usual soft whoosh as it slid shut. Once again, Damien wrapped his arm around her waist and drew her arm over his shoulder. Under different circumstances, she would be thrilled. It had been a long time since she'd dated. But these were the circumstances. This was her life. They headed back, presumably in the direction of the elevator. Above, she heard the distinctive whump-whump-whump of the hoverbikes. Two, from the sound of it. She heard a couple of pops, then a fizzing noise.

"They could have waited for us to get to the elevator before starting to fill the tunnels," she muttered.

"I don't think they're paying any attention to us."

The back of Damien's head brushed against her arm as he craned his neck to look toward the ceiling. Vaughn wanted to take off the blindfold and look at what he was seeing, but even imagining it was making her nervous.

"You really do keep the best toys here," Damien said. "Tell me about the contacts you're going to make me."

"They'll be gold, of course." She was pretty sure he was just trying to keep her mind occupied, which was absolutely fine. "And they'll need to be able to glow like a werewolf's."

"Obviously."

She paused, trying to discern if that was a joke. Damien seemed to possess a dry kind of humor. She wished she could see his face—for many reasons. The sooner they reached the elevator, the better.

"I'm thinking they should also have the detector grid installed," she said. "With scanners to identify dwellers."

"You can get that done in half an hour?"

"I can get that done in ten minutes. I also need to install a camera in them, though, with a strong feed connecting the data stream to the ranch."

"So, fifteen minutes, then?"

Vaughn laughed. "Plus another ten to make sure there are plenty of safety protocols included. Lux inhibitors for bright flashes, shielding to make sure the signal doesn't have any unexpected consequences for you."

"Unexpected consequences?"

"It's alien tech. I'm still figuring out how it interacts with human anatomy. Like with the nanites."

Damn, she had almost been feeling better until she remembered those. How was she going to get them out of Damien? The extractor should have worked, but it had glitched out. Yet another of her tools that didn't seem to be working right. No matter what else had been going on in her life, she had always been able to count on her tech. What if that was changing? Or worse, what if *she* was slipping?

It could be exhaustion, but it wasn't like she'd ever really been much of a sleeper. Sure, it had been... She wasn't sure how many days she'd been awake. But she felt fine. Mostly. Physically tired, sure. Emotionally and mentally drained... Well, yeah. But she was fine. She could handle this. All the stress was probably making it seem like things were worse than they were. She shook off the misgiving. It was just the blast making her tech a bit off. They had lost an entire sublevel from it. That was more than enough to explain the issues.

"We're here." Damien paused. After a moment, Vaughn heard the elevator doors slide open.

Surprisingly, she wasn't as eager to get inside as she expected. Sure, once they were in, she could take off the blindfold and stare at Damien to her heart's content. Okay, maybe until he thought it was creepy. But they wouldn't have a reason to be close anymore. The strength of the pang that zinged through her chest was another surprise.

Damien led him inside and the doors slid shut again. Instead of stepping away, he turned her so her back was to the wall. Even without seeing him, she could sense how close he was. The zing it was bringing on was just as strong as the other, but could end up being a lot more embarrassing. It did *not* zing through her chest.

Her cheeks burned, the flush spreading down her neck as other parts of her anatomy sparked to life. She started calculating variations of Brock's quantum signature as Damien removed the blindfold, trying to think about anything other than his closeness, his warmth and strength. Once it was off, she could see how close they were standing. Very close.

Damien pressed his hands against the wall behind her, pinning her in place. His dark gaze was so intense, she wanted to shift away—or wrap her arms around his waist and pull him closer.

"It's not all on you," he said.

"I know that."

"No, you don't. You know a lot—you're the smartest person I've ever met. But you don't know everything. You can't control everything. Not with your tech. Not with your mind." He said his next words emphasizing each one. "It's. Not. All. On. You."

Her eyes started to sting. If she cried in front of him this soon, she would never get over it. And she'd certainly not get over grabbing his sizable ribs and sobbing into his chest. Not an option.

"You say the sweetest things," she said. She'd meant it as a semi-true joke, but her voice came out raspy and tense. So much for lightening the mood. She cleared her throat and looked away. "If I'm going to get those contacts made, we should go."

Damien lingered for a few moments longer, then backed away. As she turned toward the control panel for the elevator, her heart sank even more. No matter what he said, she did feel responsible for everyone. And the more she was growing to care about Damien, the more was on the line.

Chapter Seven

"This is it." Megan pointed to a large brick building with boarded-up windows and a sagging roof.

Damien slowed the van and angled toward the curb. The lots on either side of the apartment building were vacant. Bits of withered scrub and brush dotted the ground, along with piles of trash here and there. The goblin could be hiding behind any one of them.

As soon as they were parked, Brock said, "Nice place."

"It has a lot of potential." Megan leaned toward the window, which put her closer to Damien. He did everything he could not to flinch.

It wasn't just that she was a werewolf. Not anymore, at least. The van was only dimly lit, and seeing her features silhouetted against the street outside just highlighted how much she looked like Tammie.

"Oh, sorry," Megan said, backing away quickly. "Personal space. I forgot."

Brock gripped her waist and pulled her onto his lap. "Werewolves aren't great with boundaries." He nuzzled her neck and she giggled.

Damien wanted to yank her away and shove Brock to

the street, even though they were mated. It was like being married. Stronger, even. But Damien still wanted to yell at Brock, asking what his intentions were. He had to get this under control. Megan was not Damien's sister.

Turning back to the building, Damien said, "Show some decorum, huh?"

"He's right." Megan sat up straighter. "We should behave. This is my first time in the field. I don't want to mess it up."

"We're supposed to be werewolves," Brock said, pulling her close and nuzzling her neck again. "Werewolves are affectionate."

Damien couldn't stop himself. He turned to face them and said, "If she wants you to back off, you better back the fuck off."

Everyone stilled. The energy in the van intensified a thousandfold in a split-second. Had he really just challenged an alpha werewolf... whatever-the-fuck Brock was?

Yeah. Yeah, he had. And he'd do it again.

Brock met Damien's gaze, one eye glowing bright gold and the other crackling with that eerie blue. It seemed to be putting off more sparks than usual.

"Well, this is going well." Vaughn's sudden voice in Damien's earpiece almost made him jump.

"It's okay," Megan said.

"If you tell him to stop, he stops." Damien knew he

was digging himself in deeper and did not give a single shit.

"He will," Megan said.

Damien returned his glare to Brock, knowing that holding eye contact was a challenge.

Part of this mission was a test. Damien needed to know if these really were 'the good guys.' If Brock couldn't control his werewolf nature enough to respect Megan's wishes, Damien would kill the guy on principle or die trying—which was much more likely.

"So, Vaughn here on our private channel," she said. "The feed is coming in great and I can see everything you can. Plus this overlay that I'm activating for you now."

A grid flickered over Damien's vision. Megan and Brock glowed bright red. At least, their bodies did. Brock's left eye socket—the one that held the white eye with the blue pupil—was pitch black around the edges, but glowed an intense white at the center. It was getting brighter.

"You really might want to drop your gaze," Vaughn said.

She had given Damien a crash course on subvocalizing before they left the ranch, so they could speak privately if needed. Now seemed as good a time as any to give it a try.

"No."

Starting simple. That was the way to go.

Brock smiled, his teeth gleaming in the light. His canines looked pretty damn sharp.

"Part of me wants to knock you out of the van and rip open your chest," Brock said.

Damien's heartbeat picked up at the thought. He knew he was no match for Brock.

"And the other part?" Damien asked.

Brock's smile broadened. Then he turned away, breaking eye contact first. He opened the passenger's door and slid to the ground, bringing Megan with him and setting her gently on her feet.

"You have our housewarming gift?" Brock's tone was light, as if nothing had passed between them.

"Yeah," Damien said.

"Good." Brock gestured for Megan to precede him, then slammed the passenger's door shut. He looked at Damien through the closed window for a moment, his smile still in place.

What the hell did it mean?

"I think he likes you," Vaughn said.

"Great." Damien opened the door and slid to the ground, positioning the small messenger's bag draped across his shoulder so that it wouldn't be in his way if he had to pull any of his weapons. He shut the door behind him, then followed Brock and Megan across the street.

The building was in even worse shape up close. Boards criss-crossed the front door, sealing it tight. The wood had been decorated with a bunch of really weird graffiti.

"You getting a good look at this?" Damien

subvocalized.

"Yeah." Vaughn's voice had taken on the semi-distant note that he had figured out meant she was distracted by data.

The grid was still superimposed over Damien's vision, but the lines were faint enough that they wouldn't interfere with his ability to fight if he had to. Damien couldn't see Brock and Megan's heat signatures anymore, either. Instead, lines of data started scrolling along the side of his view. It looked like there was a transparent computer screen floating a few feet away in front of him and offset a bit so his vision remained clear.

Data scrolled across the screen constantly—the angle of the boards, their density, how much pressure would need to be applied to various places to pry them off or smash them. Brock probably didn't need the data to know he could smash through the doors or even pull off the boards with his bare hands. He reached out to grab one.

"We shouldn't go in this way," Damien said.

Brock cocked his head to the side, then turned to look at Damien.

"Why not?" Brock said.

"Front doors are for humans," Damien said. "And goblins are territorial."

"He's right." Megan reached out and grasped Brock's arm. "If there are traps, they'll be here."

"I'm not worried about goblin traps," Brock said.

"Are you worried about pissing him off?" Damien said. "Because if we break down his front door and waltz through his defenses, we're weakening his den and creating a bunch of cleanup work for him."

"You're right." Brock let go of the board and stepped back. He looked up the building, then back to Damien and smiled. "Want to try the roof? I can give you a boost."

"I'll take the fire escape," Damien said.

"On this building?" Brock shook his head. "Daring."

"We'll make sure it's safe first." Megan headed toward the side of the structure. Damien let Brock go first, then followed.

Megan was standing beneath the ladder when they reached her. She stared up at the rusted metal bolted to the side of the aging building. Maybe the fire escape wasn't such a good idea. Damien craned his neck to look all the way up the zig-zagging deathtrap. It seemed like it was still moored okay. A small dish was attached at the top level, five stories up.

"Is that a satellite dish?" Brock asked.

The computer display hovering in Damien's vision centered in on the dish, then gave him a zoomed in picture of it. He didn't need the analysis to tell him it was a receiver for TV.

"Now we know what he does for entertainment," Damien said.

"Let's introduce ourselves." Megan leapt ten feet

straight into the air and grabbed the fire escape's ladder with one hand, then hung there. She gripped it with her other hand and started jerking her body back and forth.

"It's stuck." She grunted. "I can't…"

Brock laughed lightly, then grabbed one of her legs to still her. "You want to give us a hand?"

Damien approached cautiously, not sure what Brock wanted him to do. He nodded toward Megan and said, "Grab her other leg and pull."

Damien couldn't believe Brock was actually giving him permission to touch his mate. From what Damien knew of werewolves, touching the alpha female that way wouldn't even be tolerated within the pack.

"Brock," Megan said. "Damien has space issues with werewolves. Don't be mean."

"I'm not being mean," Brock said. "I'm being a team player."

Damien scowled at him. So that was his game, huh? Damien decided to call Brock's bluff. He reached up and gently grasped Megan's leg just above her knee.

"You don't have to help," she said. "Brock's just being… Brock."

The other man grinned at Damien. "You did want to see what we're like."

Vaughn's voice joined the conversation through their earpieces. "In that case, I should make a joke about pulling Megan's leg."

Brock and Megan both laughed. Damien wasn't quite there yet.

"On three," Damien said.

Megan started the count. "One, two, three!"

They pulled on her legs, and the ladder broke free.

So did the fire escape.

The computer screen in Damien's view flashed bright red warnings, arrows and diagrams pointing out the structural weaknesses that had just given out—and showing the entire structure about to come crashing down on them.

"Run," Damien yelled, pulling harder on Megan. She just stared down at him quizzically.

"Why?" Brock said.

Both werewolves jerked their heads toward the building just before Damien heard the first groan of metal.

"That's why," he said.

Megan dropped to the ground, and he grabbed her hand, pulling her after him. Which was stupid, because she could run way faster than he could. He glanced over his shoulder to see the fire escape lean away from the building, bricks raining down around it. Of course, it was falling in their direction.

Damien wrapped his arm around Megan's shoulders, urging her in front of him. They made it around the corner at the front of the building just as the fire escape crashed to the ground. He blocked as much of her body as he could, just in case some of the debris ricocheted in their direction. The satellite dish rolled out into the street, circling a few times before falling flat on its side.

"So much for not making a mess," Brock said.

"Is everyone okay?" Vaughn's voice sounded in Damien's ear again.

"Ta—" Damien shook himself. "Megan? You okay?"

"I'm fine." She smiled up at him, her eyes glowing dimly. "Thanks for looking out for me."

"Even though it was completely unnecessary," Brock said.

Megan turned to him and scowled.

"What?" Brock shrugged. "It's not like the fire escape was made of silver or anything."

Damien stood. He realized he was still holding onto Megan's elbow and quickly let her go, then stepped away.

"I'm fine, too, by the way," Brock said.

"Congratulations." Damien stepped around the side of the building to survey the damage.

The goblin was going to be pissed.

"We should have brought a better gift," Megan said.

"Oh yeah." Brock's voice dripped with sarcasm. "This is much better than going in the front."

Damien ignored him. The computer display from his contacts highlighted a section of wall. Angles and equations flashed next to it.

"Vaughn, you want to help me out here?" Damien

subvocalized.

"The fire escape falling has weakened that section of wall," she said. "You should be able to kick it in without causing any dangerous structural damage."

They'd already messed the place up so much. What was a little more? Damien walked over to the area and kicked it. The bricks fell away, grit and bits of mortar raining down from the new opening. He used his elbow on the bricks around the edges, grateful for the reinforced plating in the black leather jacket he was wearing. When he'd made a big enough hole for them to pass through, he turned back to the others. Megan's mouth was hanging open and Brock's eyebrows raised.

"You been working out, Damien?" Brock said.

Damien shrugged. "Vaughn's tech."

"All hail the IT gal," Vaughn said.

Damien wasn't sure if the comment had been just for him or on the party line until Megan and Brock laughed. It irked him somehow that they'd been included. They were on a fucking mission. Damien shouldn't be wanting Vaughn to himself.

"Any way you can make it clear when you're talking just to me?" Damien subvocalized.

Vaughn sounded a little uncertain when she replied. "Uh, sure. I could use a voice filter for our private conversations."

Damien didn't want that. He liked Vaughn's voice.

"Oh, or I can add a special signal to your contacts' display so you know when I'm talking to you directly," she said.

"That one."

A smiley-face icon appeared in the corner of the display. "How's this work for you?" she said.

Damien barely kept himself from letting out a chuckle.

"You two done?" Brock said.

Damien stiffened. He didn't have a lot of practice subvocalizing, but thought he was managing well enough to have some privacy.

"Don't worry, we weren't listening in." Brock headed for the opening in the wall.

"Then how'd you know?" Damien asked.

"You need a better poker face." Brock smirked, then ducked through the hole and vanished into the darkness of the building.

Megan started to follow, but paused next to Damien.

"Thanks for what you did back there," she said. "Trying to help me with the fire escape."

"Sure."

"But don't do it again, okay?" She reached for his arm, then flinched and quickly drew her hands back, clasping them together in front of her. "I don't want you getting hurt trying to protect me. I'm a lot tougher than I seem. I heal faster than any of the others."

"That doesn't mean I'm okay with you getting hurt,"

Damien said.

Her eyes widened and she smiled, sucking in a breath. Whatever she had been about to say, she kept it in. He could relate.

"We should go." She gestured to the opening Damien had made.

He nodded, then headed for the building. He ducked into the dark space within.

The scent of mildew and mold hit him strongly, along with even less pleasant smells. He reached for the flashlight that was built into the sleeve of his jacket, not wanting to step in anything he was smelling. Before he could switch it on, the computer display from his contacts flickered. The room around him appeared to be bathed in blue light. It was dim, but with the grid overlay, Damien could see everything clearly.

He stood slowly. "Whoa."

Brock's eyes gleamed across the space. The fizzing energy that popped out of the blue one was even more apparent in the darkness.

"Are you going to turn on your light?" Megan asked, joining him.

"I don't need it," Damien said. He pointed to his eyes.

Megan laughed. "All hail the IT gal."

This time, Damien couldn't suppress a laugh.

"Come on." Brock angled his head toward a doorframe that still had hinges attached to one side, but no door.

"There's a staircase over here. It's probably trapped, but we've busted up this guy's house already."

"We should offer to fix the damage," Vaughn said. No smiley-face, so this was the public channel.

"I don't think that's a good idea," Megan said.

It was the damndest thing. Damien could hear her in his earpiece, but nothing from standing right next to her. He couldn't wait till they had earpieces like this at his own base. If he still had a base to go back to when this was done.

He had to remember that he had his own mission here. He knew he wanted the tech, but did he really want to be a Blade? Would any of the others, once they found out about the secrets their leaders had been keeping?

"Why not?" Vaughn asked.

"These are fairies," Megan said. "We shouldn't get in too deep with them."

"I thought you said dwellers were aliens," Damien said.

"They are." Megan let out a frustrated sigh—the only sound she made as they worked their way down the hall. "But the legends humans developed around them are there for a reason. Making deals with dwellers is a bad idea."

"Present company excluded?" Damien said.

Megan stopped, then turned toward him, a stricken expression on her face. He almost felt bad for the crack. Almost.

"That's—" Megan's lips moved as she spoke, her

earpiece apparently forgotten. The floor collapsed beneath her. She let out a shriek as Damien lunged for her. He wasn't fast enough to catch her, and she disappeared through the opening.

"Meg!" Brock yelled as he jumped after her.

"Damien, don't you dare." Vaughn's voice was commanding. The smiley-face flashed into a frown.

Yeah, *that* wasn't distracting.

"Give me a moment to get some readings before you follow them," she said.

Damien scanned the floor, the walls, the ceiling with his gaze, trying to get Vaughn the data she needed. The computer display fed it all to Damien, too. There were a few other spots where the wood in the flooring had rotted enough to weaken the structure. Where Megan had fallen, though, the floor was reinforced.

"Hold your gaze right there," Vaughn said.

Damien did as he was instructed. His eyes started to ache, like the mother of all eye strain coming on all at once, but he didn't say anything. The flooring became transparent in his vision. He could see the tunnel where Megan had fallen and Brock had followed. It looked like a hollow tree. There were even branches or roots or something twining under the floorboards and creeping up the walls.

"What the hell..."

The floor beneath Damien's feet shook as the tree

moved, the roots in the floorboards pulling its massive trunk toward him.

"Shit!" He jumped over the new hole that appeared beneath his feet.

"Damien, get out of there," Vaughn said. "We have no idea what this is. I'm sending reinforcements."

Even on their bikes, it would take too long for anyone to get there to help. Damien wasn't leaving Megan in that tree thing. For all he knew, it was eating her. His stomach flipped at the thought. So did his ability to reason.

With the tree in a new spot, he could see a basement through the first hole in the floor the tree had made. Damien jumped for it. A splintered board scraped his arm on the way down and he hit the floor hard. His ankle sent a jolt of pain through him and he fell to his side.

"Damien!" Vaughn yelled.

Damien pushed himself up, vaguely registering that the basement's floor was made of packed earth. That was bad. Lots of dwellers could push up through packed earth. His ankle and arm tingled where he'd been injured. He ran his hand over the blood on the bit of his forearm exposed from where his jacket had been pushed up when he was scratched and saw nothing but smooth skin beneath. Cautiously testing his ankle, he added more weight to it till he could tell it was fine, too. Vaughn's nanites doing their work.

All hail the IT gal.

Damien could kiss Vaughn right now. For a lot of reasons. He shook his head to clear it. He might look and even heal like a werewolf, but he was still human.

"Bad dog." A crackling, deep voice came from behind him.

Damien wheeled around, palming a knife. He kept the blade hidden along his forearm.

Bad dog?

It took him a minute to remember his disguise.

"Vaughn, amp the glow on my contacts," Damien subvocalized.

"Done."

He wasn't sure how she managed it, but even though Damien could see the light from his contacts illuminating his surroundings, it didn't blind him.

"Release my pack," Damien said.

"Not until I'm sure you ain't gonna pee on my carpets," the voice said.

Damien curled up his lip and let out the closest sound to a growl he could manage.

"Down, boy."

"Goblin!" Damien shouted.

"Werewolf!" it shouted back.

Damien took a deep breath and let it out slow. He had to act the part, which meant he had to remember what werewolves were like. Real werewolves—not these weird, polite Blade versions. He pulled up the memory that he kept buried as deep as he could. Him and Tammie, huddled in the cabinet under the stairs, peeking out at the things that had killed everyone else in their family. Watching them fight over… scraps.

He shook his head again, a scream building in his chest. He channeled all the rage and horror of it into his voice, crouching low and spinning in a circle.

"Release my pack!"

"Criminy, keep it down," the goblin said. "Scarecrow is trying to sleep."

Something moved in the corner. Damien wanted to throw his knife at it, but held himself back.

Vaughn's voice came over the earpiece. "I was able to get through to Brock and Megan. There's a lot of interference, but they're okay. Just cramped. As long as they don't try to escape, the tree doesn't squeeze them. We don't want to antagonize this group. We can talk the goblin into releasing them and then I want you all to get the hell out of there."

Through gritted teeth, Damien subvocalized, "Not without what we came for."

Chapter Eight

Shit. Damien was losing it. Vaughn should never have allowed him to go along on this mission. Walking into an unknown dweller's den. What the hell was she thinking?

"'It's just a goblin,'" Vaughn parroted. "'We can handle it. Damien will be fine.'"

She blew out a breath. She had to get them back safely. All of them.

At least her nanites were working as expected. Hell, they were working beyond anything she'd dreamed. By her calculations, Damien's ankle had to have snapped when he jumped down into the goblin's den, but he was walking around just fine. And the feed from the contacts showed him wiping blood off his arm to show unmarred skin beneath. She hated that he had endured pain, but was thrilled that her tech had repaired him so quickly.

What else are they doing to him in there, though?

She pushed the thought away. Her focus had to stay on the mission. She'd figure things out when everyone was safely back at the ranch. She opened the private channel with Damien, keeping her voice utterly calm.

"Make the offer in exchange for the others, then get

out," she said.

Damien ignored her. Instead, he said, "The rest of the pack is on the way. You have three seconds to let our alphas out or we will tear this building down around your ears."

She would have closed her eyes, but she was riveted to the monitor with the feed from Damien's contacts.

"Or you could antagonize him some more, I suppose," she said.

The contacts picked up movement as something huge rolled toward Damien from a corner. At first, she thought it was a boulder, but there were spines all over it, pressed flat against its surface. It stopped in front of Damien, then popped open... like a hedgehog.

The goblin peered up at Damien with glittering, completely black eyes. He slapped his hands against the smooth sides of his head, and said, "What ears?"

Damien growled. He was really getting into his role, which was almost the scariest part. Vaughn had read his file. She knew what had happened to his family. Christ, he was going to need so much therapy after this...

The goblin grinned, a broad smile stretching his already distended face and revealing rows of sharp, serrated teeth. "Werewolves got no sense of humor."

"I want my pack."

"And I want my house in one piece." The goblin gestured around them. "Mostly. You're the ones who busted in here. I ain't lettin' anyone go till I know you're gonna stop chewing on the furniture."

That was all?

"Tell him we're just here to talk," Vaughn said.

"We don't give a fuck about your furniture." Damien stepped closer to the goblin, towering over the much shorter being.

"Then what do you want?" The spines covering the goblin's back stood up, again reminding Vaughn of a giant, really ugly hedgehog.

"You're a goblin," Damien said. "We're werewolves. Why do you think we're here? We want information."

The goblin's eyes widened briefly, then he sort of settled back down into himself. "Why didn't you just freakin' say so?"

He curled into a ball again and rolled over to the tree. When he reached it, he popped up and knocked on the trunk three times. "Spriggan. Open up."

"Spriggan?" Vaughn sat up straighter in her chair. "That's a spriggan?"

The tree's trunk split open and spread like a curtain. Brock and Megan stumbled out. Brock glanced around the room quickly, keeping Megan in his arms. She actually smiled when she saw the goblin.

"Oh, hi," Megan said.

The goblin snorted.

Behind them, the tree started to shrink. Its roots pulled

up from the packed dirt floor and its branches retreated from the exposed beams supporting the level above. Massive bursts of energy accompanied the changes, but they were outside the visual spectrum even for Brock and Megan. Vaughn's contacts were another story.

"Damn," Damien said, taking a step back.

When the spriggan was done transforming, it looked like a four-foot tall... stick. It was a couple inches around and had spindly branches coming off of it about where arms and legs would be.

"Geeze, that really took it out of me, Johnny," the spriggan said.

Johnny?

"Then get back in your pot." The goblin hooked a gnarled thumb at a large terracotta pot sitting beneath a grime-covered window.

Porter was going to freak out when he saw the footage from this mission. They'd never come across a spriggan before, but Vaughn had read the folktales about them and tried to extrapolate what they might be like. This was beyond anything she'd imagined.

Hadn't the goblin—Johnny—mentioned another dweller, though? Scarecrow. What the hell was that going to be like? Johnny curled into a ball again and rolled to a pile of clothes rumpled in the corner. He popped back up, then squatted near the ground.

He squinted at Brock, then shook his head. "Cripes,

what the hell happened to your face?"

Brock smiled, bearing many sharpening teeth. "I disagreed with something that ate me."

Johnny actually laughed, the sound sharp and abrasive. "Well, what do you want to know?"

Vaughn hit the command to talk to everyone's earpieces. "Play it cool, guys. We don't want to tip our hand too soon."

"We need some tech," Brock said.

Okay. A little direct, but that could have been worse.

"You don't need a goblin for that." Johnny waved his hand dismissively. "Check out the Internet. They even deliver."

"Not that kind of tech," Brock said. "We need something more… dweller-specific."

"You seem a little weird for a werewolf," Johnny said, "but you don't want to get messed up in curator tech. It's more trouble than it's worth."

"Curator?" Vaughn sat up straighter, then cringed when she realized she had said that over the open line.

Damn, she wanted to ask what the goblin knew. But how could she do so without blowing their cover? Or letting Damien know that she might not be as human as he thought? She pushed the need to know aside—with a lot of effort. Her team needed her focused. Luckily, Brock was all over it.

"I like trouble." Brock gave Johnny a smile that was

straight-up creepy.

"Well, that's the only advice you're gonna get for free." Johnny rubbed his index finger and thumb together.

"Damien, you're up," Vaughn said.

Damien reached into his messenger's bag and pulled out a five-pound bag of sugar. Johnny's eyes widened and he licked his lips with a thin, green tongue.

"Is that stuff pure?" Johnny asked.

"Yeah." Damien tossed the bag to the goblin.

He made the grossest snuffling sounds as he tore open a corner of the bag, then reached inside. He licked his finger after wiggling it around in the bag. His eyes closed as he let out a long sigh.

"I know we try not to judge, but yuck," Vaughn said.

Damien didn't respond. He was staring at the pile of clothes on the floor next to the goblin. Vaughn could swear she saw lights flickering over it sporadically. Damien must have noticed it, too.

"Okay, that's weird," Vaughn said, using the private channel for Damien.

"That's what I thought," Damien subvocalized.

"The tech," Brock said, still focused on the mission and oblivious to the oddly sparkling laundry pile. "Where do we find it?"

"You don't find it. It finds you. I'll put out the word that you're looking, and if you're lucky, no one will bite." A wide, menacing smile spread across his face as he opened his eyes. "If you're unlucky, someone will make contact and hook you up."

"How will they know where to find us?" Brock asked.

The goblin laughed, revealing rows of glistening, jagged teeth. "You don't have much experience with curators, do ya? They always find who or what they're looking for. That's why they are not the kind of beasties you want to fuck around with."

Vaughn let out an exasperated breath that Damien could hear over their private channel. "I have so many questions," she said.

"Another time," Damien subvocalized.

"Anyways, don't say I didn't warn ya," Johnny said.

"We won't." Brock started to turn away, but the goblin wasn't quite done.

"What's with you werewolves and curator tech, anyway?" Johnny tucked the bag of sugar somewhere under his arm. "You're the second alpha to hit me up for this info in the last month."

Megan stepped closer to Johnny. "Roy came here?"

"Meg." Brock reached out and grabbed her arm, pulling her back. Damien stepped closer to her, too.

"Meg," Johnny said. He ran a long finger under his chin. "The guy mentioned that name. But the way he told it, the tech he was after was a one-way ticket to Bluesville for you, little girl. Disintegration time."

Vaughn leaned forward in her chair. "Do you think this

guy knows why dwellers vaporize?"

"Not why we're here," Damien subvocalized.

This goblin seemed to have answers to so many of Vaughn's questions. Maybe they could come back when they weren't so crunched for time—and after she'd had a chance to order more sugar from the grocery store.

"I had other plans," Brock said.

"And you managed to bypass curator tech?" Johnny snorted. "I'll believe that when I—" His eyes widened and he jerked his head toward the corner, backing away from the pile of clothes. "Cripes…"

The lights Vaughn had been seeing on the clothing were definitely real. Small motes of white growing brighter by the moment. An energy signature was building as well. As it did, the clothes started to move.

"What the hell?" Brock backed away, ushering Megan behind him.

"Scarecrow wants to talk to you," Johnny said. "And this time of year, she's in a mood. Can't find good jack-o'-lantern heads anywhere."

Fingers made of straw poked out from the sleeves of the jacket that was rising from the floor, a pair of dark slacks beneath it. The body of whatever the hell this was flopped from side to side as it rose, becoming more solid-looking as it also became more humanoid. A burlap sack protruded from the collar of the jacket, filling out like a head as it grew.

"Holy shit," Vaughn said.

"Here's your hat." Johnny handed the scarecrow a beat-up gardening hat, the brim in tatters.

As the dweller placed the hat on her head, the lights flickered into a pattern on her face, forming triangle eyes, nose, and a broad, smiling mouth.

"What the hell am I looking at, Vaughn?" Damien subvocalized.

Ideas flooded her mind. Another interphasic creature? Something that could possess inanimate objects and make them move? There was nothing like that in the database. Nothing anywhere near this that they'd ever encountered.

"I have no idea," she said.

"Scarecrow," Brock said, angling his head slightly. "If you have information that could help, we'd—"

Scarecrow took a single step forward, then suddenly was right in front of Brock. Ripples surrounded her that made it hard to tell where she actually was. Clouds of black and blue energy swirled around her, appearing and disappearing as fast as lightning. Vaughn was having trouble getting any solid readings. The being's limbs moved strangely, a fluid movement that seemed slow, yet brought her to her destination faster than expected.

Space and time… She's manipulating one or both…

The scarecrow reached toward Brock's face with one of her straw hands and let a spark from his blue eye land on her finger. She cocked her head to the side, staring at him as she stepped even closer. The glowing lights running all over and through her body grew brighter centering on her face. Brock's eye was putting off its own light, adding to it. There was only so much data Damien's contacts could feed Vaughn, but it looked like the scarecrow was absorbing some of the energy Brock was putting off.

"You are seeing that, right?" Damien subvocalized.

"Yeah," Vaughn said. "Yeah, I am. This is going to sound crazy, but I think she's distorting the spacetime field around herself."

"That sounds like a sci-fi movie."

"Our lives are a sci-fi movie," Vaughn said. "What are the other dwellers doing?"

Damien tilted his head so Vaughn would have a view of Johnny, who was watching everything that was going on with keen interest. Even the spriggin seemed to be standing straighter in his pot. Thank the Internet the contacts were working fine and letting her see everything.

Vaughn flipped to the public channel. "I recommend nobody makes any sudden moves."

"Tell that to her," Brock subvocalized.

The scarecrow turned to look at Damien, then suddenly was in front of Megan. Megan jumped a little, but froze and stood absolutely still.

"Shit," Vaughn said. "Megan, don't move."

"Careful." Brock's tone had just enough menace that Vaughn wasn't sure if he was talking to Megan or the scarecrow.

"It's okay," Megan said. "I really like scarecrows and I'd love to bring you a new jack-o'-lantern head, just as soon as they're in season."

Vaughn added that to her ever-growing to-do list. Pumpkins and sugar. Lucky for her, with her resources, she could keep Scarecrow swimming in pumpkins. They just had to navigate this interaction, and then the Blades might just have a direct pipeline to the dweller community. The possibilities were incredible. Unfortunately, for every good scenario Vaughn's brain fed her, it also gave her a terrible outcome to this first contact.

Scarecrow reached out with one hand and gently drew her fingers along Megan's cheek, then down along the side of her neck. Vaughn's heart was racing. For the trillionth time, she wished she could be there with them. But then, what could she actually do?

Vaughn's eyes burned from keeping them open, but she didn't dare to blink. Even so, Scarecrow suddenly vanished from her spot in front of Megan and appeared before Damien. She leaned in close, cocking her head to the side as she stared into his eyes. From this vantage point, Vaughn could get tons of data—at least, she normally could. She typed in commands as quickly as she could, running every possible scan through Damien's contacts.

"Don't move," Vaughn said through their private

channel.

Damien didn't respond, as she'd expected. She wouldn't be surprised if Scarecrow could pick up the vibrations of subvocalization. Damien had probably figured that out as well. He wasn't blinking, either, holding Scarecrow's gaze to let Vaughn get her data.

The energy readouts were off the charts. Not in terms of volume but just... bizarreness. The readings were something like interphasic energy, although they went beyond that, into a realm that Vaughn had never been exposed to before. Still, it seemed strangely familiar somehow.

A field of silver energy formed over Scarecrow's face. Vaughn felt drawn in, almost like she could fall into it. Was Scarecrow doing her own scan? Vaughn wished she could check in with Damien, but he couldn't tell her anything without possibly setting this new dweller off.

Scarecrow lifted her hand. The same silver energy surrounded it. She pointed one finger at Damien's left eye, the straw close enough to brush his eyelashes. The silver energy flowed out, pausing for a moment before gently touching his contact lens.

"Don't move," Vaughn whispered. She was sitting stock-still herself, not even breathing.

The lights making up Scarecrow's mouth turned into a frown. A huge burst of the blue and black cloud energy enveloped her. She flickered, then suddenly she was across the room. The hand she'd held in front of Damien burst into flames. She stretched it far from her body, shaking it as if trying to put it out.

"Oh shit." Vaughn opened the public channel. "Everyone, get the hell out of there!"

"What the fuck did you do to Scarecrow?" Johnny yelled. He curled into a ball, the spikes on his back standing straight up. He rolled toward Damien, leaving pockmarks in the floor where his spikes pierced the dirt. Megan was between them. She shrieked as she leapt out of the way, barely avoiding the goblin's spines. Splinters of wood flew through the air, embedding themselves in Brock's chest.

"Watch the spriggin," Vaughn yelled.

Damien wheeled around just as the spriggin leapt out of his pot and charged toward him.

"We are leaving," Brock yelled, pointing at the holes above that they'd made.

Brock and Megan could easily spring out of the basement to the level above. Damien was a different matter.

"Damien can't make the jump!" Vaughn said.

"Don't worry about me, just get out." Damien ran toward the stairs.

"Damien," she said.

"I've got this." He paused briefly at the base of the stairs.

She checked his view, the computer readouts showing various areas where the wood had been intentionally weakened. He took the steps three at a time, avoiding the spaces that would spring the traps. He glanced back at the basement briefly, just in time to see Brock leap straight up through one of the gaps. Megan was already on the first floor.

The goblin was rolling around in circles, swearing, while the spriggin rooted himself in the ground and started to morph into a tree again. At the rate it was growing, it would break through to the first floor in ten seconds. Vaughn needed to get them all the hell out of there. Brock and Megan could always bust through a wall, but Damien didn't have that strength. Worse, the stairs he'd used to escape the basement didn't come out in the same hallway where Brock and Megan were.

"I'm sending you the safest route to the room where you entered the building," Vaughn said. Her fingers flew over the surface of her computer desk as she programmed in the new parameters for the display in Damien's contacts.

Damien started running. He rounded a corner and slammed into Scarecrow. Both of them toppled to the ground.

Chapter Nine

"Shit!" Vaughn yelled. "Damien!"

Damien didn't have time to respond. Scarecrow gripped him tight as they fell. He rolled to his back, kicking at the tangle of clothing and straw wrapped around him. He was not going out this way—taken out by a burlap sack in a cheap coat. He managed to get himself on top of her and pin the shoulders of her jacket to the floor. Staring down into the lights of Scarecrow's face might actually have been the weirdest experience in his very weird life. She wasn't frowning anymore, but she wasn't smiling either.

"I don't want to hurt you," Damien said. "Just let us go."

Scarecrow's eyes narrowed. She grabbed the sides of his head and held him tight as a cloud of that weird blue and black smoke burst out of her face. This time, it was filled with motes of bright light. They hit Damien in his eyes, blinding him. He yelled, shoving away from her and blinking rapidly, trying to clear his vision. His back hit the wall. Everything was bright and blurred. He couldn't make out any shapes.

"Vaughn," Damien said.

A huge burst of feedback crackled in his ear. Pain spiked through his head. He reached for the earpiece, but when he tried to take it out, the pain intensified. He felt like he was pulling out his fucking eardrum along with the device. Half-deaf and totally blind, he pulled the knife out of his boot, slashing at the space in front of him.

"He's here!" A rough voice shouted from somewhere close.

Muffled footsteps followed, and then he felt arms around him. Fur-covered arms lifting him from the floor. Whatever this was, it wasn't human. A werewolf had him and was running with him through the building. Tammie was gone. His family was gone. And the wolves were back. They'd come back to finish the job.

Damien lost it.

Pounding on the creature's back, he yelled and screamed, ripping at its fur and slashing with his knife. Silver. He needed silver.

Something struck his back and shoulder. Something solid and rough. Crashing noises surrounded him and suddenly the air shifted. The stuffy mold smell was gone. More clawed hands gripped his back and hefted him into the air. Then he was flying. Wind whipped past him. A wall of metal stopped his momentum, bringing a wave of pain over his entire back. He felt the metal cave in and bounced off of it. He landed hard, his face bouncing on asphalt. His lungs emptied as the wind was knocked from him. He couldn't breathe.

"Stop." A voice was yelling somewhere. "He's hurt and disoriented and I'm fine. Brock, I'm fine."

Damien rolled to his side, more pain lancing through his ribs and chest. He managed to push himself up on his right elbow, shifting his knife to his left hand. His mouth was full of coppery fluid. He spat it out, slashing at the air. They wouldn't play with him this time and leave him in a room full of the dead. He would force them to kill him, like they should have done all those years ago. He staggered to his feet, tingling heat spreading over his back. His eyes were on fire, his face a throbbing ball of hurt. Every part of his body ached.

"Damien, please stop." The voice didn't sound as rough anymore. It was almost human. Familiar and feminine.

"Oh my god," she said. "Look at his eyes."

Damien shook his head and slashed with his knife again, between himself and the voice.

"Stay back." The second voice was followed by a harsh growl.

They were still here. Trying to trick him.

"Damien," a third voice said. Another female.

How many fucking werewolves were there? There had been more than he could count. But at least two for each member of his family—except for him and Tammie, hiding under the stairs. The wolves had paired themselves off with their chosen prey and laughed as they'd killed everyone he loved.

"Damien." The third voice was insistent and felt almost as if it was coming from inside his own head. Her even, firm tone was comforting, even in the midst of this shitshow. Something about the way she spoke made him want to listen. He blinked again and again, trying to get the bright fog to clear. Where was he? Backing up against the metal wall, he felt it with his free hand. A van.

"We have to get you out of there," the voice in his head said. "I'm not losing a Blade today. I'm not losing you. Please."

A Blade?

That's right. Damien was a Blade. And whatever else came along with it, that meant he helped people. Even people who weren't... human. He lowered his knife. His head hurt. His thoughts were so fragmented, he didn't know what was real.

"Meg, be careful." The male was talking again, the growl gone from his voice.

"He won't hurt me." Soft hands gripped his arm, her touch gentle.

"Tammie?" Damien said.

"Meg. It's Megan." There was a hitch to her voice as she went on. "You're hurt, Damien. It's... It's bad. Please, can we get you back to the ranch? Eli can help you."

Damien nodded. He let her lead him around the van

and up into the back. She helped him onto one of the bench seats, then sat next to him, putting one arm over his shoulders. A few moments later, the van started to move.

"You're going to be okay." Her voice wavered and she sniffed loudly. "We'll find a way to fix this."

"Fix this." His uncle's stern voice made Damien jump. "Goddammit, I gave you those tools so you could learn a trade. And what do you do? You board up the windows. What is wrong with you?"

Damien clenched his teeth together, his hands tight fists at his sides. They didn't understand. They couldn't understand. Not unless they had seen...

His aunt rested her hands on Damien's shoulders and he tried not to flinch.

"Leave him be," she said. "He's been through enough."

His uncle let out an exasperated sigh. "When he was a child. He's almost a man now. He needs to move past this."

"I'll fix it," Damien said. "I'll fix it."

"I think the bleeding has stopped," a voice outside his head said. A woman's. Megan?

"What the fuck even was that thing?" A harsher voice. The man.

"I don't know!"

Vaughn...

Damien knew that voice. He clung to it.

This was real. He was real. He was Damien. Grown. A Blade. He was in a van with—

His heartbeat picked up. He sucked in a breath and held it, then let it out slow.

He was in a van with two werewolves. But they were Blades. They had fought together and they had helped him escape from the scarecrow and the others. And Megan was protecting him now. Just like Tammie had done.

"It's okay. I'm here now." Tammie wrapped her arms around Damien as they huddled in the storage space under the stairs.

He could hear Nana in the kitchen. No, not Nana...
Something else.

Damien fought against the memories. What the fuck was wrong with his head? He couldn't block anything out. All the worst moments of his life were playing out before him and he wasn't sure his sanity could take much more.

"Something is wrong," he said.

"I know, I know." Megan held him closer, stroking his head. "We're going to fix it. Vaughn can use her nanites again."

"They never left me," Damien said.

"But…"

"But what?"

"You're not healing," Megan said. "Did they stop working?"

Damien didn't know what was going on, but he did

know that he felt better than he did after hitting the van. Something had to be working inside of him. But then, why couldn't he see? And why did one of his ears feel like it was underwater? He'd always thought that being blind meant constantly seeing darkness. He was only seeing light. The pain in his ear had abated, but that entire half of his head felt numb now.

From the front of the van, Brock said, "We just need to get him back to the ranch. We can try something else when we get there."

Just like Damien had hoped to sort things out with Carey.

"You're using too much force. It's a sword, not a club. Try again." Carey stepped back and held his sword to the side, inviting Damien to attack.

It never mattered how much Damien threw himself into their sparring. He always had his ass handed to him. And he always learned.

Not a club. A sword.

Carey was right. Damien used way too many downward strokes. He lunged, swinging the sword lower, but Carey easily batted it away.

"Better," Carey said.

Damien rained down blow after blow, his shoulder hurting and his hand stinging from the reverberation as Carey parried every strike, constantly giving feedback without ever getting short of breath. He knocked away the blade every time Damien tried a thrust attack.

Until the last one.

"You're getting better," Carey said, meeting Damien's sword and using a flourish that almost sent it flying from Damien's hand. "Remember to—"

His eyes widened in surprise, and then went blank. Damien didn't register the change until it was too late. He was already thrusting with his blade. Carey didn't make a move to stop him. His sword clattered to the ground as Damien's pierced his chest, just above his heart.

Damien cried out as he tried to pull back his attack. Carey had drilled into Damien to never hold back. The blade sank into his chest. Blood welled from the wound.

"No," Damien yelled, releasing his grip on his weapon and lunging forward to catch Carey as he fell. "No!"

He lowered his mentor—his best friend—to the ground, desperately trying to remember what to do. Leave the blade in place. Don't remove it. Apply pressure. What the hell would help?

"Please," Damien shouted. "Zach! Anybody!"

He'd been about to yell again when Carey's body began to glow with a blue light. Shock had stolen Damien's breath. The light intensified, spreading through Carey, consuming him. Damien's sword clattered to the floor as Carey disappeared from out of Damien's arms.

"You should have told me you were a dweller," Damien said. "I would have understood. Now, everything's fucked up."

"Damien…" Megan pressed her forehead to his cheek.

"Where am I?" Damien said.

"You're in one of the vans. We're almost home."

"I thought I was back at the castle," he said. "I was with Carey."

"We're going to get him back," she said. "We're going to help you get better, and then we're going to get Carey back."

"You always try to help people feel better, Tammie."

"Megan," she said. "I'm Megan."

"Right." Damien shook his head, and the movement made the van seem to spin. "Right. Sorry."

"Brock," she said. "Drive faster."

He felt the van accelerate. Maybe it was the vertigo, but their inertia seemed a little touch-and-go a few times. Wasn't the ranch on a mountain, with curvy roads? Damien had just been in a wreck on those roads. He didn't want to have one again. Especially with that bogey out there.

A gaping mouth emerging from a dark shadow. Pain and claws. Fur and scales. What the hell were those things? There were so many of them…

He breathed through the memory this time, squeezing Megan's hand and anchoring himself in the van. She had been with him when it happened. She had saved his life.

Fur all along their back and sides, fading into scales

closer to their legs. And a tail.

Two sets of eyes on each face. Glowing green eyes.

A mane of black fur around a scaled, yellow-green, reptilian snout. Sharp, curved teeth, like a snake's—meant for catching and tearing flesh. Clawed feet. Elbows bending out like a giant lizard. A forked tongue.

The more Damien sat with the memory, the more details emerged. He closed his eyes, trying to focus on the imagery. Was his imagination filling things in, or was he remembering something that could help?

Black clouds streaked with blue light. They had appeared before the dwellers arrived. Sometimes, they converged, before a larger creature attacked.

"Vaughn." Damien tried subvocalizing first, but nothing happened. He wasn't surprised, after what had happened with his earpiece.

"Vaughn." This time, he said it out loud.

"Vaughn isn't here, Damien," Megan said. "But we'll be home soon."

"I need to talk to her," Damien said.

"You can talk to her at the ranch." Brock's tone held an underlying message—drop it.

Was something wrong with Vaughn? Had something happened at the ranch? Damien's heart started to pound. If she was in trouble…

I'd do what?

Damien couldn't see. Could barely hear. If Megan

wasn't holding him, he wasn't even sure he'd be able to stay upright on the bench.

"It's going to be okay," Megan said.

Damien wished he could believe her. Once again, he was the one dragging everyone down. The weakest link. It didn't matter how much muscle he packed on, how much he practiced fighting, how much he drilled himself on the Dwellers Database. When it came down to it, he was the one who failed everyone else. He closed his eyes and leaned his head against the side of the van. He wanted to help so badly.

That was the worst of it. Vaughn had to know what was going on. If she thought that her tech had let Damien down —or worse, that it had hurt him—that would kill her. It would be yet another weight on her shoulders.

I promised her I'd help.

Goddammit, Damien would not accept this.

"I think I know what they look like," he said. "The unknown dwellers that attacked us."

The van started to slow, then came to a stop. Were they already back at the ranch?

"Kind of like a pack of gigantic, black-furred, greenish-scaled, lizard-dogs?" Brock said.

Well, shit. Apparently, they didn't even need Damien's help identifying the things.

"Yeah," Damien said. "I didn't think you got a good look at them before."

"I didn't," Brock said. "I'm staring at three out the front window."

Fuck.

Something landed on top of the van with an ominous thunk. Claws scraped across the metal as it crawled toward the rear doors. Megan tightened her grip on Damien's shoulders.

"It's going to be okay," she said. "I'm here now."

The weirdest feeling skittered over his skin at her words—the same ones Tammie had used to comfort Damien time and again during their childhood. All the hairs on his arms stood on end. He felt like the van was spinning in circles, but it was just him, just his mind playing tricks on him.

"I don't think we're going to be able to drive past them," Brock said. "They could knock us off a curve and send us tumbling down the mountainside really easy."

"We can't fight them off alone," Megan said. "They'll go after Damien."

"Don't worry about me." He reached up and squeezed her arm. "Give me a weapon, and I'll defend myself."

From the front, Brock said, "No offense, but you're probably more likely to shoot us. Let us take care of this."

"Brock..." Megan's voice was thin with strain.

"We can't wait for them to find a way into the van," Brock said. "We lead them away and Vaughn uses the autopilot to drive the van back to the ranch. You copy that,

Vaughn?"

After what felt like a very long time, Vaughn's voice rasped through the van. "Yeah, I copy."

Damien had never heard her sound so torn up.

"Keep eyes on Damien," Brock said. "We're about to engage."

Megan squeezed Damien's shoulder, then leaned in and kissed his cheek. "Stay here. I'll be right back."

His stomach roiled. Not that a werewolf had kissed him, but that once again, she had said exactly what Tammie had said to him—right before she left their hiding spot. She'd even kissed his cheek.

She hadn't come back.

He heard the soft swishing of clothes, then energy filled the van. It crawled over his skin, leaving goosebumps in its wake. They must have changed. The vehicle rocked slightly. Muggy air shoved its way into the small space, thick with humidity, when they opened the van door. A moment later, it closed again.

The screeches started almost immediately, joined by the unmistakeable roars of werewolves. Part of him still felt paralyzed with fear when he heard that sound. The battle cries of the werewolves. But he forced himself to remember Megan trying to comfort him—her arms around him as she held him upright. He shoved the fear away.

These were his teammates, his allies, his… friends.

Eli had said the Blades were all family. Dammit,

Damien was not going to hide in a corner while they did the fighting. Not again. He wasn't that helpless six-year old anymore. Vaughn's nanites had helped before. They would pull through for Damien now.

'Come on, guys,' Damien thought.

His eyes started tingling, like tiny ants crawling all over them. It was the freakiest sensation. But then the haze in his eyes started to clear. The tingling spread to his ear. After a loud pop, he could hear clearly again. What he heard made his heart race. Snarls, howls, roars, and a strange crackling, almost like electricity. Interspersed in it all were thumps and crashes—bodies hitting the ground, the nearby trees, even each other.

Damien blinked a few times to clear his vision further. He couldn't believe his admonition to the nanites had done this. The timing had to be a coincidence. Vaughn's nanites just needed a chance to do their thing. And damn, had they done their thing.

He looked around the inside of the van. He could see, even in the near darkness. Instead of a computer overlay obscuring his enhanced vision he just… knew where stuff was. He could see it. He stood and opened the weapons compartment. Swords, plasma rifles, flamethrowers. A flamethrower might be useful.

"Damien, you need to stay put." Vaughn spoke over the comms. "Brock and Megan need more time to—"

Something crashed into the side of the van, nearly

knocking him off his feet. He braced his hands against the wall to steady himself and looked up to see a large dent right in front of his face.

The Blades in Providence were going through vans at an alarming rate.

His vision cut out again, white and gray static replacing the blues and blacks of the van. When it cleared this time, the world was rendered in infrared. He could see through the walls of the van.

"What the fuck?" Damien whispered.

He pulled his attention back to the weapons. After shrugging into the harness for a flamethrower, he strapped a Bowie knife to his thigh. He really hoped he wouldn't have to resort to close-quarters fighting with these things. Before he closed the compartment, he grabbed a stingray. The small pistol-shaped weapon would be the safest to use out there. Werewolves didn't like being shocked, but it wouldn't kill them if he missed.

Another impact on the side of the van had it screeching across the pavement. Staying put didn't seem like the safest option after all. Turning, he stopped with his hand on the latch to the back door. Vaughn hadn't said anything as Damien geared up. The only thing he could hear was the battle raging outside. That wasn't good. No matter what was going on out there, he had to help. He wouldn't sit in the dark, waiting to be saved—or worse, waiting for others to sacrifice themselves for him. Not again.

If Vaughn was so distracted she wasn't watching him anymore, then Brock and Megan needed all the help they could get. Even from 'just a human.' Damien pulled on the latch and opened the door to the thick night air.

Chapter Ten

Vaughn's fingers flew over her keyboard, her attention switching from monitor to monitor. Always, it went back to the screen showing the inside of the van where Damien was sitting.

Something was wrong with her tech. Something she couldn't blame on the explosion in sublevel 2. There had been little glitches here and there. She had explained them all away. 'She'd get around to fixing it.' 'She'd figure it out.' 'There were more pressing matters, and the malfunctions weren't that bad.'

Now Damien was hurt. Again.

He had let a werewolf hold him. Had taken comfort in Megan's touch. Whatever had happened to him was bad. Worse than bad. And it wasn't anywhere close to over.

Brock and Megan were fighting a pack of creatures like nothing Vaughn had ever seen before. As she watched the monitor that displayed a satellite view of the area around the van, she saw two of the creatures vanish into thin air. The space they'd occupied crackled with energy for a brief moment, then *poof*. They were gone. She couldn't explain it. And because she couldn't explain it, she couldn't predict where they were going to show up next.

She opened a communication line to Marcus's hoverbike. "Marcus, can you go any faster?"

"I'm already redlining it," Marcus said.

Dammit. They should have trained Tessa on how to pilot one of the hoverbikes. She was doing so much better, now that the psychotic werewolf who'd been manipulating her thoughts was dead. Marcus couldn't get up to maximum speed with two of them on the bike. Vaughn couldn't regret sending them both, though. From the looks of things, Megan and Brock needed all the help they could get. Plus, it wasn't like Vaughn could split up a pair of mated werewolves.

Brock and Megan were holding their own, for the moment. Every time they knocked a creature away and it ended up hitting the van, Vaughn's heart rate sped up. Damien seemed to be okay. He might even be getting better, since she noticed him standing up.

Or else he's too stubborn to stay put.

The thought made her stomach clench. It would be in keeping with Damien's psych file for him to try to join the fight, even knowing what a disadvantage he was at. The door to ops opened. Vaughn didn't look away from her monitors. She had to stay focused on the fight.

"I know what you're going to say, but we need you here," Vaughn said, even though she really wished Dexter or Porter could join the team in the field. Hell, she wished they *both* could be there.

With their link gone, they were severely limited in what they could do. For all anyone knew, they wouldn't even split if one of them was killed. It was too big of a risk. Plus, they needed someone at the ranch to keep an eye on Jon and Nathan.

She watched as Megan and Brock worked to lead the creatures away from the van. While they did, Vaughn tried to modify her algorithms to be able to detect where the things would emerge after they vanished. They were teleporting all over the battlefield. So far, she hadn't been able to discern any sort of pattern.

"If you have any ideas, I'd love to hear them," Vaughn said.

She glanced over, expecting to see Dexter or Porter or even Eli. She was not expecting the shock of white hair, heavily scarred face, and huge, hulking physique of not just Jon but also Nathan. Both replicants were in ops and there was no Dexter or Porter along as a chaperone. Vaughn swallowed hard and resisted the urge to scoot her chair a bit further away from the pair.

"Do Dexter and Porter know you're here?" she asked.

The replicants didn't respond. Then again, neither had said so much as a word since they'd…emerged. She didn't need them to answer, though. Of course Dexter and Porter didn't know. There was no way in hell they would let a single replicant from this pair near her unsupervised, let alone both of them.

They both stared at the monitors intently. More crackling sounds came over the speakers. At least the van's surveillance feeds were still working. She didn't want to turn away from the replicants in the room with her, but she had to watch over the fight and do everything in her power to help. Jon and Nathan seemed... placid. At the moment. They still made her nervous.

One of the creatures Megan and Brock were fighting vanished, then appeared a few seconds later behind Brock. It spun around, whipping Brock with its tail. Brock roared in pain as he fell forward, but he tucked himself into a roll and came up on his feet. He launched himself at the creature, arms outspread to grapple it. The creature vanished in a burst of electric light just as Brock reached it.

They were definitely using some sort of interphasic energy. Vaughn needed to figure out a way to block it in the field—and fast. At the very least, she needed to know how to track it. The ranch had defenses against interphasic energy, but those defenses involved a network of extremely complex devices on a grid that was completely separated from the rest of their base's tech. She hoped that would mean whatever was going on with the ranch tech wouldn't affect that part of their defense systems.

Back at the battle, Megan had managed to grab one of her opponents with her wickedly clawed hands. She bit down onto its neck and shook her head violently. Vaughn wasn't sure she'd be looking at Megan quite the same way when the team made it back to the base. She'd never seen Megan fight so ferociously. Vaughn had also never seen her so outmatched.

Another creature slammed into Megan's side, knocking her away from her prey. Instead of pressing its attack, it crawled over the one who was injured. Energy sparked between them, like a ball of lightning crackling on the ground. Vaughn's jaw dropped open as they merged into a single larger creature—one who was completely unharmed.

"You have got to be kidding me," Vaughn said.

It was like watching one of Brock's replicants when they split, but in reverse. Could they be a similar form of dweller?

Jon and Nathan were still staring at the monitors, their brows furrowed. Vaughn had never seen such a look of intense concentration on either replicant in this set. They only ever seemed to pay attention to Megan. Their gaze flicked from monitor to monitor, watching the movement of the fight. It wasn't going well for the werewolves on their team.

Brock was surrounded by four of the creatures. Vaughn noticed that these were smaller than the ones they'd first encountered. Two of the ones attacking Megan were also smaller, but then there was that third that was twice their size.

"Combining mass," Vaughn said. "They combine their mass when they merge. It makes them bigger and puts off a lot of energy."

She'd thought those balls of electricity that sometimes surrounded them before they vanished was them slipping into the interphasic dimension that ran alongside what most life forms on Earth could perceive. What if they were actually splitting or merging as well? That would explain why she couldn't get a good count or even a good reading on them.

She typed in more commands, tweaking algorithms and trying to boost the van's scanners to get more data. If she could determine that her theory was correct, it might help them understand this opponent better and assist with not getting their asses kicked in the future.

The lizard-dogs lunged forward. Brock swung at the closest as soon as it was in range. His fist connected. The impact sent the thing flying backwards several feet. He spun and kicked another as it neared. It hissed as it rolled, absorbing some of the blow. These things were smart. The last two leapt at Brock. One clawed his shoulder, it's back legs slashing his thigh. Blood sprayed the ground and Brock let out an ear splitting roar. A beam of bright light hit the second creature before its attack could connect, knocking it ten feet away from Brock. Vaughn recognized the energy. She had designed it.

"A stingray," she murmured. But that meant... "Damien."

She looked at the feed of the interior of the van. It was empty. The back doors were wide open.

"Shit." Vaughn checked the ETA for Marcus and Tessa again. They were still several minutes out.

Megan was doing a little better with her opponents. She was spending most of her energy dodging, it seemed. More beams of light blasted across the monitors, helping her out.

"Damien, get back in the van," Megan yelled. "They'll go after you."

"In case you haven't noticed," Brock grunted as a particularly vicious swipe raked across his side, "they're going after all of us this time."

Vaughn couldn't let herself panic. Her team needed her. *Damien* needed her.

For some reason, she couldn't get a good read on Damien's location. Why wasn't he showing up on the satellite feed clearly? At least the beams Damien was shooting were hitting their marks. She hoped that was a sign that his eyesight had been restored. In fact, it seemed like he was firing on the creatures the very instant they appeared. It was almost like he was anticipating where they would be.

Vaughn's attention went to Megan as she leapt into the air, avoiding a tail-swipe from one of the smaller creatures.

Twisting around at an insane height, she managed to land on the largest one's back. She slashed at its neck—blood, scales, and hair flying from it in the ferocity of her attack. Even still, she was barely slowing it down. And that wasn't the worst of it.

"No, no, no." Vaughn activated the external speakers on the van. "Megan, get off that thing. If it goes interphasic, it'll take you with it."

Werewolves were tough, but Vaughn had no idea what would happen to one if it went into the sub-dimension. Worse, she wasn't sure Megan would be able to make it back.

"How are we supposed to fight these things if we can't get close?" Megan yelled, still slashing at it.

She had a good point. This did not look good. Vaughn had no idea what to do. She wasn't even sure if they could escape if they ran.

Brock roared, then said, "Meg, get off that thing."

Jon—or Nathan, Vaughn couldn't tell them apart at all —turned his attention to her. A shiver passed down her spine at the replicant's cold, flat eyes. None of their eyes reflected light. It was unnerving, especially in this pair.

The replicant turned back to the monitors. Vaughn reluctantly did so as well, her anxiety spiking both from the threat in the field and in the room with her. Electricity swept over the largest lizard-dog-thing's pelt and scales. Megan kicked off from it right before the crackling energy covered its entire body. Instead of vanishing, the energy split into two spheres that elongated into the shape of the creatures. As the light faded, two more slightly smaller opponents were left behind.

"Shit," Vaughn said. She almost wished she had been wrong.

Jon and Nathan let out a low growl. She could sympathize with the frustration held in it. But then, they started tapping the keys etched into the surface of her desk.

"Hey," she snapped. "Knock it off. Those only work for me, anyway."

One of the replicants turned on her. Not *to* her, *on* her. With a snarl, he picked her up, chair and all, and flung her toward the wall. She let out a surprised scream. The chair hit the wall hardest, but then as she bounced off and hit the floor, the chair dropped onto her. One of the armrests hit her ribs, sharp pain flashing through her abdomen. Why did she have to design them to be so heavy?

She groaned as she pushed it away from her, sticking near the floor as she tried to clear her head. She needed to call for help, but one replicant was still standing in front of the computer. The other was staring at her as she scrambled to a crouching position on the floor. Vaughn would have to use her watch to call for help. Discretely.

She leaned against the wall and rubbed her bruised ribs. Pain lanced through her when she touched them. She did her best to ignore it and carefully activated her watch's comm function—broadcast only. It would play the sounds in the ops room, but wouldn't relay any returning messages. She didn't want to set Jon or Nathan off. She could only hope someone would hear her.

"Hey, Jon...nathan," she said, trying to keep her voice calm and hide the pain radiating out from her side. "If you can let me know what you're trying to do with my computer at ops, maybe I can help you. Just don't throw me across the room again."

Yeah, she wasn't the best at being subtle. If anyone was listening, they would definitely know where she was, though. And that she was in trouble.

The replicant at the computer was focused on the monitors and the controls. He kept tapping at the etchings, his movements getting more jerky and forceful as they didn't respond. The whole time, he stared at the monitors as if he could bore a hole into them with his gaze. The replicant near Vaughn growled, then let out a strange keening sound. Weirdly, it reminded her of the old tech sound that modems made. The replicant at the computer slammed his hands down on the controls, snarling as he did.

"That's not going to help any—" Vaughn's words died in her throat.

The replicant who had been watching her turned around and grabbed the shoulders of the one near the computers. Crackling electric energy burst out of his hands. It crept up his arms, spiraling around his limbs and then spreading down his torso and legs. At the same time, it spread over the replicant he was holding onto. The electric-looking energy curled around their heads, growing so intense, Vaughn had to squint against the light they were putting off. They were both making that horrible keening sound. It rose in pitch the longer it went on. Through the rippling currents, she saw their bodies merge, just like the creatures' did.

"Holy shit," she whispered.

The energy kept building. It flooded over her computer console and rolled up the walls, encasing the monitors. The tech started to make popping sounds as various parts of their systems overloaded. Sparks flew out from the sides of the screens as they went dark.

"What are you doing?" she yelled.

Even if her tech wasn't one-hundred percent working, it was better than nothing, and Jonathan was frying everything in her ops center. It wasn't like she could go to the backup in the sub-level. That one had been blown up by Megan's collar. Vaughn stood and took a painful step forward, not really sure what she planned to do. All the hairs on her arms rose. Little arcs of lightning swept in her direction. The scent of ozone flooded the room as the cloud surrounding the replicant coalesced into a blinding ball of energy.

"Oh shit," she said.

There was a moment where the only sound was the extremely high pitched keen of the newly merged replicant and Vaughn's heartbeat pounding in her ears. Instinct drove her to drop back to the floor, curling herself into the smallest ball she could.

The blast hit her the moment her arms wrapped around her head—scorching heat and waves of electricity that made her muscles spasm. The acrid scent of burnt wiring rushed into her nose. The light was so bright, it blinded her through her eyelids. Energy filled the room, buffeting her with wave after wave of agony until she finally sank into the comfort of darkness.

Chapter Eleven

We are all going to die.

Damien knew pessimism wasn't a good idea during a fight—especially one as intense as this. Then again, given the odds, it was more like being realistic. There were just so many of these... whatever the hell they were. More than he could track.

Light sparked in his vision. He prayed it wasn't a sign that his eyesight was about to go again. Instead, a display flickered into view. Vaughn's contacts must be working. The interface was a little different. She must have made some upgrades while bringing them back online. Damien was just grateful he could see.

A ball of energy started forming near Megan. Damien swung his weapon toward it. The energy coalesced into one of the creatures. She didn't react until the creature solidified. Brock cried out a warning, then leapt between her and the creature. Damien was already prepared. He fired a shot that caught the creature at the base of its neck. It convulsed as the charge rippled over its body. He needed to up the voltage. He was getting better at figuring out their anatomy before they fully manifested. The contacts were helping with that.

Another crackling outline began to coalesce. A bullseye pattern let him know where to fire. There was even a countdown timer. They might live through this encounter after all—if they weren't so outnumbered.

Megan roared, the sound laced with pain. Damien swung around, ready to fire, but Brock was faster. He slashed at the lizard-dog that had somehow managed to pin Megan to the ground, his claws raking over its scales. Blood sprayed the ground, staining the grass red. Within moments, the bright liquid glowed blue and vanished. The creature seemed mostly unfazed. It reared back, its jaws opening wide. The drool coating its teeth was viscous and tinted yellow. Damien had a terrible feeling about this. He couldn't let it bite her, but there was no clear shot.

He leapt forward, rolling on his shoulder and ending in a crouch. The interface adapted to his movements, bringing up the targeting screen before he'd even stilled. He fired the shot, not waiting to get his bearings. There was no time. A pulse exploded from the end of the stingray. It hit the creature in the side of its face, blowing a hole in its skull. The impact knocked it sideways. Megan rolled out from under it and Brock dragged her even farther away. The creature staggered a bit, then fell onto its side.

They could kill them. Damien felt the first real twinge of hope since the battle had begun—until a crackling sphere of energy appeared over it.

"Get away from it," Damien yelled.

Another lizard-dog appeared above the one that had fallen. It hissed at Brock and Megan, then dropped down so its stomach was touching the back of the maybe-dead one. Crackling energy surrounded them both. When it faded, Damien was left staring at another extra-large creature.

"You have got to be fucking kidding me," he yelled, firing another shot.

It leapt out of the way, landing close to Brock and Megan and hissing again. Narrowing its slitted eyes, it turned its attention to Damien.

"Vaughn, I hope you can hear me," he said, powering up his stingray to the maximum setting. "Because you need to know this isn't your fault. Please believe this isn't your fault."

He let out a shout and charged toward the creature. Its claws dug into the asphalt as it launched itself at him as well. The targeting system in his lenses told him to wait. Numbers and grid lines appeared, letting him know where and when to fire. Vaughn's tech wouldn't fail him. Damien just had to trust—

A sharp flare of light sent new agony through Damien's skull. He staggered, but kept his feet. Shaking his head to clear it, he blinked rapidly, looking around. The creature was reacting as well. It dropped to the ground and stumbled aside. All of them did.

"Why did they stop attacking?" Megan asked. Damien could hear the fear in her voice, even as distorted as it was from speaking in her werewolf form.

"A better question is, what are they waiting f—" Brock threw his head back and roared, the sound full of pain. Energy poured out of his right eye—his blue eye—and rippled over his body. His fur retreated and his muscles and bones shrank down. He doubled over, landing on his hands and knees.

"Brock," Megan screamed.

She reached for her mate. When her claws hit the energy surrounding him, she shrieked and was blown back, skidding across the ground. Damien ran to her as she shifted back to her human form. He pulled her against his chest, as if that could protect her from whatever the fuck was going on.

"What... What's happening?" she asked.

"I don't know."

Brock was still on all fours—still screaming. The creatures slowly circled him, Megan and Damien all but forgotten. Energy leapt from Brock's back, forming electric arcs of white-blue light.

"I have to go to him." Megan pushed against Damien's chest, but he held tight. "Let me go to him."

Whatever had happened to her must have weakened her, because Damien was able to hold on.

"Tammie, stop," he said.

"I'm Megan," she yelled back. "Stop calling me that."

What had he called her again? He shook his head, trying to clear it. His ears were ringing. No, there was a keening sound. It was all around them, coming from Brock.

Brock yelled again, dragging his fingers across the rough surface of the road as if he still had claws. His body convulsed, spittle flying from his mouth. The light surrounding him faded for a moment. Damien wished he could believe it meant whatever was happening to Brock was passing, but he knew better.

Brock threw his head back again and screamed as the light concentrated on his back, an outline of a person emerging. Arcs of energy leapt out again, blackening the pavement where it struck. Instead of fizzing out, it kept crackling, rising from the ground into the distinct shape of a man.

"Holy shit," Damien murmured.

Brock retched and moaned as the energy surrounding him lessened. The light grew brighter at each spot, then subsided, leaving behind… Jonathan.

Actually, Jonathan*s*. Half a dozen of them.

The naked replicants stepped away from Brock, forming a perfect circle around him, their movements absolutely in synch. As they pressed forward, the lizard-dogs retreated.

"Damien," Megan whispered. "What's going on?"

"I have no fucking clue."

He half-lifted Megan to her feet, the pair of them still crouching as they moved closer to Brock. There was a tendril of energy connecting the replicants and forming an actual circle around him. Another line of energy linked each replicant to Brock in the center, forming a kind of dome. The Jonathans kept stepping outward, getting closer. Damien was wary of the pale light passing between them after what had happened to Megan when she'd touched it. He brought them to a stop.

The closest replicant to them made eye contact, his white eye shining like a searchlight. Damien could see currents in the energy surrounding them. He turned, hoping to get away, but two of the lizard-dog creatures lurked behind him. Trapped between the two forces, he didn't see much choice.

"I really hope this works." He kept Megan tucked against his side and backed up to the energy field. His skin tingled where it touched him, but it didn't blast him. As soon as they were inside the dome, Megan pushed away from him, staggering toward Brock.

Brock moaned, spitting out a mouthful of blood. "I thought I was done with this bullshit," he said.

Megan dropped to her knees at his side, stroking his hair and pressing a kiss to his forehead. "It's okay," she said. "I'm here. I'm here now."

Something crackled behind them. Damien turned to see one of the creatures raking its claws against the energy field. The lizard-dog's scales sizzled and it jerked away. The field had let Damien and Megan pass, but was keeping these things out. Damien had a feeling they needed to stay inside of it.

"Vaughn, are you seeing this?" Damien subvocalized.

There wasn't a response. Maybe the energy surrounding them was cutting off their communication. He really hoped she was seeing this, though. Aside from it being really good information to have about the capabilities of their crew, it was pretty fucking amazing. He'd seen so much in the field, but nothing like this before.

The Jonathans started taking steps backward, each moving in unison. Damien huddled back with Brock and Megan. The energy thread that had been connecting Brock to the others was gone. At least, Damien couldn't see it anymore, even with Vaughn's contacts. He looked around at everything, trying to get as much data for her as he could. Just for the hell of it, he even glanced above them and almost did a double-take.

Something was there.

He tried to get a better look, but his neck cramped suddenly, forcing his gaze down to the Jonathans and the strange beasts circling them. It was almost like his body was making him look away.

What the hell did I just see?

His vision flickered and that transparent computer screen appeared again, floating a few feet away from him. This time, it gave him a playback of his survey, pausing on the thing that had caught his attention.

It was a drone. A really weird drone.

It was shaped like a donut, but with wicked spikes on its edges. They whirled around its center, looking sharp and deadly. The middle of the donut wasn't empty. There was a ball of some kind of clear quartz in it, with circles of light glowing on its surface. The video on the screen slowly stepped forward. The lights were sliding from side to side. The way they moved... It was almost organic. Like the lights were little eyes studying the battlefield.

That's not creepy at all.

Pale blue energy encapsulated the whole thing. As Damien kept staring at the display, he realized that the drone was translucent. He wasn't entirely sure how he'd seen it in the first place. He wanted to look again—with his regular eyes. But he had a feeling... He didn't think he had regular eyes anymore.

"Megan." Damien dropped down next to her and put his hand on her back, leaning close. With his mouth right at her ear, he whispered, "Look around. Look everywhere around. Tell me what you see."

"What?" She shook her head. "I, uh... I..." She glanced over her shoulders, then shook her head again. "I just see a bunch of Jonathans. And for some reason, the things we've been fighting are just circling them. They aren't attacking."

"You don't see the energy field?" Damien asked.

"What energy field?" she said.

"I see it." Brock's throat sounded wrecked. It was almost as hard to understand him as when he was transformed.

"The field?" Damien said.

"Yeah." Brock closed his eyes and sat back on his knees, taking deep breaths in through his nose and blowing them out through his mouth.

"What field?" Megan said. "I don't see anything."

Damien shifted his weight so that he was closer to Brock. He leaned in, and put his hand on the back of Brock's neck. He felt the other guy stiffen, but Brock didn't say anything.

"Don't react," Damien said, getting right next to Brock. Damien started to rub his neck, using the motion to move Brock's head where he wanted it.

"I wouldn't know how to react even if I wanted to," Brock whispered.

Damien actually chuckled. Megan was staring at him with wide, glowing golden eyes.

He leaned as close to Brock's ear as he dared and whispered, "Open your eyes. Don't react."

Brock took a particularly deep breath, then opened his

eyes. Damien felt the smallest flutter beneath his hand, still rubbing Brock's neck. Brock angled his head to the side and grunted. He turned to Damien, eyes a crackling fire of yellow and blue.

"Thanks, man," Brock said. "I'm good."

Damien nodded. He wasn't sure if that meant Brock could see it as well or not. Damien's own neck had stopped cramping. He wanted to get another look at the drone himself. Repositioning himself so he was sort of hovering over the pair of werewolves, he let himself sweep the area with a steady gaze. He hoped that it would look like he was giving everything the same level of attention while giving himself a little more time to look right at the drone.

The beasts were still circling the replicants, occasionally glancing toward each other as if they were communicating somehow. All the Jonathans stood statue-still, but Damien could see the energy field between them growing brighter. That didn't seem good. He turned his gaze upward, as if carefully scanning for threats. His blood froze when he saw the drone again. One of those little circles of light on the surface of the central crystal was pointed right at him. It looked so uncannily like an iris that the hair on the back of his neck rose.

He tore his gaze away. That was not a staring contest he wanted anything to do with.

The contacts were doing their thing. Data was scrolling

around an image of the drone with parts highlighted in bright blue gridlines. Damien just wished he could understand half of what it was saying. Even if he could read that fast, he doubted he'd understand the message. It didn't look like any language he'd ever seen.

'*It's too fast for me to read*,' he thought, wishing his nanites could hear him. '*And what the hell are those characters, anyway?*'

The image flickered again, the data feed stopping. After a few seconds, bold text appeared next to highlighted areas.

[TRANSMITTER]
[MULTI-LENS CAMERA]
[CLOAKING FIELD GENERATOR]
[ANTI-GRAVITY UNIT]
[LOCALIZED CARRIER SIGNAL]

"What the hell?" he murmured.

"Are you okay, Damien?" Megan asked, glancing at him briefly before turning her attention back to the standoff around them.

"I have no idea," he said.

He looked at the creatures surrounding them— Jonathans included.

'*What can you tell me about all of these guys?*'

The image of the drone vanished as one of the circling creatures became the new data acquisition target. It was covered in gridlines, then an image of it appeared on the screen.

[INTERPHASIC ORGANISM]

[INTERDIMENSIONAL TRANSIT CAPABLE]

[MASS REDISTRIBUTION CAPABLE]

In the top-right of his screen, [BLACK SHUCK] appeared, along with, [THREAT LEVEL - RED] in blinking red text.

'That's great, but what do we do if we can't run away? Besides die?'

After a brief pause, the screen blanked, then a gridline appeared over one of the Jonathans. His image was pulled onto the screen, just like the Shuck's.

[QUANTUM ORGANISM]

[CENTRAL PROCESSING CAPABILITY DAMAGED]

[COMMUNICATIONS ABILITY COMPROMISED]

In the upper corner, it read, [HYDRA SUB-UNIT 5 — JONATHAN]

Damien waited for it, holding his breath.

[THREAT LEVEL… ASSESSING]

Everybody seemed to have theories about Jonathan and nobody seemed to know if he was dangerous to them or not. Seemed like Vaughn's contacts were forming their own opinion.

Which was weird.

No, not his contacts… His nanites. This was going beyond feeding him data. They were reading his thoughts.

They were *communicating* with him.

The nanites had never interacted with him like this before Scarecrow's attack. Had the creature altered them in some way? They did seem to be behaving differently. He remembered Vaughn telling him that the nanites refused to leave. Damien had just thought it was a programming error, but what if they actually refused consciously? What if they had *decided* to stay in Damien and were now evolving in ways he couldn't comprehend?

'What the hell is inside of me?'

[ENERGY OVERLOAD BUILDING]

"Shit," Damien said. "Get down."

He threw himself on Megan and Brock, shoving them to the ground.

"What are you doing?" Megan yelled.

Damien glanced up in time to see the energy that had been building in the Jonathans reach a level of white-hot light. The replicants raised their arms, pointing their palms outward. The energy exploded away from them, catching the circling Black Shucks. The light burned Damien's eyes, but he forced himself to keep them open. They were going to need all the data they could get to beat these things.

As the energy hit the Shucks, they opened their long muzzles in screeching howls. Their fur stood on end, tails straightening and limbs spasming. The black clouds he had seen before they coalesced burst out from them, pulling them into the inky depths. Instead of dissipating, the clouds folded in on themselves with loud pops. The Jonathans lowered their arms and turned toward the trio huddled on the ground.

Behind the replicants in front of them, Damien saw one of the Shucks on the ground. It was lying on its side, completely still. Its scales were charred and its fur burned off. As he watched, a much more familiar blue light crept over its body, consuming it like paper that had been set on fire. Wisps of the light floated up from its corpse, fading as they rose, until nothing was left.

"What the fuck was that?" Brock said, standing on unsteady legs. Megan draped his arm over her shoulders to help stabilize him.

"That was them helping," Megan said.

The Jonathans headed toward them. Dread unfolded in the pit of Damien's stomach. The screen in his vision was analyzing the replicants again.

"Vaughn, are you seeing this?" Damien subvocalized.

There was still no response. The dread in his stomach turned to panic.

"Vaughn?" Damien said, using the regular channel.

Still no response. He was about to truly freak out when a different kind of energy lit up in the Jonathans, coursing through their bodies. This one was more like the sparkling electricity in one of those globes you could touch and make your hair stand on end. As the Jonathans converged, they moved closer to each other, until their bodies touched. As soon as they did, the energy connected. Their bodies turned into bright motes of light in Damien's view, pulled together by all those sparks, combining. Once they had all fused, a single Jonathan stood before them.

"Holy hell," Brock said.

The interface in Damien's vision flashed bright red a few times, data points scrolling faster than Damien could see once more. Everything except the dweller type and classification in the top-right.

[THREAT LEVEL - RED]

Chapter Twelve

Dzzt. Dzzzt-pop. Dzzzzzdt.

Vaughn slowly woke to the smell of scorched circuitry, melted plastic, and burnt hair. She coughed a few times before she remembered her broken ribs.

No pain.

That wasn't right. She should be in agony. She'd been thrown around, hit with a chair, then blown up. Her entire world should be pain. She was still curled in a ball, leaning against the wall of her ops center. Maybe the pain just hadn't registered yet.

Gingerly, she felt her side. The ribs seemed fine. She pressed harder. Nothing.

She had a really bad feeling the pain was going to hit when she opened her eyes. That crackling sound was one she'd heard before—the first time she'd visited sublevel 2 after the explosion. It had come from the dangling wires left behind when the ceiling plates had been blown all to hell.

But that was sublevel 2. This was her ops center. Her home.

She pried her eyes open, blinking away the blackened

bits of crusty film covering them.

What the hell?

She wiped at her eyes with her arm, then looked down and saw that her skin was coated in soot.

"That probably didn't help anything."

At least her voice sounded okay. She rose, using the wall to help support herself. Except she didn't need it. She felt fine physically. Emotionally...

"Oh no..."

She looked around at her ops center, her heart pounding. The pristine white walls were covered in black char. Remains of monitors hung from wires dangling out of their mounting racks. Some of the plastic had melted and rehardened, forming macabre drips. She'd probably inhaled enough toxic fumes to take years off her life. But her lungs felt fine, too. She took a few steps forward, surprised once again to find that nothing hurt. She wasn't even dizzy from the smells.

"Oh... Oh no..."

She lurched forward to her desk. To what was left of it.

Two handprints were melted into the surface on the places where Jon had pressed his hands next to where Vaughn's keyboard and the main interfaces had been. In between, there was nothing but slag. The metal had melted, pooling in a puddle beneath the desk. She could see some of the internal workings where the frame had melted away. The circuitry was absolutely fried.

What the hell had he done to it? Was he okay? And what about the others? They'd been fighting for their lives the last she knew. Brock and Megan and Damien were out there. They might need Vaughn. They might be hurt.

Damien…

She hung her head, blinking back tears. How could she help anyone if she didn't have her base? This was the nerve cluster of the whole ranch. She knew she could rig something up in another room, but it wouldn't be ops. It wouldn't be *hers*. She pushed away from the desk, wanting to kick something, wanting to—

A patch of white caught her attention, freezing her thoughts—a silhouette against the wall, the surface pristine, in the unmistakable shape of her curled up body. She lifted her arms and looked at them. All the hair had been burned away and they were covered in soot. She touched her face with shaking hands. Eyebrows gone. No eyelashes. Her hair was burnt to the scalp on one side—the side that had been toward the main part of the room.

Why wasn't she in pain? Why wasn't her skin blistered?

She hated to think of what she looked like. No one could see her like this. There would be so many questions. Questions she wasn't ready to answer. She ran her hands through her hair again. Movement made her jump. She held her arms out to the side as her scalp tingled. Once it stopped, she very carefully touched her head.

Her hair was back.

She touched her face again. Eyebrows, eyelashes, present and accounted for. She looked at her arms. Even the hair there was back to normal.

"How did I do that?" she said.

She looked back at the silhouette on the wall. How had she done any of this?

A loud sizzling sound came from the door to ops, making her jump. She looked over to see the metal glow blue, a line appearing down one side. Dexter and Porter. She had called them for help. They must be trying to cut through the door to get to her. The place was even more messed up than she realized.

She looked at the silhouette again. Porter couldn't see it. There were too many questions already. Too many questions in her mind. She couldn't stand it if more started to pummel her from outside.

She tore her shirt over her head and ran to the wall, using it to scuff the outline and spread more soot from the surrounding area over it. She grabbed her chair and pulled it to the most intact corner of the room, just to the side of her computer desk. The metal there hadn't melted. Maybe Porter would believe she had sheltered there during... whatever the hell had happened here.

She pulled her shirt back on and crouched down in the space. She managed to place the chair in front of her as if it had been a shield just as the door to ops fell forward into the room. Dexter leapt in, swords drawn. He spun in a quick circle. His eyes widened when he saw her in the corner.

"Porter!" Dexter sheathed his blades. He didn't wait for his twin. He grabbed the chair and shoved it aside, then knelt in front of her. "Are you okay?"

The concern in his voice shocked her. She nodded, slowly rising along with him. She was eager to give them something else to focus on instead of her miraculous survival.

"I think so," she said.

"What the hell happened here?" Porter asked, joining them. His clinical gaze raked over her, eyes narrowing.

"I'm not sure. Jon and Nathan came in during the fight." Her stomach bottomed out as she thought again of the dire circumstances the others had been in the last time she had seen them. "Is everyone okay? I lost the feeds when Jon and Nathan... did whatever they did to my computer."

"They did this?" Porter asked. "With what?"

"I don't know," she said. "Themselves? But what about the fight. Is Damien okay? Brock and Megan?"

"They're fine," Dexter said. "They should arrive any minute."

Vaughn felt a tremor shoot through her from the relief she felt. Everyone was fine. She hadn't managed to get them killed by her tech failing at the wrong moment. She looked around at the ruins of the room. They might have to go without her full tech for a while.

"Dexter, go get a scanner from the armory," Porter said. "We need to figure out how Jonathan did this."

"He can do that, but you need to prep the infirmary for Damien," Vaughn said, as Dexter exited the room. She left out, 'Again.'

Porter shook his head. "Damien is fine. Whatever caused his contacts to glitch passed."

"What?" She wasn't buying it, no matter how much she wanted to believe Damien was fine and her tech was functioning normally.

Dexter returned with one of the larger portable field scanners. He started setting up its stand. Vaughn had to know that Damien was okay. She had to see for herself. Porter grabbed her arm as she headed for the hole in the wall that was now the door to ops.

"You're the one who needs to go to the infirmary," Porter said. "Eli is there. He needs to do a full scan on you."

She wrested her arm away. "I'm fine. I don't need any scans."

"Really?" Porter shifted so he was right in her face. "So you can explain how you survived an explosion that melted your ops center without leaving you a single scratch?"

For once, she didn't back down. She stood nose-to-nose with him and said, "I don't owe you any explanations."

Dexter kept his focus on attaching the scanner to its base, but jumped into the conversation with, "You have five minutes to shower and change before Damien gets here. Unless you'd rather have him be the one asking all of these uncomfortable questions."

Vaughn glared at Porter for another moment, then turned and stepped into the hall. Instead of heading toward the garage, she turned toward the infirmary. When she entered, Eli rushed over to her.

"Are you okay?" Eli said.

Vaughn was not in the same galaxy as okay. But she still said, "I'm fine," and headed straight for the infirmary's shower. Eli started to follow her, but Vaughn picked up her pace. Over her shoulder, she said, "I just need a minute. Okay? I really am fine."

Eli didn't seem to be buying it. Still, he didn't push the issue. Having eleven non-human sons and a cyborg werewolf daughter had probably helped him know when to back off.

"Okay," he said.

Vaughn hurried into the shower, turned on the water, stripped, and then dropped her clothes in a hamper. David was still in her pocket, miraculously intact—since he'd been on the side toward the wall and her body had shielded him from the blast. She set him on the sink's edge, along with a stack of clothes for when she was done. It was a good thing she'd been keeping up with the Blades policy of storing extra clothes near their bases' infirmaries in sizes that would fit everyone living at the site.

She stood in front of the large mirror while the water heated up. Damn, she was pale. She needed to build herself a tanning bed or something since she couldn't stand to go outside. She shook her head, then ran her fingers through her hair. She leaned closer to the mirror, checking out her eyebrows and lashes.

Everything had regrown. It was like nothing had happened. But something *had* happened. Just like the time that she was attacked by a Hive Father and almost turned into a ghoul—except the parasite took one bite of her brain and died. Then there was the time she was locked in an air-tight stasis chamber for way longer than the oxygen supply should have lasted, but never even became short of breath. Now this.

How many times could she cheat death?

She stepped into the hot water and closed her eyes as it pummeled her shoulders. Leaning back, she wet her hair, then dropped her chin to her chest and let her head hang. It could have been her imagination. She could have fallen asleep and dreamt that she was in ops when it had blown up. How could she have survived that blast? It was so much easier to believe her own gaslighting.

Just like the other times.

She opened her eyes. Soot and grime pooled in the water at her feet. Streaks of black wound down her legs. This was a lot harder to explain away.

The others would be back any moment. Vaughn needed to be ready to help them, ready to help Damien. Even if the contacts were working now, they had caused a massive issue in the field. She needed to focus.

As quickly as she could, she washed her hair and body, making sure every mote of evidence was gone. She even activated the infuser system that would neutralize any lingering scents of char. Damien wasn't the only one she was worried about asking questions. If Marcus or Tessa got a good whiff of Vaughn, their pack instincts would activate and they'd be all over her, trying to reassure themselves that she was okay. She couldn't even reassure *herself* that she was okay. There was no way she could convince them.

The moment she was clean and rinsed, Vaughn leapt out of the shower and dried herself off. She pulled on the clothes she'd set out for herself, then slipped David back in his usual pocket in her cargo pants. She ran her fingers through her wet hair, turning to the mirror to make sure she looked okay. Nothing was out of place. Not a hair, not an eyelash. The same long brown hair hung down past her shoulders, darkened from the water of the shower. Her eyes were such a vivid blue, they almost seemed to glow. She leaned closer to the mirror, staring at them more intently. She'd never seen anyone with eyes as blue as hers, human or dweller. It reminded her of the color of the energy that consumed dwellers after they died.

The thought sent a chill through her. She ran the towel over her hair once more and turned away from her own reflection. There was too much to do for her to get caught up in that spiral—and she had no doubt she would drown in her suppositions before too long. She tossed the wet towel in the hamper and walked back to the infirmary.

Damien was there, sitting on an exam table with his back to her. Brock was at Damien's side, sitting shoulder-to-shoulder, while Megan fussed over them both. Eli and Porter had stethoscopes pressed against each of their patients, exchanging looks and nods as they conducted their examinations. Off to the side, Jon or Nathan stood, his arms crossed over his massive chest. Marcus and Tessa hung back, lingering in the space between the replicant and the others.

"Nice of you to join us." Dexter's smooth voice in Vaughn's ear made her jump. He was leaning against the wall next to the door to the showers, his smirk firmly in place. He'd probably been waiting for her. "Feeling better?"

"Yeah, thanks." She kept her voice flat. The way Dexter was staring at her made her feel like a mouse being stalked by a cat.

Damien twisted around on the table, staring at her with

bright golden eyes. The contacts were still working—sort of. Why hadn't they removed them, though?

"Hey," Damien said. His thick brows furrowed. "You okay?"

"Yeah." Vaughn forced her voice to be light. "I should really be asking you that, though."

He slid off the table, crowding Porter away as he stood. As Damien approached her, his eyes glowed even more intensely with that gold light from the contacts. He didn't stop until he was a breath away.

"You sure you're okay?" he asked. "We passed by ops —what's left of it—on the way in. Everything's slagged."

Right. Her last bastion of usefulness had been destroyed. The only workspace she had left that was intact was on the ship, and it couldn't do much to help them now, unless someone needed to go into stasis. She really hoped that wouldn't be necessary for a long time.

"I'm okay," she said.

"Were you in there when it happened?" Damien pressed.

"Of course not." Dexter cut in with his smooth voice, still leaning against the wall. "No one in that room could have survived the explosion. No one human, anyway."

Such a dick.

The cold gleam in Dexter's eyes chilled her. She suppressed her shiver, not letting him bait her. She turned her attention to where it needed to be right now. To

Damien.

"Why are you still wearing the contacts?" she asked.

Damien opened his mouth to speak, then closed it again. He turned back to Porter and said, "We all good here?"

"I can't find anything wrong with you," Porter said. "Vaughn's nanites have done an excellent job keeping you together."

Damien turned back to Vaughn, smirking. There was an intensity to his stare that sent a shiver of a different kind over her skin.

"Yeah, they are," Damien said. "Since the wetworks are fine, that just leaves the tech. Mind if we use your lab across the hall to check these things out?"

Porter shrugged. "Be my guest. I'll be busy trying to get Jonathan to let me examine him anyway."

"Is he okay?" Vaughn asked, as much because she was concerned as to keep the attention off of herself. She wanted to know he was alright before she kicked his ass for destroying her ops center.

"He seems as fine as he ever is, but the fact that he just teleported himself miles away by popping out of Brock in the form of half a dozen replicants, blasted our new enemies with an unknown energy pulse, and then merged into one single being bears some investigating," Porter said.

Vaughn felt her newly grown eyebrows rise. "He

what?"

That would explain why ops was destroyed. That much quantum energy... It was even more of a miracle that she survived than she realized.

"Porter and Eli have got this." Damien gently grasped her elbow, steering her toward the door. "Didn't you want to check out my contacts?"

Damn, was he doing that on purpose? Trying to distract her from Jonathan just like she'd been trying to distract everyone from herself? Unfortunately, it was working. Jonathan did seem fine, and Damien's contacts needed to come out immediately. So did the nanites.

"Porter and Eli are our doctors," Vaughn said. "They should be there if I'm going to try to remove the contacts and nanites."

"They'll be right across the hall." Damien let go of her elbow, but only to wrap his arm around her waist. Fireworks exploded in her belly, obliterating her line of thought. "And like they said," he continued, "the conventional exam is done. Now, I need the IT gal."

She caught how Dexter's smirk deepened as Damien guided her toward the door. They crossed the hallway to Porter's lab. She hesitated when it was time to press her hand to the access panel. Would it even work? Had her biometric data changed when she'd been burned—or at least should have been burned? Or had her body repaired itself to the exact state she'd been in before the blast?

Damien leaned past her, his broad chest brushing against her arm. He pressed his own palm against the scanner. Lines of blue light ran up and down and sideways on the panel, checking his data. Then the retinal scan kicked on.

"That won't work with the—" Vaughn stopped when Damien shifted even closer, turning to stare at the scanner.

As she watched, the gold coating his irises melted away, revealing the rich brown beneath. The light above the door switched to green and the door slid open.

Damien's irises flooded with gold again as he gestured toward the opening. "After you."

What *the fuck* was going on? With one more glance at him, she headed inside. The door whispered shut behind them.

"Damn," Damien said.

Vaughn turned back to him. "What's wrong?"

He looked up and down her body, then smirked. "The x-ray vision only works in the field."

She let out a half-strangled laugh. How could he make jokes? And why would he joke about that? She had sensed something between them—or, at least, thought she had. But Damien was acting almost punch-drunk. The nanites must be affecting his system.

"If you can hop up on the exam table, I'll get the portable scanner," she said.

The device was actually sitting on one of the long

counters running along the walls of the lab. She picked it up and turned around, her heart suddenly lurching against her chest. Damien was right behind her, close enough for her to feel his heat.

"I'd rather stand, if it's all the same," he said. "I don't want to think about what Porter has had on his tables."

She arched an eyebrow. "I can't argue with that. I guess I'll just..."

She lifted the scanner a bit awkwardly with the limited space between them. Blue lines appeared, outlining Damien's face like the handprint scanners outside the rooms. Vaughn slowly lowered the scanner down the front of his body, trying to ignore the lines of thick muscle pressing against his clothing—especially ignoring the thickness a bit below his belt.

"Could you..." She coughed to clear her throat. "Um, turn around for me?"

"Sure thing."

Damien slowly complied. As soon as he was looking the other way, Vaughn stared up at the ceiling, casting a silent entreaty to the universe to help her through this encounter without utterly embarrassing herself. She went back to her scans, trying even harder to ignore the view and focus on the data as she knelt to get a thorough reading. She rose, finishing her scan, then turned toward the counter and set down the machine. Her heart wouldn't calm down. It didn't help that Damien shifted even closer, his chest brushing against her back as he looked over her shoulder at the scanner's screen.

"What's the verdict?" he quipped.

"It's… weird. The nanites aren't responding to the scanner's inquiries at all." Her throat tightened as she reviewed the results, magnifying images from the scan of his eyes. She sucked in a breath. "No, this can't be right."

"What?" He rested one hand on the counter, moving closer to the screen—and her.

She shook her head, her stomach in knots. "The contacts have fused to the surface of your eyes. They're permanently affixed. I can't… I can't remove them."

"Then don't."

"How can you be so cavalier about this?" She turned around to glare at him, which put them nose-to-nose, with the way he was leaning over her. "Aside from the unknown health risks, your eyes are defaulting to gold."

He shrugged. "There are worse things than walking around looking like a werewolf."

She couldn't believe he had just said that. After what had happened to his family, he absolutely hated werewolves. Justifiably. It was stamped all over his psych profile.

She wouldn't go there. So she tried a different tack.

"Until you come up against a hunter," she said.

Again, he shrugged. "Smart ones will know to leave me be. Or is it just that you miss the brown?"

She clenched her teeth together, a muscle in her jaw twitching. Damien just smirked.

"Let me try something," he said.

As she watched, the yellow light of the contacts dimmed, the gold flooding to their edges and then running in lines along his sclera, leaving his brown irises unmasked.

"There," he said.

"How did you…"

"The nanites and I have come to an agreement."

Vaughn made a few stammering noises. So many possibilities, scenarios, and data streams poured through her mind, her thoughts tangled hopelessly. The only thing she could focus on was keeping Damien safe.

"We need to get those things out of you," she said. "Now."

She started to turn around, planning to get her tools. Damien caught her by the arm and pulled her back, leaning in closer so that she was pinned between his arms and the counter. An electric thrill coursed through her. She needed to stay focused. To help him.

"You've given me a resource that keeps me whole, makes me stronger, faster, able to see things I never could otherwise," he said. "I wouldn't let you take them out of me even if you could."

"We have no idea what the longterm effect will be of you having the nanites in your system or keeping those contacts."

His eyes seemed to smolder. Not from the nanites, just naturally. He leaned in closer and said, "Guess I better stick around then. So you can keep scanning me."

Her stomach flooded with butterflies. This had to be a side effect of the nanites, right? Or maybe wishful thinking. Hell, maybe she *had* died in the explosion or been knocked out and this was some kind of dream.

Damien leaned even closer and ran his nose along her neck. "Damn, you smell good," he said.

She swallowed hard. "I just showered."

"I could use one of those."

She needed another. A cold one.

Damien leaned back. "How about I go clean up and you make us a pizza."

"Pizza?"

"Cooking clears your head," he said. "You mentioned that during a mission when I was still back at the castle."

"Right. Yeah, it does."

"You need some 'normal.'" He half-shrugged. "And I need a shower. Head to the kitchen. We can meet up after so you can check me out more thoroughly."

The thought of being in the kitchen actually was comforting. Aside from ops, it was where she felt most at home. Even more than being in the ship. It warmed her that he understood her so well. Wait, what was that last bit he'd said?

"Sure." Her voice was high and tight, her cheeks burning. "Sounds good."

"Don't be too long." He turned and headed for the door. He paused before stepping through when it opened. Looking back over his shoulder he said, "I'm hungry."

Her eyebrows rose up her forehead. Did he mean... Was he...?

Before she could untangle her thoughts, Damien stepped into the hallway and vanished. Vaughn stood rooted in place for several minutes, trying to process what was going on.

Chapter Thirteen

An hour later, Damien was clean, dressed, and ready for company. Really ready, since it was Vaughn. He wasn't sure how long he would have to wait. Maybe he should have suggested something simpler than pizza. He'd just been so flooded with adrenaline after being out in the field. He turned on the TV and started up a movie to play in the background, but couldn't bring himself to sit down. Sweat coated his palms and his heart raced. He paced back and forth in the open space behind the couch. He hadn't been this nervous since... ever. Not outside of a fight, anyway. The big bed opposite the small kitchenette area kept catching his eye.

Too soon. Way too soon.

And yet...

They had known each other for years. Vaughn had helped Damien through countless battles. Now, he was helping her. The burden she carried was insane. Most people would have crumbled under it. She just kept shining through everything.

He shook his head. Damn, he had it bad.

A tentative knock sounded at the door. His heart leapt,

pounding vigorously in his chest as if it was trying to answer. His mouth was so dry, he didn't think he could speak. Instead, he hurried to the door, then paused to take a moment to calm himself. He tried to keep his expression neutral as he opened the door.

Vaughn stood there in a wine-dark purple shirt that gleamed in the light like silk. It was unbuttoned farther than he would have expected, revealing pale skin and perfect collarbones. She was still wearing the standard black cargos. He was sure she had that favorite tool of hers tucked into one of the pockets.

Everything about her was perfect. Those soft features and vibrant blue eyes. Butterflies exploded in his stomach. He clenched his jaw shut. What the hell was he doing, risking their friendship? Walking into battle against an unknown dweller was less terrifying than the thought of stepping aside and letting her cross the threshold into his room.

She lifted her arm, the sleeves of her shirt rolled up past her elbows and letting him see the toned muscles of her forearms. Damien could picture her in the garage working on the vehicles, sweat beading her chest and a bit of grease on her cheek. She'd be wearing a tank top to stay cool while she worked. Jesus, he needed to get his shit together.

At least for once, she seemed oblivious. Or maybe she was distracted by her own errant thoughts. She held a huge covered tray, a smirk pulling on one side of her lips, though there were lines of tension around her eyes. She pulled the lid off with a flourish, releasing the most amazing scent of freshly baked pizza he had ever smelled. His mouth had been dry before, but the moment the aroma hit him, he started salivating.

Her smirk deepened as she deftly transferred the lid to the hand that was holding the pizza tray, hooking its handle on her thumb. She leaned against the doorframe and ran one of her long, slender fingers down from the hollow of her throat, past her collarbones, and down her stomach. Damien followed the movement, enthralled. Heat exploded in his groin, his dick stirring. He curled his hands into fists to keep from grabbing her, throwing her on the bed, and keeping her there by any means necessary.

"Did you want pizza delivery?" Vaughn asked, a playful tinge to her words. "Or pizza delivery… person?"

His eyes snapped back to hers. The smile was still there, but it was brittle, like she was nervous.

You. I just want you.

The wave of emotion that rose in him trapped his breath in his chest. His skin rose in goosebumps, his heart pounding. He'd never wanted anyone more. It scared the shit out of him.

Vaughn's eyebrows furrowed, her smile faltering. Damien didn't want to scare her, too. He clamped down on his reaction and stepped aside, reaching up to push the door open wider. He left his arm in place so she had to come close to enter the room. He couldn't help himself.

Cautiously, she ducked under his arm, keeping the pizza between them. She headed for the couch right away. Damien took the moment to try to rein himself in. Vaughn set the pizza on the coffee table, then straightened, turning back to face him. Their eyes locked, and he very pointedly swung the door shut, then locked it. He watched her throat move in a long swallow, and his own lips twitched up into the ghost of a smirk.

"So... um... Romcoms?" She gestured toward the TV.

"You have a problem with romcoms?" He crossed the room to the kitchenette.

"No, I love them. I don't need any explosions or action in my off-hours." She murmured, "In a manner of speaking."

He chuckled softly as he leaned into the fridge to grab a couple of beers. He popped the caps off into the recycling bin, then joined her at the couch.

"Cheers." She took one of the bottles and tapped it against his, then sat down. Her back was stiff as she kept her spine absolutely straight, the bottle held awkwardly on her lap.

Damien sat next to her on the edge of the couch. He wanted to say something, but the pizza was making him drool so much, he thought he might choke. Instead, he grabbed a slice and took a huge bite. Flavors exploded onto his tongue. The perfect mix of cheese and sauce, the crust crisp on the edges and just the right amount of chewy otherwise. The thing was loaded with vegetables and meat that complemented each other and went flawlessly with everything else.

"Oh my god…" He hadn't meant to speak the words and barely cared. Normally, he'd have been mortified at the moans of pleasure accompanying his eating, but not with this. Not with her.

He glanced over to see her staring at him with wide eyes, her lips slightly parted. He shoved the rest of the slice in his mouth, then grabbed another. Instead of eating it, he offered it to her. She seemed mesmerized watching him chew.

"You gotta try this," he said, his words muffled.

She took the piece and sniffed it, her eyebrows rising. "It does smell pretty good." She lifted the slice, inspecting the dough's underside.

"It's even better when you examine it with your mouth." He smirked as he grabbed another slice for himself.

Vaughn sputtered a few incomprehensible sounds, her cheeks turning pink. She took a huge bite of the pizza rather than try to speak. Her eyes widened, then rolled shut.

"Oh my god," she said.

"Yup."

Her words were a little garbled as she spoke around the food in her mouth. "Okay, that is really good, even for me."

Damien chuckled, then asked, "When was the last time you ate?"

"I don't remember."

His stomach clenched at the words. This wasn't right. Vaughn took care of everyone. *Everyone.* Human and dweller alike. But who the hell took care of her?

"Sounds like you have some meals to make up for," he said.

"That might take a while."

"I don't have plans. Do you?"

"I always have plans." The color drained from her face as her lips pinched together.

"Not tonight. Tonight, it's just us. And we're not leaving this couch till you're satisfied."

Her eyes widened and she started to cough. He leaned forward, wanting to help, but she waved him away, gesturing that she was fine. She grabbed her beer and took a swig, then set it back on the table. Maybe he should cool it with the flirting. Damn, he wasn't good at this.

The drone of the movie in the background helped to make the moments that dragged on less awkward. He scarfed down his half of the pizza while she barely managed to get through two slices. She was so tense. There had to be something he could do to help her relax.

She needed a break more than anybody.

He took a big swig from his beer, then sank back, stretching his arms along the top of the couch. She stiffened rather than relaxing back into him. Every vertebra in her spine was stacked on top of each other in a perfect line. He wanted to run his fingers along it to see if that might help loosen her up. She kept eating methodically, staring down at the pizza instead of the screen.

Finally, she shook her head and said, "I guess I'm not as hungry as I thought."

"That's okay. Maybe sit back and rest?"

She half-turned toward him, one eyebrow arched as she pointedly stared at his arm. After a moment, she turned to face forward again and then stiffly leaned against the cushions. She interlaced her fingers on her lap and stared at the TV. Damien chuckled, then reached forward to grab her beer, making sure his chest brushed against her arm as he did. He handed over the beverage, then settled back again, letting his legs fall open so his thigh was against hers. For someone who had been so flirty earlier, she was wound up tight now.

Vaughn took a long drink from the beer, then chuckled and held it up, examining the label. "Did you know alcohol has no affect on me whatsoever?"

"I did not," Damien said.

"This is one of those times I really wish it did." She

shook her head and took another drink. "You know how all Blades go through a bunch of medical tests when we first sign up?"

"Yeah."

"I helped design them. I also went through them all myself. And every test says I'm one-hundred percent human."

What the hell was she trying to tell him? This was not what he'd expected from the evening—not that he minded. If she needed to talk, they would talk. He only hoped that he could help relieve some of her burden. She frowned and looked away.

"You don't seem convinced," he said.

She let out a dry laugh. "It'd be easier to believe if dwellers would stop freaking out around me and calling me a 'curator,' whatever that means."

"Curator?"

"I don't have any answers for you there," she said. "I wish I did."

She finally looked up at him. Her eyes were pinched around the edges. This wasn't helping her. It was making things worse. Why did she feel the need to talk about this now?

"Whenever a dweller decides I'm a curator, they try to kill me," she said. "They try to convince everyone around me to kill me. Apparently, curators are a 'threat to the planet' for some reason."

"You don't look that threatening to me."

"Thank you," she said. "And also, I'm a little offended."

Damien chuckled.

"Brock didn't used to look very threatening," Vaughn said.

"Brock? That guy is a fucking tank."

"Before Megan colonized him, he was bedridden. For years. We ran so many tests on him, and every single one came back saying he was one-hundred percent human."

Damien arched an eyebrow.

"Exactly my point," Vaughn said. "I don't really know what I am. Except… that *I* am what the monsters under the bed are afraid of."

She kept staring at him, eyes wide and worried.

"I'm not afraid of you," he said.

She let out a breath, but she didn't seem to be relaxing. "Thanks."

"Seriously, I don't give a shit."

She lifted an eyebrow as she cast an incredulous look his way. Damien half-shrugged.

"I've learned a lot already in the time I've been here," he said. "Things aren't always black-and-white. We need to learn to navigate the uncertainties. We're not going to do that if we can't stick together."

Vaughn nodded. She leaned forward to set down the bottle, then let out a sigh as she settled back, nestled closer against his side. Very pointedly, she lifted her right hand and rested it on his thigh. Electric energy flooded his leg and up his abdomen, hitting his dick along the way like a thermonuclear bomb. His abs tensed, his fingers tightening on his beer till he could sense micro fractures forming in the glass.

That was... new. And an unwanted distraction. There was a side table next to the couch within reach. Damien set down his beer.

"Oh good," she said. "Now at least you don't have something to whack me with if I'm being too forward."

He turned to stare at her, wishing she would look up and see how ridiculous that was, on many levels. But she was once again staring blankly at the pizza. Was that what she'd been doing, talking about being a curator? Did she want to clear the air before anything happened between them?

Damien was done playing coy. He lifted her hand from his thigh and pulled it up to his crotch, pressing it against his hard-on. That bomb of pleasure that had gone off before was nothing compared to this. He pressed harder, stifling a groan.

"You think I don't want this?" he ground out. "Want you? Come on, Vaughn. You're smarter than that."

Finally, she looked up at him with those piercing blue eyes. He released her hand, but only so he could grasp the side of her face and hold her still as he darted in. His lips crashed against hers, not as gentle as he would have liked, but her hand was still on his dick, and Damien's self control was at an all-time low.

Her lips were like silk. So was her skin beneath his calloused hand. He wanted to feel more of it, more of her. He reached up and started on the buttons, but his hand was shaking too bad and those bastards were tiny. He tore open her shirt, hoping it wasn't a favorite and vowing to help her fix it if it was. The buttons flew off, making tinking noises as they skittered across the floor. He pushed her back on the couch, plunging his tongue into her mouth. God, she tasted so fucking good.

She groaned, pushing against his stomach. He arched his back to give her space to undo his pants. She slid her hands under the waistband of his boxer-briefs and wrapped her cool, soft fingers around his aching shaft. Blinding pleasure rocketed through him, lighting up every cell in his body. He rocked against her hand, unable to stop himself, his tongue plundering her mouth. She squeezed harder, working his dick with a deftness that had the room spinning around him. It was like she knew exactly where to touch him to send him soaring. He was already throbbing, his belly tightening with need. There was no way he was going off without being buried deep in her heat.

He shifted his weight to his left arm, then reached down and clasped her wrist, pulling her hand away from his dick. His nerves let out an anguished cry, pulsing along his skin as if searching for her touch. With her onslaught on his senses temporarily paused, he tried to gather his thoughts, to make sure he wasn't going too fast for her. He met her eyes and the glimmer of doubt he saw there nearly undid him.

He pressed his hips to hers, grinding against her and ravaging her mouth once again. By the time this night was over, she would never *ever* doubt how Damien felt about her again. He moved his kisses to her neck, raking his teeth over her skin as he blazed a trail along her collarbones and down her chest.

In a breathless voice, she said, "Do you always kiss like that?"

He chuckled, nipping her skin. Of course, she would want to talk, even when they were doing this. He didn't mind. Loved it, even. He always wanted to know what she was thinking.

"Like what?" he murmured against her neck.

"Like you mean it."

Damien leaned back so he could hold her gaze. "Only when I do."

Those glacier-blue eyes of hers glittered even brighter as moisture gathered in them. But then she laughed and shook her head. She smiled up at him and said, "Cool."

Damien found himself smiling back. He never smiled with anyone. Not the other Blades, not even Carey. There was always a weight on him, pushing him down. But with Vaughn, it was becoming easier and easier to let go of every dark thing that had happened in his life. Every pain, every loss. The moments of levity she brought into every conversation, even her own burdens that she'd chosen to share with him, was like sunlight coming out from behind a cloud, warming him. Making him feel like he wasn't alone. He only hoped he was doing the same for her.

"You're the strongest, most amazing person I've ever met," he said. His stomach fluttered with nerves. "Are you sure you want to do this with me?"

"This is the part where, if I had the anatomy for a raging hard-on, I'd press your hand to it to make a point." She narrowed her eyes briefly, then looked up as if thinking. "That sounded a lot less weird in my head. Your demonstration was just really... powerful. And it's harder to come up with an equivalent—"

He leaned in and kissed her, somehow managing to laugh as he did. He hadn't known he could do that, but she was bringing so much out of him. She was showing him a world, or at least a way of looking at it, that he'd thought he lost. He wanted to show her how much she meant to him. He reached between them, sliding the back of his fingers along her stomach. He could feel his calloused knuckles catch on her smooth skin. She gasped against his mouth, lifting one of her legs to run it along his thigh.

She was wearing something dark and made of lace and

silk—definitely not Blades standard issue attire. And she'd worn it for him. A surge of pride and possessiveness blasted through him. This was his woman. *Vaughn* was his woman. At least for tonight. He couldn't believe she had chosen to share this with him. He would damn well make sure she enjoyed every moment of it.

He clasped his hand over her small breast, rubbing his thumb over her nipple. She gasped again, arching into his touch. He shifted himself down her body, raining kisses on her skin as he made his way to her other breast. When he could reach it, he grabbed the sheer fabric in his teeth and pulled it down, giving himself access to her tender flesh. He sucked her nipple into his mouth, flicking his tongue against it relentlessly. Vaughn was writhing beneath him, her hands on his neck, holding him tight.

He needed more. So much more. He slid to his knees in front of the couch, shoving the coffee table away. He quickly undid her pants, then tugged them down her thighs, bringing her panties with them and tossing them away. She had already slipped off her shoes. Without a pause, he hooked his elbows beneath each of her knees, pulling her closer to the edge of the couch and burying his face in her tawny curls. She arched her back, and let out a moan. The sound sent a jolt through him, lighting up his skin like he'd touched a live wire.

He circled her clit with his tongue and brought his hand around to capture her wetness. She was so ready for him.

He thrust two fingers into her core, stretching her, making sure she wouldn't have a moment of discomfort when he finally was able to fuck her. She grabbed the back of the couch with one hand and the cushions beneath her with another, her fingers digging into the fabric, hips bucking frantically against Damien's face. Her sheath throbbed around his fingers as she let out gasping breaths.

Damien rode it out, never easing up on the pressure, the speed, the suction. Only when she was totally spent did he release her. He half crawled on top of her, arms braced on either side of her head to support most of his weight. He leaned in and kissed her, finally able to control himself enough to be gentler, to try to convey everything he felt. This wasn't just about lust or sex. He cared about Vaughn. Deeply.

She pulled back and said, "I really, really need you to fuck me right now."

Again, he laughed, even as his nerves ratcheted up, his body on fire with the need to fill her. "Gladly."

Chapter Fourteen

Damien only paused long enough to pull his T-shirt over his head. If he hadn't, Vaughn would have torn it off, just like he'd done to her shirt. She would have tried to, anyway. She wanted to feel his skin against hers. Wanted to touch, to connect in every way possible. From everything he'd said and done, he wanted the same.

In one fluid movement, he rose up on his knees and grabbed her hips, pulling her further toward the edge of the couch. His dick found its home perfectly, finally filling her. She gasped as he stretched her to her limits, not hesitating before pulling out and ramming back into her. She wrapped her legs around his waist, bringing her arms to his neck and holding on with all her strength. Her nerves were on fire, screaming his praise, the sensations intense enough to override every other thought.

Waves of pleasure rippled over her skin, her muscles tensing to receive each thrust better. The friction was incredible. His rough hands kept a tight grip on her hips, keeping her where he wanted her, where he *needed* her. He needed this connection, too. The only thought that kept repeating through her mind, barely visible amid the scintillating pleasure, was 'Everything will be different after this.' She didn't know how, and that should have scared her, but this was Damien and she trusted him. Trusted this… whatever it was that was blossoming between them.

Another wave of pleasure crashed through her body, sweeping away the encroaching thoughts. Heat built deep in her belly. Damien shifted his arms to her back, pulling her off the couch, his dick still moving inside her like a jackhammer. She moved in time with him, tightening her grip with her legs, her arms. His warmth was all around her, his hands holding her with a gentle firmness that contrasted his passionate thrusts.

Vaughn was nearing sensory overload. She wasn't used to feeling so much, physically and emotionally. She lived in her mind, not her body. But Damien was commanding her attention, her existence coalescing on where they were joined. The heat in her abdomen became molten, energy pouring out along her nerves. She felt as though her entire body was turning into light. The energy suddenly collapsed, then expanded out in an explosion of pleasure that blanked out her thoughts and turned her vision static-white. A deep answering pulse began in his body, drawing out her ecstasy.

Damien threw his head back and yelled, "Vaughn!"

He finally stilled, his arms holding her tight as he rested his head on her shoulder. She collapsed against him, stroking the back of his head. Her stomach fluttered and her mouth went dry. She swallowed a few times so that she could manage to say what she needed to say to him.

She kissed the side of his neck, then whispered, "Lisa," against his ear. "My name is Lisa."

He stilled, not even breathing. Then he began stroking her back in gentle movements. He leaned back staring into her eyes. What she saw in his… She didn't want to name it, even though she knew, felt it reflected in her own being. His mouth parted and he reached up to smooth her hair back from her face.

"Lisa."

He breathed her name with a reverence that made her heart clench. She brought her hands to his face and kissed him, her mind too full of thoughts to parse out the right words, hoping that this would convey the depth of her feelings. Her heart beat fiercely, her chest felt overfull. When she pulled back he shook his head and smiled.

"Do you always kiss like that?" he said.

Vaughn laughed. "Only when I mean it."

A buzzing whine started in the back of her head, the lights in the room becoming brighter. She pinched her eyes shut, trying to force it away.

"Dammit," she murmured. "Not now."

"What is it?" Damien gently gripped her face in his hands.

"Another idea is coming. Ops is destroyed and I don't

trust the holoprojectors to work right anymore to record it." Images began to appear in her head. Chemical formulae, technical schematics. "Shit, I think it's about the chamber I made to help Brock split." She opened her eyes and shook her head. "It could be a way to help get Carey back."

Damien flinched ever so subtly. His eyes narrowed and a muscle in his jaw twitched.

"What do you need?" he asked.

"I need to go to the ship. Immediately, so I can make the changes before the ideas evaporate."

He grasped her waist and lifted her as he rose. Vaughn squealed and wrapped her arms around his neck to hold on. Damien was smiling when she looked back at him.

"Then let's get you to the ship."

She didn't want to go to the ship. She wanted to stay with Damien. They hadn't even made it to the bed yet. Hell, she hadn't even managed to get him naked. All because of the weirdness of being her—which was getting harder and harder to write off as just eccentricities. And here was Damien, being the most unbelievably supportive guy she could have ever dreamed of, even though he had every reason not to be.

"What did I ever do to deserve someone as wonderful as you?" She hadn't meant to speak the question out loud.

Damien didn't hesitate when he replied, "You didn't have to do anything. Just being you is enough."

"You're kind of making my case for me here." Vaughn laughed, but there was a bitter edge to it. "I don't even know what I am."

He leveled a serious look at her—as usual. "That doesn't matter. You know *who* you are. That's what matters."

"And who am I?"

"The IT gal."

The biggest smile she had ever seen on him spread across Damien's face.

"A joke? Seriously?" She laughed. "Okay, I guess I'm being a better influence on you than I thought."

"Then let me be a good influence on you. I mean it when I say it doesn't matter. You have a good heart. You use everything you have, everything about yourself, to try to help people. To help everyone, even people you'll never meet. Working with the Blades, it's all about keeping people safe."

"Even the people who aren't human?" She was afraid of what his answer would be, but she had to know. He was quiet for long enough that her heart started to hammer in her chest.

"Coming here has helped me see things better," he said. "And I'm not just talking about the contacts."

She chuckled and shook her head.

"I'm serious, though," he went on. "I always knew we were trying to make the world a better place for everyone.

Trying to find a way for humans and dwellers to coexist safely. I was worried when I found out about Carey that maybe there were ulterior motives involved."

"And now?"

"Now I'm *sure* there are ulterior motives involved. But that doesn't mean they're bad motives. That doesn't mean that what we're doing isn't the right thing to do."

"What changed your mind?"

"A lot of things. But mostly you."

Her throat was tight, heart pounding. "Because I'm not —"

"Because you are." He cut in before she could finish. "Because you're you. That's enough for me. It always has been."

Her eyes filled with tears. She smiled and wiped them away, then leaned in and kissed him—tenderly at first, but then he deepened the kiss, walking them to the door and pressing her against it. He groaned as he pulled back.

"If we don't go now, I'm not sure I'll be strong enough to stop," he said.

"That makes two of us."

Vaughn released her hold on his waist, straightening her legs and sliding down his body. He kept his grip on her hand until the last possible moment as she walked away from him, heading for her clothes. Damien fixed his pants and joined her, picking up his T-shirt. He waited till she had pulled on her panties and jeans, then handed his shirt to her.

"I'll mend the other one," he said.

"I'm not worried about it, especially if I get to wear your shirts instead." She let it fall over her, closing her eyes and inhaling deeply as Damien's scent surrounded her. When she opened her eyes again, he was staring at her with an intensity that made her skin rise in goosebumps. "We really better go."

"Yeah." He headed to his closet and pulled out a fresh T-shirt. Vaughn practically salivated as she watched him put it on, the thick muscles of his waist rippling with each movement. He smirked as he approached her. When he was close enough, he ducked down, catching her in her middle and throwing her over his shoulder.

"What are you doing?" She squealed, then laughed as he walked out the door.

"I'm taking you to the ship so we can get whatever you need to do over with and head back to one of our rooms."

Vaughn laughed the entire time as he walked to the elevator. She managed to input some commands into her watch to get it to drop faster than usual, her stomach doing flips. If Damien was nervous about it, he didn't say anything. She was as eager to get back to what they'd been doing as he was. Maybe even more. But first, she had to get these modifications out of her head and into the stasis chamber.

The elevator door opened, revealing the cave. A wave

of unease flowed through her, but didn't linger. She closed her eyes, trusting Damien to keep her safe. Before long, he was setting her on her feet in front of the hatch. The cavern really hadn't bothered her much at all. She kept her focus on the data pad built into the hull that would enable her to open the door. The moment it opened, she hurried through, Damien on her heels.

"That didn't seem to go too badly," he said.

"Well, you've given me a lot to focus on instead of my agoraphobia."

He chuckled. "And I'll gladly give you even more to think about once we're back upstairs. Let's get this done."

She nodded, then hurried down the corridor to the engineering bay that held the stasis chambers. The biofluid mix was off. She needed to change the chemical configuration, saturating it with a reactive element that could hold more quantum energy. Reprogramming the infusion units wouldn't take too long, but she had to do it from within the chamber.

David was in her pocket, and her other tools were already right there, waiting since the last time she'd been down here. It hadn't been that long, but it seemed like forever. She pointedly didn't look at the stasis chamber where she'd hidden when a rogue werewolf had managed to infiltrate the ship and had almost killed her. Even so, a shudder trembled through her.

"You okay?" Damien asked, standing near Zach's stasis

chamber.

"Yeah. This place just holds some bad memories for me."

"You want to talk about it?"

"Not really." She cast a reassuring smile at him. "I just want to get this done."

She wished she could say more. Maybe add something about how much she wanted to be in his arms in her bed. But her mind kept circling his question. She should talk to him about it. He should know more about her before things progressed. The trouble was, *she* didn't know more about herself. How she had survived hiding in an airtight stasis chamber for longer than the oxygen within should have lasted. How she had walked away unscathed after her ops room blew up. How a dweller had tried to colonize her, and she had somehow killed it, just with her biochemistry—biochemistry that still said she was one-hundred percent human. What could she tell him when she didn't have answers herself?

She focused on her work instead. Adjusting the feeds from the various chemicals stored in the wall behind the tank. Making sure the enormous reservoir of purified water that would be the primary agent filling the tank was still pristine and full. Reprogramming the integration network so that the chemicals could be infused with quantum energy.

That was yet another mystery driving her crazy. She

knew what she was doing would work, but she didn't know exactly how. The ideas and formulae would come to her like visions, and she would follow what they said. They had never let her down before. That didn't change the fact that she didn't know how she knew what she knew. She felt like she barely understood what she was doing and yet understood it almost on a genetic level.

Another shiver skittered down her spine. She probably did understand it on a genetic level. That's why it felt so strange on a conscious and subconscious level. Her DNA was feeding her information and her brain was processing it. That wasn't how it was supposed to work. Not for humans, anyway. Maybe that's what a curator was. Someone who was really good with technology. But if she was genetically programmed to be good with alien tech, did that make her—

Clink.

Vaughn froze, not wanting to make a single noise. She should not have heard that. The tank should not have made that sound. She didn't want to change any of the settings on her tools. Didn't want to alter how they were interacting with the tank in that moment at all. With how strangely her tech had been acting up recently, she had no idea what would happen. But the feeling in her gut told a different story. That unknown—that *alien*—part of her speaking up again.

The problems in the ranch had made it to the ship. The

errors and malfunctions that would happen at the worst time with the worst possible ramifications. Her heart sped up and her skin felt electrified. Something terrible was about to happen.

Clink.

She spun around as fast as she could, flinging herself toward the exit to the tank. She wasn't fast enough. The door slid shut in her face. She grabbed at the curved, transparent material, but couldn't get any purchase. She was trapped.

Damien was on the other side of the door in an instant. His eyes narrowed with worry. He pressed his hands against the transparent material, his mouth moving with words she couldn't hear but could discern from the pattern his lips made.

"What's wrong? Vaughn, what's wrong?"

She shook her head curtly, backing away from him. The foreboding in her gut became a screaming terror as she heard the unmistakable sound of water moving in the pipes behind her. Damien looked at her feet, his eyes widening, pupils dilating with his own fear. She didn't have to look down to know what was happening. She could feel it.

The tank was filling with water. Quickly.

He pressed himself closer to the door, fingers desperate for purchase, but finding none. Their eyes met and he mouthed, "Lisa."

Vaughn pinched her eyes shut. This wasn't happening. This couldn't be happening—not when they'd both been so happy just a moment ago. She spun around, unable to see the fear in his eyes and fight off her own as well.

Shut off the water. Shut it off, and then she'd have time to figure out how to get the door to open. The diodes on her tools that let her know they had power and were working flickered and went out.

"Fuck," she muttered. Her stomach felt like it was dropping through her body. The room—the tank—spun around her. "Keep it together, Vaughn. You're the IT gal. You've got this."

Behind her, she could hear Damien pounding on the glass. He was going to hurt himself at this rate. She turned around and forced a smile, trying to reassure him when all she felt was a building terror. Looking at him was a mistake. His rugged features were contorted with his own fear. The crease between his eyebrows had never been deeper, his mouth was open as he drew in panting breaths, the lines around his eyes deepened as the muscles pinched, his entire body tensing, wanting to help, wanting to… save her.

The water was up past her knees.

She turned back to the water-tight control panels built into the back of the tank. Damien would not watch her die like this. He would not see her drown. He wouldn't see… He wouldn't see her come back if she did.

Oh god... I'll come back.

How many times had she been in situations that should have killed her? How long till her luck ran out? Except, it wasn't luck. It was genetic. Part of her nature—what it meant to be a curator, maybe? The thought calmed her enough to help her think more clearly. She was more and more certain that she would come out of this alive—though she doubted it would be pleasant.

She reached into the water and pulled out tool after tool, trying to find one that still had power, wondering how she could use it without exposing it to whatever glitch or virus was obviously in the system. Not that any human computer virus could breach the alien-based tech defenses she'd programmed into everything.

Alien tech...

Shit, how could she have missed that? Theories and images sprang up in her mind, blinding her to her surroundings as they took over her cognitive function. All of her systems had security defenses. She worked with alien tech every day—tech that could do near miraculous things. No malicious programming should be able to get through.

But she had just recently learned that she wasn't the only one making inventions based on alien tech. Megan's collar had proven that. That collar hadn't been Vaughn's tech exactly, but it was obviously based off of the same foundation.

She was operating on an outdated assumption. Not just that she was the only one with access to alien tech, but that she was the best at interpreting it and making new inventions based on it.

What if she wasn't? What if the other curator had a better understanding of the alien tech?

They could have planted a virus within Megan's collar. It could have breached Vaughn's systems without her knowing it. She had scanned Megan's collar in the boom room, right before the collar exploded. The virus could have jumped to her favorite tool then. Vaughn could have been spreading it everywhere she went as she tweaked things or made repairs. Hell, the collar could have spread nanoparticles through the ranch that were designed to infiltrate deeper into her systems when it exploded.

The entire ranch was compromised. Her *home*. And now, the ship was compromised as well.

She forced her attention back to where she was, to her physical body and instantly regretted it. The water was up to her chest. She had two tools in her hands. Both were shiny, slippery chrome. The one shaped a bit like a stingray could emit electric charges and be used for small welding jobs. The other—her favorite, that she used on everything all the time—was a long cylinder made to resemble a tool from her one of her favorite sci-fi shows. She had nicknamed it David.

David emitted energy in different wavelengths that

would interact with the command panel and should be able to make the modifications she needed to stop the water flow. One tool had power, the other didn't. Of course, the one with power wasn't the one she needed to override the water supply. The blue light that was supposed to shine on David remained dark.

"Come on, David," she said. "You've never let me down before."

She tried to reconfigure the one working tool so that it wouldn't be receptive to any new programming. It barely had any security protocols built in for her to adjust. Why would her tools need that? She had never envisioned a situation like this one. Even if she could lock down its programming, if the other curator was using nanites to spread the malicious code, there was no way she could block that.

Vaughn lifted her arms higher to keep the tools out of the rising water. Maybe if she activated the working tool's repair function, she could somehow force the virus out of David and transfer the power from the working tool into him.

Water was lapping at her ears. She tilted her head back, entered the necessary commands as she held the tools high above her head, desperate to put her plan into motion. A spark flew between the tools, the current strong enough to zap her hands and make them go numb. Both devices fell into the water.

Dammit!

Tears flowed down her face. She had known it was a longshot, but she had at least wanted to try. There wasn't enough space left for her to try again. Her toes were about to lift off the bottom of the tank to keep herself in the shrinking pocket of air. Trying to fix her tools while treading water wasn't possible. There was no way out of this. Nothing she could do.

Damien was about to watch her die.

Chapter Fifteen

Fuck fuck fuck.

What the hell was happening? Vaughn was up to her ears in water and the tank was still filling, the water level rising with a terrifying speed. The door to the thing curved out into the room, making the tank a huge cylinder. It was made out of a smooth transparent material that Damien couldn't get a grip on, no matter how hard he tried. He darted from one side of the door to the other, running his fingers along the seams, trying to force his fingers into the cracks so he could rip it open. His nails broke and his fingertips bled, but he barely registered the pain over his growing panic. Nothing was working.

There was a communication panel on the wall near the tank. He ran to it and slammed his hand on the security scanner.

"Help," he screamed. "Vaughn is stuck in the tank and I can't get it to open. It's filling with water and I can't get her out."

The device made a garbled beep, then flashed red. Had the message gone through? Damien wiped the blood from his hand onto his pant leg, then lifted his shirt to clean the panel. He pressed his hand against it again. Nothing. Not even a sound of dismissal.

"Fuck!" He turned back to the room, looking for a weapon, a tool, anything that he could use to break through the glass. Everything around him was built into the walls or bolted down. Bile rose in his throat and his stomach heaved. This was not happening.

He ran back to the tank. Vaughn was standing on her tip-toes, her head tilted back as she gasped in air. She held two tools above her, trying to do something with them. A flash of light burned his eyes for a moment, then the tools fell from her hands.

"Shit!" He pressed himself against the glass, as if he could somehow reach through it and pick up the tools and hand them back to her. All she had to do was take a breath and dive under to get them and try again. Except she didn't. His heart seized painfully as he looked back at her. The pain and sadness in her eyes, the despair, made his blood turn to ice.

She couldn't be giving up. This was Vaughn. She was more full of hope than anyone he had ever met. She would never give up, unless… Unless it really was hopeless.

His eyes burned with tears. He didn't give a shit if she saw him cry. He *wanted* her to, especially if that meant she would start fighting again. Start trying.

"Please," he said, pressing his hands against the glass. "Please, baby, you have to pick up your tools. You have to try again. You can do this." He let out a laugh that turned into a sob. "You're the IT gal. Come on. Be the IT gal."

Her feet weren't touching the floor anymore. She was treading water, her head bumping up against the top of the tank as her movements caused ripples in the liquid. She was running out of room. Running out of air. Running out of time.

"No. Please, no," he whispered. "You can't do this to me. You can't leave me. Lisa, please."

She pinched her eyes shut and turned away.

"Lisa," he yelled. "Lisa!"

He pounded on the glass separating them. The skin of his knuckles split on impact, but he didn't care. He hit harder. Bones splintered. He could feel his nanites rushing to the areas, healing them. There was no way they could fix him if she... If she died. His mind shied away from the thought like it was fire. There had to be something he could do. She had changed him, saved him. He had to be able to save her.

Wait, she *had* changed him—given him nanites. He ran to the external control panel built into the wall next to the tank and pressed his bloody hand to it. That was good. The blood would help the nanites move, wouldn't it? They were already there, already close, healing him.

'Don't help me,' he thought desperately. *'Help her. Leave me. Go into the control panel. Open the tank or drain it or call for help.'*

His skin sealed and one of his fingers that was bent at an unnatural angle popped back into place.

'*Stop!*' he screamed in his mind. '*Stop healing me and get into the panel. You have to help Vaughn. Please! Please, I can't lose her.*'

Nothing changed. Nothing.

He was just as helpless as he'd been as a child when the wolves had come for his family. Just as powerless. Vaughn had only been in the tank to try to bring back Carey. To try to help Damien get his best friend back. She was doing this for him, just like what Tammie had done. Vaughn was about to sacrifice herself for him, and there wasn't a damn thing Damien could do about it.

Rage rose like a fire within him, building to an inferno. He screamed, then punched the control panel as hard as he could. Pain seared up along his arm, but the panel cracked. If the panel cracked, surely he could break the tank. He ran back to it and struck it with all his might, trying to ignore Vaughn's legs kicking, keeping her up at the tiny layer of air at the top of the tank—the only thing that was keeping her alive. A loud cracking noise gave him a moment of hope before the pain registered, a thousandfold worse than before. His right hand was at an angle it shouldn't be on his wrist. Damien didn't care. He had another.

Everything he did, everything he worked for was to be strong enough to protect the people he loved. To be able to fight for them. To save them. He had to be strong enough now. He couldn't lose Vaughn.

He pounded on the glass with his left hand, waiting for the nanites to heal his right. Blood smeared the glass, obscuring his view of Vaughn as she swam to him. Her eyes were narrowed with effort, a few bubbles escaping her lips as she grimaced. There was no more air in the tank. No more time.

Damien slammed his fists into the glass again, but Vaughn shook her head. She kicked her legs, getting as close to the glass as she could on her side. Damien pressed himself against it, too, trying to be as close to her as he could. She pressed her hand against the glass and looked at it pointedly, then at him.

His chest was so tight. His heart felt as though it was about to explode. He ran his hand over his face, wiping away some of the tears and sweat. His breath came out in a sob.

Vaughn was smiling. *Lisa* was smiling at him. His Lisa.

Damien pressed his hand to the tank above hers as if they could touch through the glass. He forced himself to smile back, even though his heart was breaking.

He couldn't save her. But he could try to give her comfort through this, even though it was rending his soul into a thousand pieces.

She slid down the tank till she was kneeling on the floor and he dropped to his knees in front of her. More bubbles escaped her mouth. Her eyes pinched with strain as she tried to hold on. Her lungs must be burning. God, how was he supposed to watch this? How could he be strong enough?

She managed to smile at him through the water, then mouthed, "I love you."

His chest seized. He couldn't breathe. He curled forward, resting his head against the glass. It felt like his heart was turning into a black hole, sucking in all of his energy, all of his hope, all of his light. But he managed to whisper back, "I love you, too."

She smiled and laughed, precious air leaking out from the edges of her lips. Then she closed her eyes and bowed her head. He saw her shudder, her body spasming as the last her air escaped, as the first water entered her lungs. He rose up on his knees, but kept his hand pressed to the glass above hers.

"Lisa. Lisa!"

Her hand floated away from the glass, then drifted down to settle into her lap.

Pain unlike anything he had ever felt racked his body. It transcended the physical. Pressure built within him, his heart pounding fiercely in his chest as if wanting to punish him for his failure. Every molecule in his body felt as though it was unraveling, and he didn't care. No, he *did* care. He welcomed it. He deserved it. If he couldn't keep the people he loved safe, what was the point of him even existing?

He couldn't save his family. He couldn't save Tammie. He couldn't bring back Carey. He couldn't break through the tank to save Vaughn. He couldn't call for help. He couldn't even get the damned door to open. He couldn't hold her. God, he wanted to hold her. He wrapped his arms around the cylinder as much as he could and sobbed against it, slowly banging his head on its transparent surface.

There was no more fight in him. There was nothing left of him at all.

He slid down to the floor and sat, staring at nothing. His forehead was millimeters away from Vaughn's as she rested in the same position. So close, and yet there might as well have been a universe between them. Damien let his hands drop to his lap, mirroring her. Wishing he could go with her to wherever she had gone. He let his tears flow freely, not feeling them. Not feeling anything. There was nothing left for him here.

Movement stirred in his periphery. Probably an optical illusion from the water in his eyes. It didn't matter. Nothing mattered.

Vaughn's hand twitched, then suddenly slammed against the glass. Adrenaline fired through Damien's system, lighting him up as if he'd been struck by lightning. How was she moving? What the hell was going on?

He sprang up on his knees, pressing his hand to the glass above hers, letting her know he was still with her.

God, he'd be with her through anything, for as long as she had on this world. She rose to her knees as well, her other hand reaching up to support her against the tank's door. Damien matched her movements, willing her to look at him, begging her silently to let him know what was going on.

"Vaughn," he said. "Vaughn, can you hear me?"

She lowered her head, not letting him see her face. Did that mean she could hear him? She'd just come back from the dead. Who the hell knew what else she could do?

"Please, baby," he said. "Please, look at me. Let me see you."

She shook her head, lowering it further. Her chest was expanding and contracting, as if she was breathing, but she was still submerged.

"Lisa, please," he pleaded. "I'm begging you."

Her hands curled into fists, but she kept them against the glass. And then she looked at him.

Her skin had turned silver-gray. White lines made large, irregular shapes resembling scale-like patterns on all of her he could see. Her pupils were huge, and the bright blue of her irises completely flooded her sclera. Her hair flowed around her head like a soft crown. With her hair out of the way, Damien could see the most beautiful change, the most miraculous. Rows of gills opened and closed along the sides of her neck, in time with the movements of her chest as she breathed—as she *breathed*

—underwater.

"Oh my god," Damien whispered.

She flexed her hands, expanding them against the glass once more. Webbing stretched between her fingers. She jerked her arms back, staring at the slight claws at the ends of her fingertips. She spread her hands wide, staring at the changes, her eyes roving up along her arms, taking in the scale-like pattern on her skin. Wincing, she pushed herself away from the glass and huddled in the back, curled into a ball. It was as if she didn't want him to see her.

"It's okay," he said, rising up higher on his knees. "Lisa, it's okay. I swear to you. If this is what you are, it saved you. I don't care if you're a dweller. I don't care what you are, as long as you're safe. As long as you're here with me. Please, Lisa. I love you."

She glanced over at him, her eyes casting an eerie blue light into the water between them. He swallowed hard, willing her to believe. She was just starting to move forward when footsteps started pounding down the hallway. Vaughn perked up, staring at the open door, then shook her head and buried her face in her knees, hugging them close to her chest.

"Dammit," Damien said. He rose, ready to face whoever the hell had interrupted their moment.

Dexter was the first into the room, followed closely by Porter. Porter ran to the command panel next to the tank while Dexter stood just within the door, scanning the area for threats. His eyes lingered briefly on the blood covering the walls near the tank and smeared all over its surface. He looked Damien over with the same cold focus. Tessa and Marcus tore into the room behind them. They blew past Dexter and ran straight to the tank itself.

"I can't get the tank to open or drain," Porter said. "It's not accepting my commands."

"Jesus Christ, Vaughn is in there." Marcus was looking all around, as if trying to find a button or a handle that would open it.

"It's okay," Damien began.

Before he could say more, blue light rippled over Tessa's body. Fur sprouted from her skin. Her face elongated, along with her limbs—even the cybernetic arm Vaughn had made.

Fuck, this was not going to be good.

"Just wait a minute," Damien yelled.

"While she drowns?" Marcus yelled back.

"She already drowned, but—"

Tessa let out a deafening roar. She flung Marcus away from the front of the tank, right at Damien. Even in his human form, Marcus was big enough to almost knock Damien from his feet. Before he could catch his breath to say more, Tessa punched through the glass of the tank with her cybernetic arm.

The water that had terrified Damien with its presence moments ago poured out of the tank from the hole she'd made. A new fear rose up in him. What if Vaughn couldn't change back? What if she needed to be in water now to survive?

"Tessa, stop!" Damien ran at Tessa, but she backhanded him. He flew across the room and slammed into the far wall. His head struck the metal bulkhead with a loud crack. He fell forward onto his face, fighting to stay conscious. Blood filled his mouth and the room faded in and out. Tessa was still attacking the tank. He had to stop her.

'*You guys better earn your keep,*' Damien thought, pushing himself up to his knees. He rose on unsteady feet, not waiting to regain his equilibrium before staggering toward Tessa. The floor of the room was slick with water.

"Stop her," Damien yelled.

"Why the fuck would I do that?" Marcus was still in his human form, but his eyes were glowing bright gold. Vaughn was part of his pack. More than that, they were best friends. Damien understood why he was upset, but dammit, Marcus didn't know what was going on.

"She's changed. She might need the water to—" Damien's heart sank as Tessa struck the tank's door one more time with her metal arm, shattering it completely. Water rushed out into the room, carrying Vaughn with it.

"Fuck!" Damien yelled.

He ran past Marcus and shoved Tessa out of the way. He dropped to his knees next to Vaughn, ignoring the growling werewolf hovering over them both. Damien turned Vaughn over as he pulled her into his lap. Her eyes were wide and she was gasping for air as if she couldn't breathe. The gills in her neck were flapping rapidly, but there was no water for them to filter oxygen from.

"Holy shit," Marcus said. "What happened to her?"

"Nothing happened to her," Damien snapped. "This is who she is."

'*Help me,*' he thought. '*Please, help me help her.*'

An interface flickered to life in his vision. Gridlines covered Vaughn's body in his view, dim enough to not obscure his vision, but bright enough to see. Data scrolled alongside arrows pointing out different features, the words written in those alien characters again.

'*About fucking time,*' Damien thought. '*You need to use my language, remember?*'

The characters flickered, then changed to English. Vaughn's body temperature was low. Much lower than it would be in a normal human. Her oxygen saturation was dropping, the numbers flashing orange, then red. Shit, she did need water to survive. He had to find a bathtub or something to put her in.

'*Fuck, what do I do?*'

In the upper-right of his field of view, more of the alien text appeared, bigger and flashing in and out, as if to draw his attention. The words changed to English.

[...CLASSIFICATION...]

[…]

[…TRACTUS…]

'Tractus? What the hell is a Tractus?' He'd never heard that word in any of his studies of folklore, trying to be ready to face unknowns in the field.

[…CORRUPTED…]

'Corrupted? What do you mean?'

[…GENETICALLY… MODIFIED…]

[…EXTRA…EXTRA…]

His eyes burned, the alien text taking longer and longer to translate. He needed their help now, dammit. He took a deep breath and blew it out slowly.

'I just need to know how to help her,' Damien thought. *'Please.'*

The burning subsided as the screen in his vision blanked. Damien willed the nanites to tell him what to do, desperate to help Vaughn.

[…]

[ASSISTANCE NOT REQUIRED]

'She can't breathe.'

[ADAPTATION IN PROGRESS]

'I don't understand. Tell me in a way that I can understand.'

[…]

[CLASSIFICATION: SURVIVAL-BASED SHAPESHIFTER]

A shapeshifter? Finally, some information that was

actually helpful. He'd never heard of anything like this in the Dwellers Database. If Vaughn's shifting was based on survival, then she should change back. She just had to understand how to be who she was. *What* she was. She had changed once. She could change again. She had to.

"It's okay." Damien smoothed Vaughn's hair away from her face. "You can do this. Just relax. You've got this."

Vaughn looked up at him, her eyes pinched with pain. Her mouth opened and closed as she kept gasping, her chest moving like a bellows.

"I know," he said. "I know. But I'm right here with you. I'm not going anywhere, and dammit, Vaughn, neither are you. You can figure this out. If anyone can figure this out, it's you." He leaned closer and kissed the side of her head. "Please, figure this out."

She closed her eyes and closed her mouth. Her breathing slowed and calmed. The silver-gray of her skin began to turn pink in the centers of each of the scale patterns, the color spreading out to fill them. Her gills sealed, leaving the sides of her neck smooth once more. The white outline of the scale pattern filled in, leaving her looking like... Vaughn. She opened her eyes, and as Damien watched, the color that flooded her sclera receded till he was staring at the brilliant blue irises he loved.

'*Is she okay now?*' he thought. '*Is she safe?*'

[ANALYZING...]

The readouts were changing. Everything was becoming green again. Body temperature, blood oxygen levels. The numbers flashed several times, then the display faded completely after one last message appeared.

[ADAPTATION COMPLETE]

Damien laughed. He couldn't help it. Relief flooded him, making him almost giddy. Or maybe it was the concussion. He leaned down and kissed Vaughn's forehead, then pulled her close against his chest as she clung to his arms. Blue light reflected off the water on the floor marking Tessa changing back to her human form. For one brief moment, Damien felt a peace unlike anything he'd experienced in his life.

"What the fuck was that?" Tessa yelled.

And then it was over.

"That was Vaughn surviving." Damien stood, lifting Vaughn to her feet as he did. He kept his arms around her, not ready to let her go. The way she clung to him, her own arms tight around his waist, gripping fistfuls of his shirt at his back, let him know she felt the same.

"Surviving what?" Tessa growled, stepping closer to Damien. Marcus reached out to place a hand on her shoulder, but from the way his eyes glowed, he was just as worked up as she was. "Why the hell was she in that chamber when it was full of water?"

"There's a virus." Vaughn's voice sounded strange, a hollow echo to it that made it reflect around the room. Had her throat not completely changed back yet? She coughed a few times, then said, "A virus in the system," in her normal voice.

"A virus?" Dexter stepped closer now, eyeing the machinery around them as if it might come to life at any moment and attack them. Hell, for all Damien knew, it could.

"It explains everything," Vaughn said. "The glitches in the ranch. My tech not working."

"But it doesn't explain what just happened to you." Porter also stepped closer, his focus intent on Vaughn in a way that made Damien's hackles rise. He tightened his embrace, angling her away. Porter's attention slid to Damien. "I'm going to need some samples. And we need to run a battery of tests."

"Fuck off," Damien said.

"He's right." Vaughn let out a breath that might have been a laugh in some universe, but sounded more like an expulsion of pent up fear. Still, she pulled away from Damien, turning to face the others, though she wouldn't meet their eyes. "The sooner we gather samples, the more likely we are to figure out what I am."

"We all saw what you are." Tessa shrugged. "You're a Creature from the Black Lagoon."

Vaughn winced. Damien lost it.

He'd just watched Vaughn die. She had *drowned*, right in front of him. And there wasn't a damn thing he could do to stop it. She might have survived somehow, but it had been tortuous. He had seen her pain, watched her body go limp after she lost her battle with the water. There was no way he was going to stand by and watch somebody— anybody—make flippant remarks about what she'd just been through. What they'd *both* been though.

He lunged forward, getting right in Tessa's face. "Shut the fuck up."

The werewolf snarled at him, her eyes glowing bright. Her lips peeled back from her sharpening teeth.

"Tessa…" Marcus said.

Damien swore the air in the room became thinner as everyone else sucked in a breath and held it. He didn't give a shit that they were scared. Tessa had hurt Vaughn with that callous remark. If she did it again, he would kick her ass.

Somehow.

"I know you've been through some serious shit," Damien said. "And that's going to give you a pass for a lot. But we just went through…" His voice actually cracked. Christ, that hadn't happened since he was a kid. He didn't give a damn. This was too important. He stepped closer to Tessa, till they were nose-to-nose. "We just went through some serious shit, too. Vaughn and me. You have no idea what you walked in on. She just fucking drowned, right in front of me. She *drowned*."

"Damien." Vaughn clasped his elbow gently. "It's okay.

I'm okay."

"*I'm not.*" Damien turned to her, his chest feeling like it might explode as the memory of watching her drift away from him kept replaying in his mind. He thought it might drive him crazy. He needed something else to think about, he needed to reassure himself that Vaughn really was okay.

"Everybody out." Tessa smiled at him. Somehow, the sight was more unnerving than when she'd been staring at him like she wanted to dig out his spleen with a toothpick. "Vaughn and Damien need some time alone to… process things."

"But, my samples—" Porter said.

"You need to get back upstairs and keep helping Eli with the tests he's running on Brock." Marcus grabbed Porter by one arm and started steering him from the room.

Dexter smirked at Damien and shook his head, but followed the others. Damien held Tessa's gaze as the room emptied.

"Don't be long," Tessa said. "We have work to do."

"We'll take as long as we need," Damien said.

Tessa's smile grew broader. It still had an unhinged edge to it, but it didn't scare him like it once had. He had to respect how well she was holding herself together.

"Welcome to the family," she said. And then she was gone, leaving Damien and Vaughn alone.

Chapter Sixteen

Shit shit shit.

Had Damien really seen Vaughn change into... something else? Her fingers had been webbed with claws at the ends. Her skin had turned silver and, even though it didn't have scales, there were markings that made irregular somewhat oval patterns that looked almost like shields all over what she could see of her body. But *he* had the better view. What had he seen? How else had she changed?

"We probably should have let Porter examine me," Vaughn said, her voice small.

"Next time."

Dread bottomed out her stomach. "Next time?"

He stared at her, his eyes pinched at the corners. His chest started to heave as his breathing quickened. His hands flexed and fisted at his sides. Whatever he had seen, it must have really freaked him out. The intensity in his expression froze her in place. She couldn't even think. He reached up and clasped her face in both hands, then brought his lips to hers in a crushing kiss. His tongue thrust into her mouth, demanding proximity. From this close, she could feel a tremor wrack his body. Was he repulsed by her now? Was he only doing this to make her feel better?

He moved his lips to her neck, kissing the area where she was pretty sure there had been gills a few minutes ago. One hand moved to the small of her back while the other gripped the side of her neck he wasn't kissing, his thumb stroking her skin.

Her stomach roiled.

"You don't have to—" He cut her off before she could say more.

"That scared the shit out of me," Damien said. "I thought I lost you."

"I…" She didn't know what to say. Was he accepting her, even after what he'd seen?

He pulled back enough to cradle her face in his hands again. Tears streaked his cheeks. The same pain she had seen through the water and specialized glass marred his strong features.

"I couldn't do anything," he said. Another tremor shook his huge frame. "I couldn't save you."

"It's okay." Vaughn shook her head and finally let herself wrap her arms around his neck. "I'm okay."

He bent down so their foreheads touched, gripping her hips tightly. "I can't lose you."

"You won't."

If only he knew how many times she should have died, but hadn't. She should tell him, reassure him, but she wasn't ready. Instead, she reassured him without words, craning her neck so she could bring her lips to his. He groaned, as if savoring the feel of her as his mouth moved against hers. This time, when he delved into her, it was more a loving caress. His hands flexed on her hips, moving around to cup her backside. Every touch, every breath, made her feel more grounded in her body. In *this* body. This form.

With a gasp, he broke off the kiss, and said, "I need..."

She nodded. "Me, too."

He dragged his shirt over his head and tossed it away, then gripped hers and tore it in half. He bent to one breast as he tugged the tattered fabric down her arms, taking her nipple in his mouth and sucking hard. As soon as her shirt was gone, he undid her bra and threw it aside. He clutched her back, his lips roving over one breast and then the other, nipping at her skin, grazing her nipples with his teeth with just enough pressure to electrify her nerve-endings.

He dropped to his knees, quickly undoing the fastener for her cargos. He pulled them down, along with her panties, grunting in frustration when he reached her shoes. She helped him get them off, then shimmied the rest of the way out of her pants. The moment her legs were free, Damien grabbed one of her calves and pulled her leg up over his shoulder. He buried his mouth in her silken folds, finding her clit and circling it with his tongue.

Pleasure arced through her. She was already so keyed

up from everything, her nerves lit up like dry kindling. Her skin rose in gooseflesh, her muscles tensed. She could barely keep her balance. She clung to his shoulders as he continued his relentless attentions. Damien reached up to stabilize her with one arm. With his free hand, he gathered her wetness, then slid two fingers deep within her, massaging her channel. The pleasure he was building in her grew like a tsunami. He added a third finger, pumping them faster, increasing the pressure with his tongue. The wave of ecstasy crashed down on her, flooding her body with bliss. She threw her head back and screamed his name.

Damien let out a pained grunt as he rose. He grabbed her arms and walked her back to the nearest wall, claiming her lips again in a searing kiss. She wrapped her legs around his waist as he lifted her from her feet. He reached between them to undo his jeans and jerk them down, then lined up his shaft and plunged into her, stretching her sheath to its limits. She held onto his immense shoulders, her fingertips digging into his muscles as he pounded into her.

His thrusts were nearly frenzied, his hands gripping her ass tightly as he pounded into her over and over again. She was still pulsing from her first climax, but the friction, the heat, the desperate passion between them set her nerves singing again. Molten fire exploded through her being, her vision going white. Her core clenched around him, urging him to his own release. She felt an answering pulse as he spilled himself in her, letting out a guttural roar. He finally slowed, then stopped, buried deep within her.

Still gasping, he angled his hips to keep her pinned against the wall, then reached up to hold her face in his hands. He kissed her again, slow, tender, and deep. Warmth spread through her, her chest filled with something like hope, but brighter. He broke off the kiss, but kept gazing into her eyes, his calloused thumbs tracing her cheekbones. His chest heaved with panting breaths.

Had she changed again? Was something different about her? She didn't know how he could be staring at her so intensely. He pressed a kiss to her forehead, then rested his against hers, his breath starting to even out.

"I love you, Lisa," he said. "With everything that I am."

A choking sob burst out of her as her eyes filled with tears. How could he love her when there was so much they didn't understand?

"But can you love everything that *I* am?" she asked. "When I don't even know—"

"*I* know," he cut in "I know you. And I love you. All of you."

Tenderly, he kissed one eyebrow and then the next. He tilted her face up so that he could do the same to her cheekbones, her nose, her jaw. His lips whispered a gentle promise against her skin. He paused with his mouth just above hers, close enough that she could feel the ghost of its touch.

"I love every part of you," he said. "All that you are."

He pressed his lips to hers, kissing her gently, letting her process his words. It was so hard for her to believe. After everything he'd been through in his life, how could he love a dweller? If that was even what she was. They'd never encountered anything like her before. What if she was dangerous? What if being with her like this could hurt Damien?

He deepened the kiss, reached between them to cup one of her breasts, massaging it, flicking the rough skin of his thumb over her nipple. She gasped in a breath as more pleasure flooded her awareness, pushing out her thoughts, bringing her back to this moment, to his touch. Had he done that on purpose? She wouldn't be surprised. He knew her so well already. Better than anyone ever had. And he loved her. Despite everything. Maybe even because of it.

She tightened her grip on his shoulders, tilted her head to give him better access. He was already hardening again within her. How the hell had he managed that? Not that she was complaining.

He rocked his hips against hers slowly, letting her savor the delicious friction as he pulled himself almost all the way from her, then plunged back in. He mirrored the movements with his tongue, claiming her mouth with leisurely strokes that somehow let her know he wasn't going anywhere. Her skin prickled with awareness, feeling his warmth, the rippling movement of his muscles as he brought them this pleasure, this connection.

He still had one hand on her ass, holding her up as her back pressed against the wall. With the other, he kept coaxing more pleasure from her breast, pinching her nipple, flicking it with his thumb, lifting its small weight in his huge hand and massaging it. His chest moved against hers with each thrust, so much of their skin touching. Heat built deep in her belly, spreading out along her limbs. She didn't know her pleasure centers could handle so much.

Electric arcs sparked along her nerves again, spreading through her. She moaned his name and he quickened his pace, landed harder, thrust deeper. The sparks suddenly exploded into an inferno, saturating her senses with pleasure. Damien was right there with her, his hands supporting her hips as he pounded into her, pushing her higher, till all she knew was this ecstasy.

"Lisa," he yelled, the pulses of his dick keeping time with her own climax.

This time, when he stopped, his arms were wrapped around her, holding her tight as close to him as he could. With their chests pressed together, she could feel the pounding of his heart through his rib cage, so close to her own. She clung to his shoulders, breathing in his scent, trying to remember everything about this one perfect moment—the sheen of sweat on his shoulders, the strength of his hands supporting her, the feel of him still buried deep within her.

"Are you alright?" he asked after a few lingering moments.

"No one has ever called out my name like that." Her stomach fluttered a bit. "I mean, it's probably not the best time to talk about that, but just... I've never told anyone my name before."

He leaned back enough to meet her eyes. "Not even Tony?"

Her eyebrows rose. "Okay, I guess nothing is off limits, even in moments like these."

How did he remember her talking about the one serious relationship she'd had in her life? She barely remembered the conversation herself.

"You can tell me anything anytime," Damien said.

"Most people wouldn't want to talk about exes while they're like literally still fucking. Sort of."

Damien only laughed, then he kissed her, deep and passionate. He pulled back again and said, "The first kiss isn't as important as the last."

Her stomach fluttered again, but in a much more pleasant way. "You really are perfect. You know that, right?"

He shook his head. "Far from it."

"Well, you're perfect to me."

"You're perfect to me, too." He smiled, and the sight sent her heart racing. He shifted his hips as their bodies 'disengaged,' but kept holding her up, staying as close as he possibly could. "Thank you for trusting me with who you are."

Her breath caught. She hadn't really thought of it that way, but he was right. That's what she was doing. What she'd been doing pretty much since he reached the ranch. Opening up to him a little bit more every time they talked. Sharing more each time she was met with his warmth and acceptance. Finding herself growing braver, knowing she had him at her side.

She gazed into his rich chestnut eyes and noticed flickering golden lights at the edges of the contacts that were now permanently fused to his corneas. Some of his nanites must be lingering near the surface so they could continuously scan Damien's environment. Vaughn had programmed them to heal his body whenever he was injured, but they seemed to be taking it a step farther and were insisting on keeping him safe.

The thought should make her uneasy, but instead she was grateful. It was just one more layer of protection for him. One more way to keep him safe when he was out in the field and she was stuck at ops. Well, at what used to be ops. She wasn't sure where she'd be stuck now. Maybe in the ship? Except, the virus that was plaguing the ranch had reached the ship now. There was no other explanation for what had gone wrong in the tank. She'd probably brought it along with her in her tools.

Until encountering Megan's collar, Vaughn had been absolutely certain of her place at the top of Earth's technical food chain. No one had tech or knowledge anywhere close to hers—except whoever had made that device. A device that had exploded and taken out an entire sublevel. And that was after she had interacted with it using her favorite tool. It would have been easy for someone with that level of technical expertise to lace the collar with a virus. She didn't have protocols for dealing with such scenario. It had never occurred to her.

The odds of one spaceship crashing on Earth were astronomical. Two was out of the question. Perhaps it was an escape pod or shuttle? She hadn't had a chance to thoroughly explore the ship and discover those resources. That needed to happen as soon as possible. Damien could go with her, though she might want Porter there was well. But that would only help them know more about what *had* happened—if her theory was even correct. She was more concerned with what was going to happen next. How could they get rid of the virus plaguing their systems?

Thank god Damien's nanites didn't seem to be affected. Vaughn had made them before the incident with the collar, back when Tessa had first come to the ranch and joined the Blades—after she had cut off her arm to save them all. The nanites in Damien had been created to connect Tessa's cybernetic hand with her biological arm. They were the test prototypes. Vaughn had stored them in an absolutely pristine environment not connected to any of the ranch's other systems, so they should be safe from the virus at least.

But then, Vaughn had made his contacts. Those had been created after the collar blew up. After the virus was introduced. And she had used David—her favorite tool—when creating them. It was probable that they had been exposed to the virus, the nanites carrying it within them like people transmitting the common cold.

Damien's contacts had well and truly glitched when they blinded him in the field, but Vaughn had thought that was more about his interaction with the dweller called Scarecrow. They had self-corrected shortly afterwards, probably thanks to his nanites. At least his nanites seemed to be working fine, aside from their persistent behavior of ignoring her commands for them to leave his body. The little bastards seemed to have developed a mind of their own, which was yet another concerning thought. Or maybe a helpful one...

Damien said that he and his nanites had come to an agreement. It really seemed like he could communicate with them. If the nanites were in the process of creating a sort of collective consciousness, maybe they could help Vaughn figure out how to defeat the virus. They were still following their primary objective of keeping Damien in one piece. If she could communicate with them somehow and explain that getting rid of the virus would help keep him safe, maybe she could get them to help her.

"Is the eye contact helping?" Damien asked in a low voice.

"What?"

"You've been staring at my eyes for about five minutes now. I figure you're sorting something out."

"Trying to." Vaughn laughed again. "It seems like you've already figured me out."

"I pay attention, especially to what I care about."

A little zing of warmth flowed through her at his words. Her brain was too fixated on this new problem to let her enjoy it, though.

"Are you still feeling okay?" she asked. "With your nanites and the contacts, I mean?"

"Never better. We had a little trouble dealing with whatever Scarecrow blew into my eyes, but it's resolved itself now."

"Wait, nothing malfunctioned until the interaction with Scarecrow?"

Damien shook his head. "Everything was perfect before that."

"And after? When the issue resolved, did you notice anything weird?"

His eyes widened slightly and his lips parted, but then he snapped his mouth shut. Something was going on, and he didn't want to tell her about it.

"Damien, you have to tell me," she said. "I think there might be a virus infecting all the tech on the ranch and now even in the ship."

"You'll sort it out."

"Megan's collar was made by another curator." Vaughn loved his faith in her, but he needed to understand what they were up against. "It might have had tech in it that could bypass my defenses and breach my systems."

"Shit," Damien said.

"If I'm right, your contacts would have been affected. So if they're acting weird, I need to know—not just for you, but for all of our safety."

He let out a sigh, then said, "The nanites have started communicating with me. Like talking to me directly."

She felt her eyebrows hitch up her forehead. "They what?"

"They respond to my thoughts. Mostly in the data feed from the contacts."

"Holy—"

"Don't freak out. They've been really helpful."

"I'm not— Okay, well, I am freaking out a bit. But that is just... I don't understand. How exactly do they respond?"

"I ask them to give me data and they scan things and tell me about them. Like the drone that was watching us back when we were fighting the Black Shucks."

"What drone? And what Black Shucks?" She let out an exasperated sound, then said, "Put me down, please."

He released his hold and lowered her from the wall. Her feet splashed in the water at their feet. She should be freezing, standing there naked with wet hair, but she was actually comfortable. She filed that factoid away to examine later. Right now, there were more important things to think about. She started picking her clothing up from the water, squeezing out what she could and shimmying into the wet clothes.

"We forgot to tell you about the drone, didn't we?" Damien said.

"Yeah." Her shirt was in tatters. Damien's had actually landed on a workbench and was dry. Vaughn grabbed it and pulled it over her head. More out of habit than anything, she picked up David and slid him into her back pocket. She wouldn't use him on anything, but having him close would still be a comfort.

"There was a lot going on." Damien shrugged. "When the Black Shucks attacked, there was a drone watching the fight. It was cloaked and had an anti-gravity generator active."

Vaughn closed her eyes, her mind flooding with images, data, and scenarios as she parsed the new information he was giving her. The disjointed pieces didn't match up. Too much was missing.

She shook her head and said, "Okay, how do you know

it had an anti-gravity generator and why are you calling those creatures Black Shucks? There's not an entry for that legend in the Dwellers Database yet."

"My nanites told me. There was a readout in my field of vision that gave me information about everything that was going on. The Black Shucks were listed as interphasic and there was something about interdimensional travel and mass redistribution. Oh, and they're threat level red, unsurprisingly."

Holy crap, that was a lot of information. Great information, only some of which Vaughn had already figured out.

"What about the drone?" she asked.

"It looked like a spiky donut with a crystal suspended in the center that had lights that I think were sensors or cameras. Only Brock and I could see it and the van's cameras didn't pick it up."

Fuck.

"I know we should have probably said something before, but there was a lot going on," Damien said. "Brock and Jonathan did that really freaky split-teleporting thing and ops was blown to hell when we got back. I was more concerned with making sure you were okay."

"I guess I was distracted, too," she said, letting the new data settle in. "I want to be sure I have this straight. Someone was observing the fight with super advanced tech. Let's assume it's the same asshole who made

Megan's collar and designed the virus that's attacking our systems."

"They could be behind the Black Shuck attacks, too," Damien said. "Those things seem targeted."

"That would mean they can control them, which actually tracks. The crazy werewolf who attacked us and sent Megan here in the first place wearing the collar was working with more trolls than I knew existed on the planet. They dug out the ship for him so he could get to Brock, even though thousands of them died in the process."

"So the trolls were being controlled."

"Undoubtedly."

"And maybe the Shucks are as well."

"It seems likely," Vaughn said.

"If we can interrupt that control, maybe we can break the link and get them to leave us alone."

"But the top priority still needs to be defeating the virus. If our weapons fail or the vehicles malfunction, you're sitting ducks out there."

"My nanites seem to be doing fine."

"Aside from blinding and deafening you and making you hallucinate."

"Hey." He lifted his hands to her arms, gently gripping her elbows. "That wasn't your fault. And they were fine till Scarecrow sneezed on me or whatever. Unless part of their glitching is what made her hands catch fire."

"Wait, that's right. Her hands did catch fire after she waved them in front of your eyes."

"She didn't just wave them in front of my eyes," he said. "I'm pretty sure she was scanning my contacts somehow."

Vaughn closed her eyes and took a deep breath, letting it out slowly. She had so many of the pieces. Now, she just needed to let her brain do its thing. She had seen the data from Damien's contacts when he first encountered Scarecrow. The dweller was filled with tiny motes of energy that somehow could animate the clothing she wore and the straw that made up her limbs and body. The motes of light actually reminded Vaughn a lot of her nanites. What if they were something similar? Similar enough for the virus that was most likely latent in Damien's contacts to affect?

Vaughn had been theorizing that Scarecrow was some kind of energy matrix. With another curator in the mix, anything was possible when it came to what the virus could interact with. It would explain why Scarecrow had combusted her own hands immediately after doing her own scan of Damien's lenses. Checking out the tech and then making sure it couldn't infect her with the virus. Since dwellers apparently had a thing against curators and 'curator tech,' maybe that was why Scarecrow had attacked Damien.

Something didn't feel right about that, though.

Scarecrow had blown something into Damien's face—into his eyes. He'd been hurt badly for a while, but then he'd fully recovered and then some. If the virus could interact with Scarecrow, did that mean that Scarecrow could interact with it? When she blew that cloud of energy or nanoparticles into Damien's eyes, had she been attacking Damien or the virus?

The information Damien had shared went beyond the capabilities of the contacts Vaughn had designed. She doubted the virus would improve on their tech when it seemed more interested in destroying everything. What if Scarecrow had somehow reprogrammed Damien's nanites to help them push out the virus? And to do even more?

If she had, Vaughn might already have the template she needed for defeating the virus. It was in Damien—in his nanites. She just had to figure out how to get them to share that information with her.

"I think I know what I have to do." She looked up into Damien's eyes and stared intently at the glowing lights flickering within them.

"Damn." He cast a chagrined grin at her, then started to fasten up his cargos. "I'm guessing from your expression it doesn't involve more fucking?"

"Unfortunately, no." She laughed, some of her unease dissipating, though the strange excitement laced with fear remained. "We'll have to save that for when we're done."

"Done doing what?"

"Kicking this virus's ass. There's only room for one curator's tech around here, and it's mine."

Chapter Seventeen

"I don't have a shirt." Damien paused just inside the door that led to the cavern outside.

"Well, you keep tearing mine to pieces, so I'm keeping this one," Vaughn said.

She laughed as if she hadn't a care in the world, even though she'd just basically died and discovered she wasn't really human. Damien didn't give a shit about her being a 'survival-based shapeshifter.' Actually, he loved that. If it helped her get through things like what had just happened back in the stasis chamber room, he was all for it. But he didn't think he'd ever get over seeing her drown.

He pushed that dread way down, waiting till they had finished fixing whatever the hell this was before truly freaking out. If he put it off long enough, maybe he'd never have to deal with it. That and telling her what his nanites had said about her. Maybe she knew what a Tractus was.

"Let me tear a little off the hem," he said.

"No." She swatted his hands away when he reached for the shirt. "Seriously, what is it with you and tearing my clothes off? Not that I mind, actually."

"I'm just trying to tear a little from this one." He shifted his weight, then clasped her arms carefully. "We're going out into the cavern. I thought you'd be more comfortable with a blindfold."

Her brow furrowed for a moment, then she laughed again. She reached up, wrapping her arms around his neck, and pulled him close for a kiss. He let his hands drift to her hips, walking her back against the bulkhead and pinning her there with his body. Her fingers grazed his shoulders, tracing the lines of his muscles and leaving trails of goosebumps in their wake. Finally, she pulled back.

"I should have known better than to start something like that," she said.

"Give me a few minutes and I can finish it for you."

She laughed again, the sound as beautiful as anything he'd ever heard before. "Later. We need to get back upstairs."

She ducked under his arm and stood in front of the door. After a deep breath, she reached out and pressed her palm against the access panel. The hull slid open in front of them. She looked up at him and smiled, then took his hand and stepped outside. She walked forward cautiously, looking all around. The cave was huge, stretching for hundreds of yards in every direction. There were small hills and dips here and there, but the view could still only be called expansive. Vaughn took another deep breath and blew it out through pursed lips. Then she tilted her head back and stared at the cavern's ceiling high, high above.

Damien's heart started pounding. He held his breath as he waited for her to react, wondered what he could do to help. Her eyes didn't widen, and her breath seemed fast, but calm. Her lips parted as if in wonder. She didn't cringe or gasp or hyperventilate. She didn't even flinch. The only reaction he could detect aside from what he'd call cautious curiosity was that her grip tightened on his hand.

"You okay?" he asked.

Vaughn smiled. "Never better."

"How are you doing this? Not freaking out?"

"Perihelion." Vaughn stared at him as if that explained everything.

That word sounded familiar, but not. There was something she had told him earlier, but he couldn't quite remember.

"You used a word like that when you showed me the ship for the first time."

"Aphelion," she said. "The farthest spot in a planet or moon's orbit to what they're orbiting."

"And perihelion is?"

"The closest."

He considered the words for a moment, but couldn't figure out how they applied to their current situation. Finally he shook his head.

"I'm lost," he said.

"So was I." She smiled and let out a little laugh. "I told

you that I felt like I lived my life in aphelion. Always stuck at the farthest point from everyone and everything in my life. All the things I was orbiting."

"And now?"

"Now, I realize that I was in the wrong orbit. Always thinking of missions and the impossible stakes we deal with. Feeling like it was all on me to keep everyone safe."

He squeezed her hand reflexively. "It's not."

She nodded, but then shrugged and looked away. "Well, it kind of is. A lot of it, anyway."

"We all know the chances we take when we sign up for —"

She pulled her hand from his, but only so she could grab his face and lean in to kiss him again. He pulled her closer, more confused than ever, but grateful to have something else to think about. More like something to get him to not think at all. She broke off the kiss, one arm still around his shoulders and the other tracing his cheek. Her soft fingers sent a jolt of electric awareness through him.

"I don't care if it sounds cheesy," she said. "You are the center of my orbit. The one thing in all the universe that I feel I can actually reach, can actually touch. The one person that makes me feel a pull toward closeness and safety."

"Perihelion," he said.

"It's the strangest thing." She shrugged again and shook her head, but she was smiling. "I just... I realized that I've never felt safe before. But when I'm with you, when I'm near you, I don't feel like gravity is going to switch off at any moment and I'm going to go hurtling into space. I don't feel like I need reinforced walls around me when I know I can run into your arms." She groaned and said, "Okay, that was really cheesy."

He captured her lips with his, holding her close, delving into her mouth with his tongue. His hands went to her ass, pulling her up against him as he kissed her thoroughly. She matched his passion, clinging to him as if he really was what kept her tethered to the Earth. They were both breathless when he finally let her go.

"That wasn't cheesy," he said. "It was beautiful."

"See, there you go again," she said. "Being my own personal source of gravity."

"I'll be your own personal source of whatever you want if you keep kissing me like that."

"Let's get to Porter's lab. I want to deal with this virus ASAP so we can find the curator behind it and kick their ass and then get back to our real priority."

"Which is?"

"Finally having sex in a bed."

"That is a project I can get behind." He laughed, then took her hand in his as they walked along the winding path that led to the elevator that would take them up to the ranch. "Please tell me you think the elevator is safe. I don't want to have to climb all those stairs."

"I think it's fine." She pressed her hand against the access panel, then keyed in the command to bring it to their level. "The elevator has extra safeguards, and I haven't worked on it for a while."

"What difference would that make?"

"Remember David?" She pulled her favorite tool from her pocket and held it up.

"How could I forget?" Damien stared at it and said, "How's it going, man?"

"He's not sentient or anything—I just like naming things."

Damien laughed. "I never really know with you."

"That's fair. David here is my absolute favorite tool to use for just about everything. And I'm pretty sure he's infected and has been spreading the virus anywhere I've worked."

"I can see where that would be a problem."

The doors to the elevator opened. They shared a look, then stepped through the opening together. Vaughn took a deep breath, then pressed the button for sublevel 1. He didn't see her let it out as she watched the numbers that denoted each level light up. It was easy to tell, since he was holding his breath, too. Even though the elevator was actually covering a huge distance at an incredible speed, it seemed to take forever for them to reach sublevel 1. The moment the doors opened, they both hopped out. Vaughn let out her breath in a huge gasp, pulling in fresh air right after. Damien tried to be a little more surreptitious as he started to breathe again.

"I'll definitely double-check the elevator's systems as soon as we get things cleared up," she said. "That was nerve-wracking."

"How do you plan to defeat the virus?" He walked after her as she headed toward Porter's lab.

"By doing what I do best. I'm going to reverse-engineer whatever your nanites did to purge your contacts of the virus. Since you can communicate with them, we might even be able to get them to help us."

"Sounds like a plan."

The door to Porter's lab opened. Vaughn had already stepped through, so Damien followed, even though a feeling of misgiving shuddered through his limbs. He pulled her back against his chest as soon as they crossed the threshold.

A long, spindly branch was standing on one of the office chairs, clinging to its back with a hand made of sticks. It used another wooden limb to push against the counter the chair sat next to, spinning it around in dizzying circles as it said, "Wheee!" over and over. Crouched next to it, half-curled in a ball, a goblin chuckled, scratching at his cheek with claw-tipped fingers.

"Oh shit," Vaughn said.

Johnny grunted, then leaned forward. "About time you got here. You always keep company waiting this long? It's rude."

"Mind your manners," Spriggan said, spinning its chair so forcefully that the inertia made it start to slide from the seat. "Whoa."

"How... What..." Vaughn stammered.

Damien stepped in front of her. "What the hell are you doing here?"

"Sheesh, you really *don't* have any manners, do ya?" Johnny reached out and grabbed Spriggan's chair, stopping it suddenly. The little tree-creature lost its grip and flew off the chair, landing on a counter and knocking over several beakers. Johnny bellowed with laughter. Spriggan sat up on the counter and rubbed its head, then joined in with a high, tittering sound.

"Hey, don't do that." Vaughn darted out from behind Damien, running toward Spriggan. "Are you okay?"

"Aw, see that?" Spriggan said, with what Damien thought was probably its face pointed toward Johnny. "This curator has to be something special for Scarecrow to bring us all the way out here to help her."

"You're here to help me?" Vaughn asked, turning her attention to Johnny. "Is Scarecrow here?"

Johnny pointed at the wall behind them. Vaughn looked over Damien's shoulder, her eyes growing wide. He forced himself to turn slowly, even though he wanted to whip around and maybe jump back a few feet as well. Scarecrow stood inside the room just next to the door. She had flattened herself against the wall to the point that she almost looked two dimensional. Hell, with the freaky way she moved, maybe she *had* made herself two dimensional.

As he watched, she started to gain depth, her jacket and slacks inflating. She peeled herself from the wall and took a few jerky steps forward, heading toward Vaughn. Damien couldn't help himself. He held out his arm between them, even though he was pretty damned sure it wouldn't make a difference if Scarecrow really wanted at his girl.

"We're not going to have a problem, right?" Damien said.

Scarecrow stared at him, her mouth lit up in a frown. Behind him, Johnny started to laugh again.

"You think Scarecrow here is the problem?" Johnny said. "You don't have a clue, do ya?"

Damien kept himself absolutely still as Scarecrow sized him up again. At least, on the outside. His heart pounded, memories of the last time she'd been this close playing through his head. Things were different now, though. He was different. And he had Scarecrow to thank for that, at least in part. Vaughn's nanites had kept him in one piece before, but he hadn't been able to communicate with them like he could now, and that was a game-changer in the field.

Come to think of it...

'*Can you hear me?*' he thought.

A display opened, overlayed in his vision.

[…]

'Is there anything you can tell me about what's going on here? About Scarecrow?'

[…]

[NO SCARECROW DETECTED]

'She's right there. The thing with the burlap sack for a head.'

[…]

[NOT FOUND]

'Not found? She's right in front of us.'

[NO LIFEFORM DETECTED]

No lifeform? Was Scarecrow not actually alive? Or was she something so alien that his nanites couldn't even register her existence? Hell, with that freaky way she had of moving around, maybe she was constantly in some sort of dimensional flux or something and that made it so his nanites couldn't see her. He'd be sure to ask Vaughn what she thought about it as soon as he had a chance. If he kept up this line of speculation, Damien was going to be the one who couldn't go out into the field. It was one thing to face off against tangible monsters while he was out on patrol. Dealing with beings that might not exist in his plane of existence was some next-level shit.

The lights that made up Scarecrow's eyes brightened as she stared at him, the cloud of energy that surrounded her swirling faster. Her mouth curved up in a smile. That was good, right? The next instant, she disappeared. Damien heard a little 'eep' from behind him. He spun around to see Scarecrow leaning over Vaughn, her smile lit up like a neon sign. Vaughn did not look as happy.

"N... Nice to meet you," Vaughn said. "I'm Vaughn. Apparently, I'm a curator, but I don't know what that means. I th... think that's important for you to know and just want to be up front about it."

Scarecrow tilted her head to the side, the lights of her eyes brightening. She stepped back and lifted both arms. The cloud of energy surrounding her swirled, thickening into a rectangular shape that looked like a floating monitor. Motes of light skittered over its surface before forming geometric shapes that looked like they might be words written in what should have been an utterly alien language. *Should* have been.

Oh shit...

'Can you translate that for me?' he thought, even though he already knew the answer. Whatever language Scarecrow was displaying, it was the same one his nanites had started using when feeding him data after she'd blown that cloud of whatever into his face.

Lights flickered in his vision, his own display becoming visible just for him.

[SAMPLE]

'Sample? What the hell does that mean?'

Scarecrow stepped to the side of the floating screen and

held out one gangly arm. Her hand was curled into a fist, but then she extended her makeshift index finger, pointing at Vaughn.

His nanites responded, but the first word that appeared was just the same weird characters, with [FRAGMENT REQUESTS SAMPLE] after it.

'Fragment?'

The weird characters flashed red several times. More of the alien language scrolled in his view. An image of the scarecrow formed next to the data feed, her energy cloud much more pronounced. It was almost like reality was flipped, with her corporeal form being barely visible and the cloud filled with light particles being clearer and almost opaque.

"I don't understand," Vaughn said. "What does she want? I'm sorry, I can't read whatever that says."

"She wants a sample," Damien said.

"A sample?" Vaughn turned to him, her eyebrows furrowed. "Wait, how do you know that?"

"Whatever that language is, my nanites can read it."

Vaughn's lips pressed into a thin line. She stared at him intently for a few moments, then nodded and turned back to the scarecrow. She took a deep breath, then held out her hand.

"Careful, Vaughn." Damien took a step forward.

"I think we all need to be careful about now, huh?" Johnny's voice was low and menacing.

"It's okay," Vaughn said. Under her breath, she added, "I just hope this isn't going to hurt."

A thin beam of light extended from Scarecrow's finger to the center of Vaughn's palm. After a few seconds, the light took on a reddish hue. It condensed until a single drop of blood spun, suspended between them. The light retracted into Scarecrow's finger, bringing the sample with it. Scarecrow pulled her arm back and stood stock-still, her mouth turning into a frown as the display she'd made vanished. Minutes ticked on.

"How long are we just going to stand here?" Damien asked.

"As long as it takes her to process the new data she's received," Vaughn said. "We need her help to purge our systems of the virus before it causes some real damage."

As if Vaughn drowning wasn't damage enough? Damien kept the thought to himself, but his skin prickled with the need to do something.

Scarecrow straightened. Not hunched over, she was even taller than Damien had thought—as tall as he was. She took several more steps backward. Was she making room to attack? To run away? She lifted both arms, like a conductor about to start a symphony. The gesture was weirdly familiar, but he couldn't quite place it.

"I'd say we should get ready to run, but she's blocking the door." Damien's heart pounded in his chest.

Lights started to flicker between Scarecrow's hands,

forming a swirling ball of crackling energy. The lights extended into lines, creating a complex pattern made up of grids. It took a few moments for Damien to recognize the shape.

"That's my ship." Vaughn stepped forward, her gaze focused on the holoprojection as the last lines connected. She laughed, then reached out to touch one of the sections of the hull. It vanished when she tapped it, revealing furnishings and little command stations within.

That was where Damien had seen Scarecrow's gesture before. It was exactly like what Vaughn had done when she was interacting with the holoprojection back at the ranch. And this creation was identical to her own.

"This part is wrong, though." Vaughn moved to the front of the ship, where the impact from the crash had torn a hole in the hull. She touched the lines, maintaining contact to manipulate the image—again, just like back at the ranch. When she was done, a huge section of the hull was gone, the metal peeled back around it. She pointed at the section and said, "This is what it looks like now."

Scarecrow's eyes were wide. Her mouth actually formed a little 'O' as she stared at Vaughn. The lights that made up her features glowed brighter. The holoprojection of the ship vanished.

"Please, I need your help," Vaughn said. "There's a virus attacking our base. It's made it into the ship. I think it's still dormant in a lot of our systems, but when it activates, I'm pretty sure it's going to try to kill everyone around it. It was in Damien's contacts when he met you earlier, and you did something that neutralized it. If you can just point me in the right direction, give me any sort of clue about how to fight it…"

Scarecrow turned to Damien, her eyes angled down and her mouth turned in a frown. How could a burlap sack be so expressive? The lights making up her features turned to a bright yellow. More of the alien characters appeared in his field of vision, only these were in the same color as the lights of Scarecrow's face.

[CURATOR APPROACHING] appeared in the regular white he was used to. Was that his nanites translating for him still?

"Vaughn doesn't mean you any harm," Damien said, shifting to stand closer to Vaughn.

"Why did you just say that?" Vaughn looked back and forth between them. "Wait, are you talking to her directly?"

"I think so," Damien said.

"What did she say?"

"She said, 'curator approaching,'" Damien said.

"But I'm not approaching—I'm already here." Vaughn's brow furrowed for a moment, then her eyes widened and her mouth dropped open. "Unless…. she's not talking about me. She's talking about whoever made the virus. The other curator."

"That would make sense," Damien said. "But anybody who shows up here is going to get their ass handed to them, between Jonathan and the pack and your defense... systems..."

His heart started to pound. If the systems had been infected by the virus, were their defenses even working anymore? If they were, how did this trio make it into the ranch?

"No, no." Vaughn stepped closer to Scarecrow, panic making her voice tremble. "Please, how do I defeat the virus? How do I protect my ship?"

"Protect your ship?" Damien said. "What do you mean?"

"The curator who made Megan's collar could see and hear everything Roy could," Vaughn said. "They know about the ship."

"Fuck." It was all clear now. The Black Shuck attacking. The malfunctions in the ranch. "They're trying to kill us off and take over the ranch so they can get to the ship."

"And if these three made it in without any of my alarms going off, the virus must have taken out the ranch's defenses. You said Scarecrow is interphasic. So are the Black Shucks. If she made it this deep into the ranch, all of our defenses must be down."

Dread flooded Damien's stomach, making the hairs on his arms stand on end. "We should have seen someone on our way here. Where is everybody?"

"Now, that's a smart question," Johnny said. "My guess is, they're all out on the lawn fighting the Black Shuck that's been sent after ya."

Damien was already bolting for the door when Vaughn caught his arm. He'd managed to drag her a few paces before he could stop himself. She looked up at him, her eyes wide with panic.

"None of us stand a chance against that thing without my tech," she said. "They at least have Jonathan to protect them. If we can purge the virus from the system, I can bring the interphasic disruptors back online."

"Then do it," he said. "I'm going to go join the fight."

"I can't do it without you. I literally can not do it without your help."

He clenched his jaw, wanting to argue, but if Vaughn said she needed him, she needed him. He trusted her completely. The thought of leaving everyone else out there to fight made his skin crawl. How the hell had he gone from hating werewolves with every fiber of his being just a few days ago to being desperate to fight alongside them now?

"Tell me what to do," he said.

She turned back to the odd trio of dwellers that had made themselves at home in Porter's lab, then pulled that shiny silver cylinder out of her back pocket. 'David.'

"I was going to try to study the nanites in your system

and your contacts to see how they had fought off the virus," she said. "But with Scarecrow here, I'm hoping we can find a more direct solution." She turned to Damien and said, "Can you translate for me?"

"I'll do what I can."

Vaughn smiled and nodded at him, then she focused her attention back on Scarecrow. Cautiously, Vaughn stepped forward, holding David on her flattened palm. She was probably trying to make sure it didn't look like she was approaching with a weapon.

"There is a virus in our systems," Vaughn said. "But you probably already know that. We need to get rid of it. Whatever you did to Damien's contacts, to the nanites in his body, it enabled them to fight the virus off. I need your help to do the same for the systems in the ranch and the ship. Please, help me save my friends. My home."

"Cripes," Johnny said. "Almost brings a tear to your eye."

"Quiet, Johnny," the spriggan said. "We need to help them out. We don't want the Curator getting her hands on the ship, do we?"

"I've had my hands on the ship for years," Vaughn said. "And I've only used what I've learned to help people —dwellers and humans alike. I swear, that's all I want to keep doing."

"Yeah, but you're just a knock-off," Johnny said. "We're talking about the real deal. If the Curator got her hands on the ship, it'd be bad news for all of us."

"What do you mean, I'm a knock-off?" Vaughn said.

"I thought all you mini-curators were supposed to be smart," Johnny said. "No wonder she keeps having to make more copies, trying to get the right mix."

"Copies?" Vaughn started forward, but Scarecrow suddenly flickered again, this time appearing right next to Vaughn.

Damien reached out to grab her elbow. He managed to not pull her away. The movement had been instinct, but he had enough sense to know that acting like Scarecrow was a threat was not the best way to earn her trust and get her help. Scarecrow held her hand over the cylinder, her palm parallel to Vaughn's. An aura appeared around Scarecrow, the same dark nebula expanding from her burlap sack and second-hand clothes. Motes of light glittered within them. The lights dropped down from the cloud, landing on the tool. Scarecrow pulled her hand back.

"Is that it?" Vaughn asked, her voice trembling. "Can I use David—I mean, my tool safely?"

"It took some time for my contacts to start working again," Damien said. "It might take time for whatever she did to really kick in."

"We don't have time to wait." There was a note of anguish in Vaughn's tone that resonated with him. "Isn't there something she can do to speed things up?"

Damien turned to Scarecrow, not really sure what to do.

He settled on following his gut and getting right to the point.

'*Can you bring up the display we use to communicate, but make it visible to others?*' he thought. He wasn't really sure how this whole thing worked, but he'd seen enough to know that the alien tech could practically perform miracles. Projecting a hologram didn't seem like too big of an ask.

His hand started to burn, itching and stinging enough to make him flinch. He lifted his left arm and saw that his palm had turned bright red. Silver lights flashed beneath his skin. Maybe it was a bigger ask than he'd thought.

Beams of light erupted from his hand, somehow creating a glowing rectangle that looked a lot like the one Scarecrow had created, if smaller. The pain subsided, leaving a tingling in its wake. Vaughn's eyes were wide, her mouth hanging open. Behind her, Scarecrow's burlap sack was decorated with a smile big enough to make her triangular jack-o'-lantern eyes narrow at the corners. Damien glanced at Johnny to see that the goblin had also narrowed his eyes, but he wasn't smiling. He was rubbing his fingers over his chin, the rough skin making a grating sound as he did.

"Lookit that!" Spriggan hopped down off of its chair and approached, the small wooden creature prancing around Damien, not even coming up to his waist. "We got ourselves a full-blown cyborg here. I wonder what else your new nanites are up to in there." It picked at Damien's pant leg with two twiggy fingers. Damien ignored it.

'*We need Scarecrow to fix our systems, both in the ranch and the ship so I can go join the others against the Shuck. And I know Vaughn is going to need more answers about what Johnny said.*' He was relieved that his thoughts didn't appear on the screen. '*Can you convince Scarecrow to help us?*'

[UNNECESSARY] His nanites' reply appeared in his field of vision, not on the screen.

'*What do you mean?*'

[ALL FRAGMENT PROGRAMMING REQUIRES ELIMINATION OF THREATS TO SHIP SYSTEMS]

'*What?*' Suddenly, he wished Vaughn could see this. She would have a better idea of what his nanites were talking about. Then again, so would Scarecrow, probably.

"You have to help us with the ship," Damien said.

Words scrolled on the screen in the alien text, the color letting him know his nanites were the ones 'speaking.'

"What does that say?" Vaughn asked.

"What I'm saying." He nodded toward the screen. "My nanites are translating for us to make sure we're clear."

"Well, you should ask politely." Vaughn frowned at him. "It's not like we can order her to do what we want."

"We don't have to," Damien said. "She's programmed to protect the ship."

"What's that now?" Johnny sat up straighter, still

scowling.

"Programmed?" Vaughn angled her head to the side as she stared at Scarecrow. Damien knew the look by now. Vaughn was working through things, putting the pieces together.

Pieces...

"My nanites also say she isn't a life form," Damien said. "And they're calling her a 'fragment.'"

Johnny tucked himself into a ball and rolled toward Damien, spines poking out all over his body. Damien held himself completely still, even when Johnny stopped just inches away. The goblin popped himself out of his ball-form and stood as tall as he could—which wasn't all that much taller than Spriggan. He reached up and poked Damien in the chest with one spindly finger.

"You tell your nanites to fuck off," Johnny said. "Scarecrow is family. Wraiths might not be alive like you and me, but she's still a life form and she deserves some respect."

Damien felt his lips twitch at the corners, but he suppressed his urge to smile. Johnny obviously cared about Scarecrow. Warmth flooded Damien at the thought that family was universal, even a strange found family like this one. Dweller or not, the need to protect and belong was an emotion that crossed all barriers of existence. The thought was a comfort, even with everything else going on.

"Nobody in this room respects Scarecrow more than I do," Damien said. "I'm the one who took a face full of her nanites. I know not to piss her off."

Johnny's eyes narrowed again and he frowned. He let out a low grunt, then nodded, as if Damien's words had satisfied him. The goblin rolled backwards, tucking himself in a ball again and giving Damien some space. Their exchange had also given Vaughn something she needed—time to process all the new data. When Damien looked at her again, she was beaming.

"I knew that complex of a ship had to have some sort of AI to control its various systems, but could never find any sign of the operating system beyond basic code," Vaughn said, her eyes wide with wonder. "You're part of the ship's programming. A fragment of it. And if you're a wraith and there are multiple wraiths in the world, that means there are more fragments out there." She stepped forward excitedly. "Which systems do you control? There are so many, I can't even begin to guess. Unless you're part of the security protocols? Is that how you're able to defeat the virus, or is that code so fundamental that it's part of every wraith?"

"You're part of the ship?" Spriggan's voice was even thinner than usual, so quiet, Damien barely heard it speak. "You're part of the prison that brought our ancestors here?"

Scarecrow's features winked in and out of existence. As

unnerving as it was to see her jack-o'-lantern face, seeing the blank burlap sack was even worse. When her face returned, she was frowning and her eyes were downturned in what looked like sadness.

"The ship is a prison?" Vaughn said.

"Enough bullshitting around," Johnny yelled. "Your friends are out there fighting for their lives. Probably. Scarecrow can fix your systems, and then we're outta here. Go fight or die together. Whatever. Just leave us be."

Relief flooded Damien at the thought of finally taking some action. He wanted to pat Johnny's shoulder, but didn't think that'd go over well. The spines would probably stab him, anyway. Before Damien could head to the armory, his display flashed—the one visible to everyone. The characters were Scarecrow's gold, letting him know she was the one talking. Beneath it, his nanites translated in glowing white characters.

[CURATOR CONTROLS BLACK SHUCK]

Vaughn's brow furrowed. "I figured as much. They controlled the trolls that dug out the ship as well."

"Dug it out?" Johnny asked.

"It was buried in a cavern beneath us," Vaughn said, her voice tight with unease. "The ranch was attacked recently by thousands of trolls. Most of them died digging it out. We knew something had to be controlling them to make them do that."

"She's making her move," Johnny muttered. Spriggan

ran across the room and clung to his side, its fingers wrapped around the sharp spikes covering Johnny's hide.

Scarecrow took a step forward. She actually walked, instead of that weird flickering thing. She pointed at Damien's display, then at Vaughn.

[CURATOR CONTROLS BLACK SHUCK] appeared again.

"Yes, the other curator is the one sending things against us," Vaughn said. "And we get that they're after the ship."

"She," Damien said. When Vaughn stared at him quizzically, he explained, "Johnny just said, 'She's making her move.' The other curator is female, like you."

"Like me…" Again, Vaughn's eyes got that distant, unfocused look. "Wait, you keep saying 'a' curator when you're talking about me, but you call her 'the' curator. Like *the* Curator. Capital-C."

"She's the original," Johnny said. "Prisoner Zero. All of us—the things we evolved from and the things that could survive on this dump in their original forms—were evidence to be used in her trial."

"That's why they called her 'the Curator.'" Spriggan's voice was a low whisper, like it was telling a ghost story around a campfire. It wiggled its twig-fingers for spooky effect, which was really unnecessary. Its words were the scariest part. "Cause she was collecting genetic samples from all over the galaxy and performing weird experiments on us."

Vaughn grew even paler than usual. Her lips were pressed together so tight, they were nearly bloodless. Her voice grew thin as she forced herself to speak. "And you said— You said she's making copies... of herself. And I'm one of them?"

Johnny hesitated for a moment, then said, "Yeah. Sorry, kid."

Damien was still holding her elbow. He shifted closer, putting his free arm around her while keeping the palm that was projecting the holoscreen facing up. He needed to keep his line of communication open with Scarecrow, but couldn't not comfort Vaughn as well.

"No need to be sorry." Vaughn took a deep breath and blew it out. She looked over at Scarecrow, resolution entering her features, even though her voice trembled. "I get it now. I think I know what I need to do."

Chapter Eighteen

"Vaughn…"

The gentle note in Damien's voice made Vaughn walk even faster down the hall. She couldn't get into it now. Couldn't even let herself think of what she'd learned about herself. So what if she was a clone. A clone of a criminal. Space criminal. And she'd thought her life was as weird as it could get.

Oh god, does that mean I'm an actual *alien? Not a hybrid, like a dweller? Am I not human at all?*

She shoved the thought aside. There was no time to have an existential crisis. She needed to help her friends.

"We need to hit the armory," Damien said.

He pressed his hand against the access panel and the door slid open. Damien hissed in a breath. he stood in the doorway as if trying to block her sight.

"What's wrong?" She ducked under his arm and stepped into the small room. "Oh my god."

It had been absolutely ransacked. Claw marks carved deep gouges in the metal walls. Metal that could withstand a plasma torch. The weapons that were normally hung in neat rows were scattered around the floor, smashed beyond any usefulness. Scorch marks covered the walls where some of the heavier artillery had exploded. Thank god she'd reinforced the walls of the room or the entire sublevel might have been taken out.

Damien entered the room after her, his mouth a grim line. He picked up the remains of a pulse rifle and moved to stand in front of a partially melted glass display case. With the butt of the gun, he smashed the glass, using it to clear the small space so that he could access the swords inside. He dropped the broken weapon in favor of one of the early katanas Vaughn had forged for Dexter. She'd refined the mix in the metal so that the ones he used now were much sturdier. These were only meant to be decorative. She'd never been more grateful for her nostalgic streak.

Damien lifted a second sword from its mounting, then turned, one in each hand. Vaughn's breath caught in her chest, shivers of gooseflesh flowing over her and heat blooming deep in her belly. Holy shit, he was gorgeous and terrifying. The skin stretched over his huge muscles glistened, patterns of light criss-crossing his bare chest. His eyes were glowing silver. Spriggan had called Damien a cyborg. What the hell were his nanites doing to him?

She didn't have time to worry about that now. They would keep him alive. That had to be enough.

"These will have to do," he said. "Come on."

She nodded, then turned and ran to the garage in the

sublevel. The others hadn't even closed the door from the corridor. Whatever had happened, it hadn't given them time for even the smallest security protocols—not that any of those really mattered now that the ranch was defenseless. She scanned the area, taking in as much data as she could, perversely grateful to have something to push out thoughts of what Johnny had said. The vans were still in place, but two of the hover bikes were gone. Had the others fled the ranch? And if they had, what the hell were she and Damien about to walk into?

A roar thundered from outside, the battle cry of a werewolf. Not everyone had left, then. Vaughn and Damien had to do everything they could to help. She ran up the ramp to the converted barn that made up the ground level of the garage. The doors were open wide here as well. Lightning flashed on the walls from outside, the sound of torrential rain a backdrop to the battle. The sun should be rising, but the sky was still dark as midnight.

Damien caught up with her as she ran into the driveway and slid to a stop. Chunks of asphalt had been torn up, leaving deep pits. Marcus stood next to one of the piles, a huge piece of the driveway held above his head. He roared as he threw it. Vaughn's gaze followed its trajectory, her brain short-circuiting as she saw what he was aiming at.

One Black Shuck stood before her. A single dweller that was as big as the barn behind her. A long, sinuous tongue flicked out from between rows of razor-sharp teeth that were as long as she was tall. The dull yellow-green of its scales gleamed in the light pouring out from the open doors behind her. Lightning flooded the sky, coalescing above the creature before streaking down and striking it. The energy lit up the Shuck's skin beneath the wet hair matting its body, illuminating each scale. It turned its muzzle toward Vaughn, closing its mouth briefly. A clicking noise came from deep in its throat.

"Look out!" One of the werewolves rammed into her, knocking the wind from her lungs. Two golden eyes—Marcus. He lifted Vaughn from her feet and lurched toward Damien.

"I'm good," he yelled, dodging to the side.

The creature opened its mouth, angling its head to follow Marcus. Electricity spewed from deep in its throat, burning a line of dark black along the barn. The wood was designed to resist fire, but it still smoldered under the onslaught of heat.

"Fuuuuck," Marcus yelled, the Shuck's lightning breath practically singing his pelt.

Vaughn felt his muscles bunch beneath her, then they were airborne, hurtling through the air as he leapt impossibly high. She saw the shingles of the barn's roof, the weathervane spinning wildly in the storm.

We aren't going to stop. We're going to keep going, up into the stars. The vacuum of space will kill us or the cold or...

She clamped down on the familiar panic. Her friends needed her. Damien needed her. He was here, on the Earth, fighting for his life. She wasn't going anywhere. She just needed Marcus to get them back down to the ground without letting the Shuck fry them with the lightning still coming out of its mouth, carving a burning line across the side of the barn.

Marcus touched down on the wet roof for the briefest of seconds, launching them higher into the air. Too high, even for a werewolf. Then the ground was flying up toward them. She screamed as they fell, not sure if Marcus could absorb enough of the impact to keep himself safe, let alone her.

Can I survive a fall from this height?

At the last minute, he twisted, pushing her up into the air. He hit the ground with a sickening crunch just before she landed on top of him, most of her inertia dissipated. Marcus let out a grunt of pain. His chest was heaving with his panting breath. Vaughn rolled off of him, then rose on her knees. His hips and legs were twisted so that he was facing backwards, his spine broken.

"Oh god, Marcus," she said. "How do I fix this?"

"I'll… heal." Marcus grunted again as he clawed at the ground, dragging himself away from her, his legs useless behind him. His body wasn't realigning itself. Maybe if Vaughn grabbed his feet, she could help him straighten out and speed up the healing process. The battle raged on behind them, grunts and roars and the ringing of metal piercing the heavy rain.

"What do I do?" she said, tears clouding her vision as she reached for her best friend. The rain had dampened his fur, making it stick to his frame in an odd pattern. "Please, tell me what to do."

Marcus shook his head. His lips peeled back from his teeth in a growl. He lashed out, his teeth clacking loudly millimeters from her face. She screamed and fell backwards, landing hard.

"Run!" he yelled.

Instinct took over where reason had abandoned her, the panic returning, blocking out thought. She scrambled for purchase on the wet ground, finally getting to her feet and running toward the side of the barn, away from the battle. She crouched down, sobbing uncontrollably.

Stop. Stop. STOP!

She grabbed fistfuls of her hair and pulled, shaking her head, trying to get the fear to leave her alone just for a moment. She only needed a moment to gather her thoughts and be of use to someone. But the thoughts that came only pushed her down further into despair.

Of course Marcus told me to run. How could I help him? He's always the one protecting me. I'm too weak to fight. Now, I can't even fix my tech.

No wonder the Curator—the original curator—had to make more copies of herself. More clones.

They can always find another one—another me. A better one.

The Curator could probably fix things. Especially since she was the one who had fucking broken everything. She was the one who had made Vaughn. What did that make her? Make them?

My mom was Stephanie Vaughn. She raised me. She birthed me.

Christ, did she even know? Did she know that her daughter wasn't actually hers? Knowing everything Vaughn knew, she didn't want to think about how the Curator could have made Vaughn come to be. What she could have done to Vaughn's mom. The whole fucking ship was a prison just for the Curator. Prisoner Zero. What atrocities had she done to warrant that? What had she done to Vaughn's mom?

I thought she died of cancer.

She had. That's what the doctors had said, the disease they had treated. Vaughn had been too young to learn all the details, but she had figured out the systems affected. Of course she always knew the systems.

Her reproductive systems. It killed her. Whatever the Curator did to my mom... It killed her to have me.

Tears streaked Vaughn's cheeks. She grabbed her knees and hugged them against her chest, rocking as sobs tore through her.

The Curator had done this. Had taken Vaughn's mom.

Now, she was destroying Vaughn's home. Threatening her friends—all the family she had left. All because *Prisoner Zero* wanted the ship. Wanted her prison and whatever power it could grant her on this planet. *Vaughn's planet.*

Vaughn would give the ship to her. She would ram it down her fucking throat.

But first, she needed assets. First, she needed an army.

She used the barn's wall to push herself to her feet, then wiped away the tears and rain soaking her face. She peered around the corner of the building, stunned at the ongoing battle. Megan and Tessa were on the Black Shuck's back, holding on to handfuls of the thing's shaggy hair. Meg clawed at the creature frantically, but didn't seem to have any effect. Sparks flew where Tessa's cybernetic claws raked the creature, its scales deflecting the damage.

Brock dodged in and out of the Shuck's range, his blue eye leaving a strange afterimage suspended in the air. Jonathan flanked the massive beast on its other side, firing blasts from what looked like a stingray. The weapon was small, but could melt the alloy that Vaughn had used to build most of the sublevels—an alloy stronger and with a higher melting point than tungsten. Vaughn couldn't see where the energy beams were doing more than annoying it.

Marcus was probably still healing. Spine injuries were no joke, even for dwellers that healed as quickly as werewolves. But where were Dexter and Porter? Where was Eli?

Where was Damien?

Jonathan managed to hit the beast on the side of its face, the Shuck twisted toward him, lashing out at him with his long tail. Jonathan threw himself backward, tucking into a roll and coming up in a crouch. Why wasn't he using his quantum energy abilities? Did he need time for it to recharge after how he'd used it earlier? He held still rather than trying to attack again or gain distance. It was a gambit. He was luring the beast toward him. Vaughn's heart caught in her throat when she saw why.

Damien darted forward, keeping low to the ground. Streaks of blue light lined his arms and chest, bright enough to reflect off of his swords and illuminate the rain falling near him. The design was just like the lights on the hoverbikes and in Tessa's arm. Jonathan fired at the Shuck's face again. Damien launched himself up under the creature while it was distracted, carving a long line in the beast's underbelly.

The Shuck let out a deafening bellow. Instead of turning its attention to Damien, it kept focusing on Jonathan. It swung at Jonathan with one of its front feet. Jonathan hesitated for a second too long. One of its talons impaled him through his stomach.

Brock roared, running forward so fast he blurred in Vaughn's vision. He jumped onto the Shuck's muzzle, clawing at the creature's eyes. It shook Jonathan free from its foot, but only so it could claw at its face, trying to dislodge Brock.

Vaughn could stop this. She *needed* to stop this. They were going to ruin everything.

This was her fucking planet. Her ship. Her family.

The Curator wanted to take everything from Vaughn. Vaughn would take everything from her.

She ran forward with a purpose unlike anything she'd ever felt. Her legs pumped strongly beneath her, her lungs pulled in oxygen. She ran beneath a cloudy sky, as fleet as a deer. Gravity was no obstacle. The pull of this planet was pitifully low. Her vision brightened, a blue cast making everything glow.

Gridlines appeared over everything before her, data scrolling in her view. The outlines of her allies, their status. Something… Something was wrong. She couldn't parse the data and maintain the calculations she needed for her plan to work. Her heart gave a painful lurch, a sob threatening to steal her breath. She didn't dare let it. She would deal with the grief and the guilt later. Now, she needed to take action, before she had more to mourn.

She let out a keening wail that she hadn't known she could make. The Shuck turned toward the sound. Brock took advantage of its distraction, ramming his clawed hand into one of the Shuck's right eyes.

No, no, don't blind it. I need it whole.

It screamed in pain, its mouth open wide. Perfect.

Calculations flooded her mind, angle of trajectory, force of launch, pull of gravity. Vaughn coiled her strength within her, grinding her teeth together. With a guttural shout, she threw herself into the air, straight into the thing's gaping maw. She vaguely registered Damien screaming, "Lisa!" just before the beast clamped its mouth shut.

The stench was incredible, burning her lungs with its fumes. She forced her lips to stay shut, trying to ignore the pain searing her chest. Viscous saliva dripped around her, peeling her skin where it touched her flesh. Her feet slipped on the creature's tongue as it tried to smash her against the roof of its mouth. She stifled a scream as it pressed her against the rows of sharp teeth lining its mouth, their rough surface flaying her arms.

Change. Come on, change.

Her skin was bathed in blue light. Was it coming from her eyes? The scale pattern emerged, her wounds starting to knit. Before they could seal completely, she flung herself onto the creature's tongue, wiping her blood on as much of its surface as she could. The stench blanked out to nothing, the burning pain vanishing with it. Her skin finished healing, the pattern becoming more pronounced as the scales thickened, protecting her from the acidic venom of the creature's saliva.

This has to work. Please, this has to work.

The Curator would not work with a beast that could harm her. Vaughn was certain of that. You didn't play god at this level without having a narcissistic streak as wide as the solar system. She was certain she would survive— physically anyway. She did not want to endure the trauma of passing through this thing's digestive system. And what would happen if it started going interphasic? The idea sent a thrill through her, a cold fascination at the concept taking root in her mind.

If her plan worked, the creature would recognize her DNA as that of the Curator, its master. Its *former* master, if Vaughn had her way. And then she could perform as many experiments on it as she wanted. Perhaps it could break into sub-components and she could use each in a different manner. Some wouldn't survive, but there was plenty of biomass in the subject for her to pursue many lines of inquiry.

Vaughn recoiled from her own thoughts, the cold, clinical, *alien* nature of them. She would never do that to another living being. She could never be so cruel.

I'm sorry. She willed the dweller to understand her thoughts, even though it hadn't been privy to them. To feel her regret. *I'm sorry I even considered it.*

Its mouth opened. Vaughn rolled off its tongue onto the wet earth. She let the rain pour over her body, cleansing her of the creature's venom. She looked down at herself to see that her clothes had disintegrated. The scale pattern was paler on her chest and stomach. Her torso was completely smooth, like a mannequin. A thin line ran along her stomach, parallel to the ground. Was that a… pouch? Just how different was her anatomy? Was this her true form?

"Lisa!" Damien screamed, running toward her.

Vaughn managed to lift her arm, warding him off. She pushed herself up on all fours, then stood on shaky legs. Her feet had lengthened and lifted, making it more comfortable for her to walk on her toes. The Shuck was staring at her with its three remaining eyes, its mouth closed as a low rumbling sounded from deep in its throat. Tessa and Meg were still clawing at its back, trying to find a weak spot. Brock pulled his arm back, prepared to claw out one of the creature's other eyes.

"Stop!" Vaughn yelled.

A wave of power flowed out with the word, blue light erupting from her middle in a sphere around her. The shockwave hit Damien first, knocking him from his feet. Brock was launched off of the Shuck's muzzle. He flew through the air, hitting the ground hard and rolling to a stop. Tessa and Megan managed to keep their holds, but they had stopped trying to hurt the beast at least.

Vaughn gentled her voice and said, "Stop," again.

The Black Shuck lowered its head to the ground and let out a low, rumbling groan. Vaughn approached it slowly. When she was close enough to touch it, she lifted her arm and placed it on its muzzle, close to one of its massive nostrils.

"I'm so sorry she did this to you," Vaughn said. "That she made you do this. But you don't have to fight anymore. You can rest."

It let out a huge sigh, its warm breath blowing past her. A shudder trembled through its body as its eyes rolled shut. A swirling cloud of plasma burst into being behind the right eyelid of the eye that had been damaged. Vaughn wasn't sure how she could perceive it, but knew it was there—just as she somehow knew that its eye had returned, fully healed.

"What the hell just happened?" Tessa said.

"We came to an understanding." Vaughn kept her hand on its muzzle, her heart heavy with sadness for what the beast had been through. What they'd all endured.

Tessa leapt down from its back. Megan followed, then ran to Brock. He was already on his feet, hunched over with his clawed hands flexing, as if he wasn't ready for the fight to be over yet. A blue glow flowed over Megan's body as she ran toward Damien. He had also recovered from whatever Vaughn had done. He stood with his swords pointing at the ground, beautiful lights flowing down his arms and making mesmerizing patterns on his chest. He was breathing heavy, and there was blood running down his face from a wound at his temple. Vaughn didn't need whatever interface she'd used a moment ago to tell her he would be fine. She wasn't as sure about Jonathan.

"Megan." Vaughn forced herself to remain calm, which strangely wasn't that difficult at the moment. She felt an odd detachment from everything, as if she was viewing what was going on from far away. She wasn't sure if it was disassociation or an artifact of inhabiting this form. That clinical perspective was lurking just beneath her conscious thought, urging her to give in to it, to let her logic take over and wipe out everything else. "Check on Jonathan, please."

"Jonathan!" Megan ran to the other side of the Shuck. Brock followed more slowly, keeping a wary eye on the creature Vaughn was still trying to soothe. Megan dropped to her knees next to Jonathan. "Oh god, I don't know where to apply pressure. His stomach…"

Rippling blue light spread over Brock as he also resumed his human form. He crouched next to her, assessing Jonathan with a grim expression. He reached out to rest a shaking hand on Jonathan's forehead.

"Christ, I'm so sorry," he said.

"What do we do?" Megan asked. When Brock didn't say anything, she turned to the others, finally locking eyes with Vaughn. "What do we do?"

The Black Shuck had healed itself, just as it could heal its smaller units when it broke itself down into its multi-form. Jonathan was a similar lifeform. A being of quantum energy. He just didn't know how to harness his full power yet. Not like the Shuck could.

Vaughn leaned forward and whispered, "You know what to do, don't you? You know how to fix him. How he can fix himself. He's depleted now, but he just needs a jumpstart. I'm so sorry to ask, but can you help us?"

"What the fuck did you just say?" Brock demanded.

Had they not understood her? The language she'd used felt so natural. It didn't matter. All that mattered was that the Shuck understood. It made another of those low rumbling noises as arcs of electricity crackled along its body, flowing down its spine to the tip of its tail. It lifted its tail a few feet off the ground and moved it over to where Jonathan lay still on the ground.

"Do not interfere," Vaughn said, consciously choosing their language.

Brock and Megan held still as the Shuck slowly lowered its tail onto Jonathan's chest. The energy that crackled along its spine flowed into him, filling him, until his body glowed with it. The gaping hole in his stomach filled in, the skin above the wound sealing. His eyes fluttered open.

"It worked!" Megan leaned forward and wrapped her arms around Jonathan's neck, helping him to sit up. "I can't believe it."

As the Shuck pulled its tail away, Brock hooked his arms under Jonathan's and helped him to his feet. The three of them backed away, still eyeing the Shuck warily.

Brock cast the same suspicious gaze at Vaughn as well.

It should have bothered her. Somewhere deep inside, it might. But she was most concerned with the beast—*her* beast. The first member of the army she would raise to fight the Curator. To take her revenge. Jonathan would join them as well, in time, as would the rest of the Blades. They already followed her instructions. She only needed to modify their objective.

"Vaughn." Damien's low voice caused a frisson to flow along Vaughn's spine. Her skin had been cleansed of the creature's venom from the rain, so she didn't pull away when he dropped his swords and reached for her. She didn't lean into his embrace, either.

His skin felt odd against hers. Soft and weak, even with the cybernetic reinforcements that she could sense his nanites forging all throughout his flesh.

"Vaughn, look at me," he pleaded. He turned her to face him. She didn't see the harm in meeting his gaze.

The furrow between his brows had deepened. Lines of strain creased the corners of his eyes. The nanites had sealed his wound, and the rain had cleansed him as well. She let her gaze rove over his massive chest, following the streams of nanites tracing paths of light just beneath his skin. She lifted her fingertips to him, following their path.

Another excellent specimen. Another who would serve her.

He pulled her closer and crushed his lips to hers. Heat

and energy erupted within her, pushing away the cold detachment that had encroached on her consciousness again. Her arms wrapped around his neck, her body pressed against him. She kissed him with all the passion she could, desperate to reconnect to that part of her that was human. That part that loved him.

That wasn't me. That isn't me.

Except it was. Part of her, anyway.

The rain became colder, but Damien's arms were around her, keeping her warm. She dared to pull back, checking the skin of her own arms. They had reverted to their usual pale color. No scale pattern. And the cold consciousness—the alien self within her—had retreated. At least for now. For this one moment, she let herself feel the safety and comfort of his embrace.

"Brock!" Tessa's screeching call shattered Vaughn's calm, a heart-pounding panic taking its place. What could make a werewolf sound like that?

"Where's Marcus?" Vaughn's voice hitched as the question sprang forth without thought.

"Brock!" Tessa screamed again. "Dad! Bring back Dad!"

Brock let go of Jonathan and bolted in the direction of Tessa's voice. Megan kept supporting Jonathan as they hurried after him as quickly as they could. The last Vaughn had seen of Marcus, he'd been clear of the fight. He'd been injured, but she had seen him shake off worse dozens of times. What if she'd missed something? What if this whole time he'd been out there hurt? Or worse?

"Damien..." Her voice cracked on his name.

"Come on." He grabbed her hand and pulled her along, ducking down to pick something up off the ground before running after the others.

They managed to reach Tessa before Megan and Jonathan. Brock was already there, kneeling in a copse of tall grass near his sister. Brock's eyes were wide enough to show the whites all around his glowing irises, the blue eye crackling with energy. His hands were lifted at his sides as if he didn't know what to do with them. Tessa was hunched over something, sobbing softly and murmuring to herself.

Vaughn's heart pounded in her chest. Marcus couldn't be... He just couldn't. Tessa would have already completely snapped if that had happened. And if he wasn't... gone... there was still hope. Vaughn stepped closer, drawing on Damien's strength at her side, dread coiling in her belly like a serpent.

"Jesus Christ," Damien muttered. He tightened his grip on Vaughn's hand, but she pulled away, stepping closer to the group.

Marcus was lying in the grass, his skin reflecting the pale light of dawn filtering through the thick cloud cover above. The rain had finally stopped. His eyes were closed, but his chest heaved in quick breaths, as if he was hyperventilating. A huge gash ran along his back. The skin along the edge of the gash looked like it had been melted by acid and had a yellowish cast. The wound wasn't bleeding, but the flesh within was blackened.

Vaughn's gaze roved lower and her mind recoiled, unable to process what she was seeing. She ran a few feet away and threw up in the grass. Damien was at her side in an instant, rubbing her back and gripping her arm tight enough to let her know he was just as freaked out. Tessa was making strange little broken noises behind them. Vaughn swore she heard her say, "daddy," and her heart nearly broke.

"Keep it together," Damien said. "He needs you. We all do."

Vaughn nodded, wiping her mouth and trying to get her breathing back under control. That cold detachment looked pretty good right now, but she couldn't trust herself to do the right thing for Marcus if she let it take hold.

"Brock." Vaughn hurried to Brock and rested her hand on his shoulder. She squeezed as hard as she could, trying to snap him out of his shock. She tried not to focus on Marcus in her periphery, but it was hard. Her mind was still reeling from how his body twisted at an unnatural angle at his waist. Had he healed at all? Had he healed... wrong?

How could she not have realized how badly he was hurt? The rain had dampened his pelt, hiding the gash, but

Vaughn had seen how badly his back had broken—broken while saving her life. The way he had snapped at her, she should have known he was half-mad with pain. How could she have missed this?

Keep it together.

She repeated Damien's words in her mind, focused on the feel of him close. Marcus might be Tessa's mate, but he was Vaughn's best friend. They'd been best friends for years. Vaughn had always taken care of him, always made sure he made it back from the field. She wasn't about to let him down now.

Megan and Jonathan finally reached them. Megan's eyes widened, then filled with tears. Jonathan brought up his arm to shield her vision, pulling her against his chest. Brock was so focused on Marcus, he didn't even complain.

"Marcus needs a doctor," Vaughn said. "Now. Where are Eli and Porter?"

"Dexter and Porter took Dad away on the hoverbikes," Brock said. "To keep them safe during the fight."

"Then we need to call them back." She glanced around at the group, only then registering that almost everyone was naked, including herself. Damien had pants and Jonathan was fully dressed, though his shirt was in tatters from being impaled by the Shuck. "Does anybody have a communicator? Anyone?"

Jonathan stared at her with a bleak expression. Vaughn

already knew Damien didn't have one, unless his nanites had somehow installed one within him—which she doubted was their priority with all the fighting going on. Her watch was long gone, probably back in the tank or something. She scanned the area, trying to find any sign of her tech.

"Daddy can fix it," Tessa was chanting. "Just hold on. Hold on to me, Marcus. Please."

Her hands were resting on his back. The one of flesh and the one of metal.

Vaughn darted forward, grabbing Tessa's cybernetic arm. Tessa was so fucked up, she didn't even fight it. She just looked up at Vaughn with wild eyes. She'd never seen anyone look so lost. Vaughn ran her fingertip along an access port and popped it open. How the hell was she supposed to do this without her tools?

Something glinted in her periphery. She looked over to see Damien holding her favorite tool within reach.

"David!" She grabbed the tool and hugged it to her chest briefly. "Okay, let's do this. Steady her arm for me."

Damien dropped down next to them and gripped Tessa's arm, supporting it so that it wasn't shaking as much. She seemed a pale echo of the fierce werewolf Vaughn was used to.

Tessa looked up at Vaughn and, in that small, broken voice, said, "I can't feel him. I can't feel him in my mind anymore."

Vaughn's stomach bottomed out. Only death could break the bond of a mated pair of werewolves. Marcus was still alive, so something else was going on. Vaughn glanced back to her best friend, remembered how protective he'd always been, even while grievously injured.

"He's blocking you," Vaughn said. "He doesn't want you to share his pain."

Tessa let out a heart-wrenching groan, doubling over as if Vaughn's words had dealt her a blow. She looked back to Marcus, smoothing his hair away from his brow with her free hand.

"Marcus, I'm strong," she said. "I can take it. I can help you. Please let me in."

"I don't think he can hear you," Brock said. "I can't reach him either."

"It doesn't matter," Vaughn said, making adjustments to Tessa's arm. "We've never lost a Blade before. We're not losing one Blade today. You hear me, Marcus? This started with you and me. The pack within the Blades. We were the first pack. You and me. Just the two of us. If you try to leave it before me, I will never let you hear the end of it. You hear me? Leave me here and I'll find a way to haunt *you* in the afterlife. And you know I could figure it out. Just like… this."

Tessa's arm emitted a long, high beep. Vaughn grabbed it and said, "Dexter! Turn your ass around and get Porter and Eli back to the ranch immediately."

"Vaughn?" Dexter sounded genuinely surprised.

"You think a barn-sized, interphasic dweller is more than I can handle after drowning, being blown up, suffocating, and having an alien parasite try to eat my brain?" she said. "Please."

Damien stiffened next to her. "When the hell did all that happen to you?"

"It's been an eventful couple of months." Vaughn shrugged. "And it's not showing any sign of slowing down."

Chapter Nineteen

"Dexter, what's your ETA?" Vaughn's voice was flat and calm, but it didn't have that cold edge that she'd spoken with while in her other form. Her alien form.

Damien suppressed a shudder at the memory. Not at how she'd looked, but how she acted. How she *felt*. That person, whoever she was, wasn't Vaughn. That was the Curator.

"Five minutes," Dexter said through the comm system Vaughn had jury-rigged in Tessa's arm.

"Drop off Porter and Eli here, then head to the ranch and drive the main van out to these coordinates." Vaughn messed with Tessa's arm some more, presumably to transmit their location. "Bring the van that still has a stasis chamber in it. We need an emergency transport."

"Tell Damien to hold on," Dexter said. "He's pulled through before."

"It's not Damien." Vaughn looked up at Damien briefly. Pain haunted her gaze. "It's Marcus."

"Did he get hit with silver or something?" Dexter asked, an odd note to his tone.

"The Shuck bit him," Vaughn said. "I think it's

interfering with his ability to heal. He's hurt. It's… It's really bad."

Dexter's voice was cold and controlled when he spoke again. "I'll be there in two, with the van."

"How—" Before Vaughn could finish her question, they heard a sonic boom overhead. Damien looked up to see a blue streak in the sky. He hadn't known the hoverbikes could go that fast. It didn't seem safe to do so with a passenger. Dexter must have been pushing it past its limits.

I think we can all relate.

"Please let me in, Marcus." Tessa pulled her arm away. Her hands were shaking as she stroked Marcus's hair. "Let me help you bear this. I can do it. I'm strong enough now. Please, my mind is my own. Let me share it with you. I can help." She stared at him intently, as if she was trying to break down whatever mental barrier Marcus had put up between them. She looked at Brock with tears streaking her face. "What do I do? I can't get through to him."

"Neither can I." Brock's voice was so small, Damien barely heard it. "I've been trying."

"You're the alpha," Vaughn said. "You're the progenitor. How can you not get through to him?"

Brock shook his head. "He's too far away. Wherever he's gone, I can't reach him."

"Gone?" Tessa made another little whimpering noise. Damien felt his heart breaking for her.

"I… I don't know," Brock said.

"Stop it." Megan cut in, her voice sharp and commanding. She stood behind Brock, resting one hand on his shoulders. "Marcus is still here. He's still with us. He's just gone to the safe space in his mind. I've done it hundreds of times, when the pain was too much to handle. He'll find his way back to us."

Tessa broke into sobs. She bent over, resting her forehead against his cheek.

Damien tore his gaze away as he heard two engines approaching. One from the lightening sky to the east, still far away, and one from the west. Dexter was driving the van through the field, the vehicle lurching and pitching on the uneven terrain. Vaughn must have reinforced its frame for it to handle how hard Dexter was pushing it. He drove slightly past the group, turning so that the back doors were lined up with them. The driver's door slammed shut just before he raced around the side of the van, joining them.

"I got here as quick as I—" His voice dropped off as he saw Marcus. Dexter's eyes widened and his mouth dropped open. He slowed his pace, his hands clenching into fists at his sides. "How the fuck did this happen?"

"It was the Black Shuck," Vaughn said. "But I've taken care of it now."

"You?" Dexter turned his baleful glare on her. "You took care of it? Who the fuck took care of Marcus?" He lurched forward, getting right in her face. Vaughn backed up a few paces, and he followed. Damien grabbed his arm, but Dexter shook him off. He stalked back to the group and bit out each word. "Who. Let. This. Happen?"

"I'm the alpha," Brock said, standing. "It's on me."

"No shit, it's on you," Dexter said. "You're the asshole who ordered me to leave. Porter could have taken Dad to safety. I could have stayed. I could have fought."

"You're vulnerable," Brock shot back. "You both keep saying you're 'diminished.' We don't even know if you'd split if one of you dies. It was too big of a risk."

"Too big of a risk?" Dexter's voice grew thick, his features conveying his exasperation as clearly as his words. "We're Blades. We all know tomorrow isn't guaranteed. We still fight. We still stand together."

Brock strode over to Dexter, stabbing his finger into the replicant's chest. "And you still take my fucking orders."

Dexter grabbed his wrist and twisted it, stepping forward and lifting Brock's elbow, locking both joints. Lightning fast, he kicked the back of Brock's knee, taking him to the ground. He kept his hold on Brock's wrist and elbow, using his grip to shove his arm up farther than anyone's could go. Damien heard something pop in Brock's shoulder. Dexter kept applying pressure, twisting Brock's arm at an unnatural angle.

"Dexter!" Megan yelled.

Dexter leaned in close, his teeth right next to Brock's ear, and said, "Do I seem *diminished* to you?"

He shoved Brock hard, releasing him as he stepped back. Brock caught himself with the arm that hadn't just had its shoulder dislocated. He stood, growling low in his throat. Reaching across his body, he popped his shoulder back into its joint, glaring at Dexter the entire time. The replicant didn't seem to notice the danger he was in. That or he didn't care.

"Marcus grew up in this shitshow," Dexter said. "Because of you. You're the one who had something to prove to your stupid human hunter mom. A woman who would be trying to kill us all if she was still alive—even Tessa."

"What the fuck are you talking about?" Brock said.

"I'm talking about your stupid Blades of Janus," Dexter yelled. "We did what you asked. *I* did everything you asked of me. And that included keeping Marcus in line. Making sure he didn't snap. Taking care of him. You dropped this poor kid with me and told me to keep him safe, to keep him sane. I had to fucking finish raising him. And even with everything he was fighting, with a fucking psychopath inside his head, telling him to take me out, he always had my back. *Always*. And where the fuck were you?"

The rage evaporated from Brock's features, replaced with shock. Megan came to stand at his side, holding onto his arm, but she didn't say anything. Not in his defense. There was nothing she could say.

"Even in the good days, when you could still fight," Dexter continued. "You were always off doing your thing. You gave us orders and then ignored us, because you knew we were good little soldiers. But you also gave me a goddammed kid, when I was barely more than a kid myself. You left me to finish raising him, to keep him from going crazy, and I did. I did every fucking thing you ever told me to do. Even tonight, when you told me to leave him. And I trusted you. I trusted you to keep him safe. To have his back, like he always had mine. Now look at him."

Dexter lashed out again, grabbing Brock's head and turning it so that he was facing Marcus. Brock didn't even resist. His body was shaking. Damien couldn't tell if he was about to change or what. His skin felt electrified. This was a powder keg about to explode, and that wouldn't help anyone. But Damien had no idea how to to diffuse it. Vaughn was staring with wide eyes, one hand clamped over her mouth and her other arm wrapped around her middle, hugging herself tight.

"Fucking look at him, Brock!" Dexter yelled.

Brock let out a horrible sound, a half-choking sob. Damien had only heard something like it once—from himself, when he'd watched Vaughn drown. Brock fell to his hands and knees, shaking his head.

"We heal," he said. "Werewolves heal. We're supposed to heal. I didn't think he'd get hurt. Not like this."

Megan crouched next to him, holding his shoulders as

his body was wracked with sobs.

'*There has to be something we can do for him,*' Damien thought. '*Anything.*'

[SCANNING]

Was there actually something he could do? He didn't dare to breathe, waiting to see what his nanites could come up with, barely daring to let himself hope.

[HEALING SYSTEM OVERLOAD DETECTED]

'*What does that mean?*'

An image of Marcus's body appeared overlaid in Damien's vision. His stomach tried to revolt as details his regular vision couldn't detect were presented with a horrifying clarity. Marcus's hips and legs were rotated almost one-hundred and eighty degrees from his upper torso. Blue lights highlighted his spine where it had healed —backwards.

"Shit," Damien murmured.

"No kidding," Dexter snapped at him. He turned to Jonathan and said, "Make yourself useful. Go get the stretcher from the van and bring it here next to Marcus. Vaughn, check the stasis chamber in the van and make sure there's no virus in any of its systems."

"The virus shouldn't have made it to the van," she said.

"*I* don't take chances," Dexter said. "Do it."

Vaughn nodded. Her gaze locked with Damien's for a moment, then she ran to the van. At least she knew her main tool didn't have the virus in it. Damien returned his attention to the data his nanites were feeding him. It wasn't good.

Lines of sickly green crept out from the wound, occasionally spreading a bit, but then being pushed back by a pale blue light that he was pretty sure represented Marcus's werewolf-enhanced immune system. It looked like a battle was going on within him. Whatever toxic goo was in the Black Shuck's mouth had gotten into Marcus's body and he was trying to fight it off. From the looks of it, he was losing.

The nanites zoomed in on Marcus's spine. A timestamp appeared next to the injury, scrolling backwards. The blue light turned red, showing the spinal column very obviously severed. The image scrolled up to his back, where a huge gash throbbed with that sickly green light, just around the edges of the wound. More blue light pressed against it, but was being pushed back.

The image zoomed out, his nanites highlighting Marcus's spine again as the blue light converged there. The red faded away as his spine reconnected. His body must have healed what it could, not having the resources to straighten his spine out first. Damien's stomach lurched again. If they were going to help Marcus, they were going to have to break his back again.

A hover bike landed in the field several yards away, two men riding it—Porter and Eli. It looked like Eli was already trying to jump off before Porter even stopped the thing. The moment they pulled up near the group, Eli was off and running toward them.

"Oh, dear god…" His face blanched as he took in the scene, then his features hardened. He crouched next to Marcus and started tapping in commands on his watch, then slowly passed his arm over Marcus's body, letting the device scan him. "Tell me what happened."

Tessa looked up at him with her reddened eyes. "You have to help him."

He reached out and squeezed her shoulder. "I will, sweetie. I will."

"I thought you said we shouldn't make empty promises." Porter was standing over his shoulder, the grimmest expression Damien had ever seen on his face.

Eli ignored him, continuing his exam. He held his wrist over Marcus's spine for several moments.

"That's not the problem," Damien said.

"You're a doctor now?" Dexter quipped, standing to the side with his arms crossed over his chest.

"A cyborg, actually." Damien moved closer. "The spinal injury has been healed."

"How can you say that?" Megan gasped. "I mean, look at him."

"It didn't heal properly, but we can deal with that later." Damien held up his hand, his palm toward the sky, and thought, '*Do your thing. Please.*' Light burst out of his palm, projecting a hologram of Marcus's body for them all to see. "The venom is the problem."

Just then, Vaughn and Jonathan hurried over to the group. Jonathan was carrying a stretcher, and Vaughn had a stack of clothing with several blankets on top. She had already dressed in the standard Blades' field outfit.

"The stasis chamber and the van are all clear," Vaughn said. She handed the clothing to Megan. "Did I hear you say something about venom?"

"The Shuck bit him," Damien said. "It looks like it was a glancing wound, but enough to transmit some of its venom."

"We need to make an anti-venom," Porter said.

"That'll take time." Eli was studying Damien's holoprojection. "It looks like Marcus is still fighting it off, but the stuff is trying to spread."

"The stasis chamber suspends all biological functions." Porter turned his attention to Vaughn. "We made it to suspend our particular energies as well. Will that be enough to stop whatever this is? That dweller is unlike anything we've ever faced before."

"Actually it isn't," Vaughn said. "It has a similar quantum signature to Jonathan's. He might have come out a little different, but he's still fundamentally the same as you. He's still a replicant. He's just a little more obvious with his... idiosyncrasies." She glanced over at Jonathan, who was staring at Marcus with a blank expression, still holding the stretcher. "It should stop the spread of the venom, even if it isn't purely a biological toxin."

"Then let's get him in the chamber." Damien took the stretcher from Jonathan and set it down near Marcus. He angled his head toward Tessa, and said, "Megan."

Megan nodded, then walked over to Tessa. Megan had already dressed, as had Brock. She draped one of the blankets over Tessa's shoulders, and urged her to stand.

"They're going to help Marcus, now," Megan said. "But you need to give them room to work."

"But…" Tessa looked up at her, confusion etched in her features. Shock must be setting in. They would have to watch her carefully after everything she'd been through. Tessa let Megan help her to her feet. They walked a few paces away, Tessa staring intently at everything they were doing to Marcus.

Damien moved the stretcher closer. "Brock, you support his back, I'll get his head. Jonathan, you get his feet."

The replicant cocked his head to the side, then moved to crouch near Marcus's feet. When they were all in position, Eli started the count.

"On three," he said. "One, two, three."

They all carefully hefted Marcus onto the stretcher. Damien nodded toward Jonathan. Together, they lifted the stretcher and started toward the van. Vaughn ran ahead of them, Porter at her side and Eli lagging a few steps behind as he trotted alongside the stretcher.

"Hang on, son," Eli said. "We are going to fix this. I don't make empty promises." He said the last loud enough that Porter could hear.

"Here's hoping." Porter jumped up into the van with Vaughn. The pair set to work prepping the stasis chamber.

"Balance him out," Damien said to Jonathan. "I'll stay down here and lift as high as I can. Keep him level."

Jonathan placed his grips for the stretcher on the van's floor, then jumped up. He carefully matched his movements to Damien's, keeping Marcus level. Damien walked forward as far as he could.

"I've got this." Dexter patted Damien's shoulder, then leapt up into the van. He took over holding up the stretcher near Marcus's head.

Damien wanted to climb in after him, but the van was already crowded. He stood just outside, watching them work. The pair placed the stretcher inside the stasis chamber, then stepped away.

"Okay, everyone except Porter and Vaughn, out." Eli was at Damien's side. "Jonathan, Dexter, go help comfort your sister." The two men filed out of the van and leapt to the ground. Dexter lingered for a moment. Eli put his hand on Dexter's shoulder and gave it a squeeze. "He'll be okay. You raised a fighter."

Dexter's lips thinned. He put his hand on top of Eli's for a moment, then nodded and walked away.

"What can I do?" Damien had noticed that Eli didn't

order him away.

"Help an old man up into this thing?" Eli chuckled.

"Absolutely." Damien half-lifted Eli into the van, almost managing a smile at the other man's gasp as he was momentarily—safely—airborne.

"Thanks." Eli straightened his shirt, his eyebrows high on his forehead. He shook his head, then turned to Vaughn and Porter.

"Activating anti-gravity," Vaughn said.

Light flickered in the stasis chamber. Marcus's body slowly rose. When he was clear, Vaughn reached in and grasped the stretcher, pulling it out from under him.

"How's he doing?" she asked.

Porter was staring intently at a display screen. "Baseline readings are unchanged."

"Okay, let's freeze him." She tapped a few more commands on the stasis chamber's main control panel.

"You're not actually freezing him, right?" Damien asked.

"No, that's just an expression," Porter said. "What we are doing is hitting the pause button on all of his biological functions. And since he's a dweller, there are other, more numinous functions we need to suspend as well."

"Keep an eye on that venom," Vaughn said. "We don't know how his body will react to being in stasis with that stuff in him. If his immune system goes dormant first, I don't want it taking the chance to spread."

"I'm watching." Porter entered a few commands of his own, frowning deeply in concentration.

"Porter?" Vaughn's voice was tight.

Porter's brow relaxed. He turned to her and smiled.

"Stasis achieved," he said. "We just managed to buy ourselves some time."

Vaughn let out a huge breath that was as much a sob as a laugh. She threw her arms around Porter's neck and hugged him. His eyes widened in surprise, but then he hugged her back. Vaughn released him, then hugged Eli as well, before turning toward Damien.

"We did it," she said. "He'll be safe while we figure this out." Her forehead crinkled as the tears started again. "And he won't be suffering while we do."

Damien put his hands on the floor of the van and launched himself up into it. He grabbed Vaughn and pulled her against his chest, hugging her tight while she cried.

"I should have seen," she said. "I should have known that he was already hurt. He broke his back saving me."

Damien straightened enough to cradle her face in his hands. "You're the one who stopped the Shuck. You saved us all when you did that."

She shuddered, her hands fisting in his shirt. Her arms tightened around him. If only he could hold her like this forever. But they had work still to do.

"About that..." Porter broke in to their moment. "We're going to need a sample of its venom if we're going to create an anti-venom. Anyone have any ideas of how we get that without being eaten?"

Vaughn angled her head toward Porter, though she kept her grip on Damien. "I can get it for you."

"You?" Porter's eyebrows hitched up again. "How?"

She shrugged. "I figure I'll just ask."

"Ask?" Porter repeated.

"I think we might have missed something important," Eli said. "Why don't you walk us through it?"

"I found out what a curator is." She looked up at Damien, her eyes pinched with pain.

He smoothed her hair away from her face. "*What* you are isn't *who* you are."

She let out another of those bursts of emotion that was equal parts relief and despair. God, he wished he could shield her from this. He reached up and wiped the fresh tears from her cheeks, then kissed her forehead. Hugging her close, he brought his lips to her ears and whispered, "You're the IT gal."

She actually laughed. The sound helped loosen some of the tightness in Damien's own chest. They had all been through hell, but they weren't out of it yet.

"Are you ready to get to work?" he asked.

She finally let go of his shirt and pulled away, nodding. She wiped her nose and eyes once more, sniffing and looking around as if getting her bearings.

"I can explain on the way back to the barn," she said.

"Let's get Tessa in here so she can be close to Marcus."

"Megan and Brock can ride up front with me." Damien walked to the back of the van and jumped to the ground.

The pack wasn't far away, clustered in a trio and hugging each other. Damien didn't know who was comforting whom. Brock was almost as torn up as Tessa. And damn, after that dressing-down Dexter had given him, it was no surprise. The real surprise was how much the replicant seemed to actually care about Marcus. Damien would not have put money on that happening in a million years.

Even with his short time with this team, he was pretty sure no one had a clue how Dexter really felt. Hell, maybe Dexter hadn't even known until he was stuck in a single body, without anyone else's thoughts to distract him—or keep him company. That kind of sudden isolation had to cause some self-reflection. Eli had told Dexter to go help comfort the others, but who the hell was comforting him?

Scanning the area, Damien saw Jonathan and Dexter standing near the hoverbikes. Dexter met Damien's eyes and straightened. Damien nodded in what he hoped was a reassuring manner. Dexter's shoulders lowered a bit. Guess Damien pulled it off. He signaled for them to get ready to roll out. Dexter turned to Jonathan and said something. A moment later, the pair mounted the bikes and started them up.

That got the pack's attention. They hurried over to the

van, Megan reaching Damien first while Brock and Tessa followed, their arms around each other's middles. At some point, Tessa and Brock had dressed, which was a relief. Being around werewolves involved a lot of nudity. Then again, Vaughn had been naked a little bit ago as well, after whatever the fuck had happened inside the Black Shuck's mouth.

He shuddered, the too-recent memory rising up. She had been fearless as she approached the beast, leaping into its mouth. It had snapped her up in one bite. He'd thought she was as good as dead—again. The despair he'd felt in that moment had brought him to his knees.

But then, the creature had spit her back out. She'd emerged... different. Not just physically, but the way she acted, the coldness in her eyes. He didn't give a shit about the alien physique. He loved her for her mind, for her heart. The trouble was, those had been affected, too.

He couldn't lose her. He *wouldn't*.

"Tessa, you're riding in the back with Marcus," he said. "Brock and Megan, you're up front in the passenger's seat. I'm driving."

As Tessa started past him, he clasped her arm gently. Her golden eyes were dull and unfocused, her pupils blown. He stepped closer, gripping the side of her neck and angling her face up to his.

"Marcus needs you, Tessa," he said. "He also needs everybody inside of that van intact and unharmed."

"I… I'm better," she said.

"I know, and that's why I'm trusting you to be in here with us." He let out a sigh. "You're stronger than you know. That can be a blessing or a curse. Be careful when you touch the others with your emotions so high. You could hurt them without even meaning to when you're this worked up."

"I won't." She shook her head. "I won't touch them."

"You will," he said. "You should. They need it as much as you do. I'm just saying, be careful about it. Be strong, but be aware of your strength. Make it a blessing."

She nodded, tears glinting in her eyes. Damien pulled her against his chest and hugged her. Hugged a werewolf. He couldn't believe it, but this was his life now. Without really thinking, he kissed the top of her head, then turned and guided her to the open doors of the van. She jumped in, her back straight as she walked toward the stasis chamber holding Marcus.

"Thank you." Brock spoke in a low voice. "That couldn't have been easy for you."

Damien shook his head. "As easy as breathing. Let's go."

Chapter Twenty

The van's floor vibrated beneath Vaughn's feet, letting her know it was moving forward. The uneven ground of the field would have tested a normal suspension, but she had designed this one. She barely felt a thing as Damien headed toward the barn, probably quite a bit more cautiously than Dexter had driven it to them a few moments ago. Brock was in the passenger's seat, Megan curled up in his lap.

"Systems nominal," Vaughn said, checking the readout again. Could she think of it as 'again' if she was never taking her eyes off of it?

Porter was just as entranced by the scrolling numbers and data feeds. That didn't stop him from talking, though.

"You realize that I am going to run even more tests on you when we get back to the ranch, right?" he said. "Maybe try to get this other form of yours to manifest."

"And you realize that the only times I've changed was when I was either in life-threatening danger or actually died, right?"

In her periphery, she saw him shrug. "I'm sure we can find a way to make you comfortable."

"How magnanimous of you." She glanced over at him, which was a mistake. Not because of any glitches in the systems. Thankfully, everything was working just as she'd hoped.

Tessa was standing between them, staring at Marcus through the transparent window above his face. Even in stasis, the corners of his eyes were pinched with strain. He shouldn't be feeling anything—Vaughn prayed he wasn't feeling anything. It was as if the lines were permanently etched there. Tessa was hugging herself, her lips pressed together.

"You okay?" Vaughn asked, in a low gentle voice. She immediately realized the idiocy of her question.

Tessa's mate was grievously injured, to the point that he had blocked their mental link. As much as Porter casually spoke of making an anti-venom, they had no idea how that would work. They were applying human solutions to an alien problem. Vaughn only hoped that they had similar enough physiologies that they could figure out something that would work.

"I'm so sorry," Vaughn said. "That was stupid—"

"It's okay." Tessa glanced over at her briefly, forcing a tight smile. "I'm—" Her forehead scrunched up as her voice broke. She shook her head and covered her mouth with her cybernetic hand.

"Tessa—" Before Vaughn could reach out to her, Eli stepped forward and put his hand on Tessa's shoulder.

"Pumpkin," he said.

Tessa burst into tears. She spun around and wrapped her arms around Eli's middle. Porter took a step toward them, but paused. Vaughn held her breath as they watched the pair, looking for any sign of discomfort or unease from Eli.

Tessa had only ridded herself of Roy, the psychotic werewolf who had been the previous alpha of their pack, a few days ago. Before they'd managed to take Roy out, he'd twisted the mental bond packs used to communicate telepathically to try to get her to kill everyone—including Eli. Vaughn hadn't seen the two embrace like this since Brock and Eli had arrived at the ranch, even though they'd both thought the other was dead for years.

Tessa had had her first psychotic break before Brock had even been wheeled out of the van. But Tessa had been fine ever since they'd killed Roy. Everyone was still on edge around her, especially Vaughn. The previous alpha had been especially keen on killing curators. After what had happened with the Shuck, Vaughn was beginning to see why.

Seeing the father and daughter embracing now brought fresh tears to Vaughn's eyes, especially when they started to speak.

"Daddy." Tessa's voice hitched.

Eli's eyebrows rose in surprise, but his arms wrapped around her without hesitation. His eyes closed and he smiled, pulling her tighter.

"I'm here, baby," he said. "I promise, I won't ever leave you again. And I won't let Marcus leave you, either. You've lost enough."

Tessa let out a sob. Her body trembled, but Eli just kept holding her. He didn't show any signs that she might be holding him too tight. Vaughn turned back to the stasis chamber. None of the numbers had changed.

The van slowed to a stop. Vaughn pressed the access sequence that opened one of the storage cabins in the back and pulled out the field sample collection kit within. She lifted its strap over her shoulder, then opened the doors to the van and jumped down.

"Where are you going?" Porter asked.

"I need to get to the Shuck and collect some of its venom," she said.

"I can do it." He walked to the edge of the interior of the van. "You can get Marcus down to the stasis room."

Vaughn shook her head. "Marcus stays right here till I have a chance to talk to Scarecrow and make sure the virus has been completely purged from all our systems, both on the ranch and in the ship."

"Scarecrow?" he said.

"Oh, did I forget to mention that when I was filling you in about being an alien clone?" She forced herself to smile, kept her voice light. "Silly me. Yeah, Scarecrow is in the ranch—or maybe she's already done here and moved on to the ship. I don't know how long she'll need. But she's purging all our systems of the virus for us. Super helpful. And she brought along her friends, the goblin and the spriggan."

Porter made a little choking sound, his eyebrows high up on his forehead. It must feel like Christmas and he was getting his very own pony. Vaughn let out a deep sigh.

"And before you say anything, no, you can't try to get samples from them or run any tests," she said.

"What if they agree to—"

"No." She didn't let him finish. "There is no polite way to say, 'Excuse me, do you mind if I run potentially dangerous and painful tests on you so I can gather data since any samples I remove from you will vaporize in a few seconds? Oh, don't worry, though. Your body would vaporize, too, if I killed you, so I'll do my best not to let that happen because I want to keep experimenting on you.'"

If only dweller poison vaporized as well. Marcus wouldn't be fighting for his life. But the poison itself wouldn't be as effective if it vanished as soon as it left their bodies.

Porter scowled. "Well, when you say it like that…"

Vaughn actually managed to laugh a bit. Damien joined them just as Dexter and Jonathan pulled into the garage and parked their bikes.

"I was serious with my offer to get the sample,

though," Porter said. "If you've tamed it, as you say, it would spare you from having to go outside again."

Vaughn's stomach lurched. She tried to cover it with yet another fake smile. There was a lot of that going around at the moment.

"I'm not afraid of going outside anymore," she said. "I know where my fear was coming from. I can handle it."

Damien threaded her fingers with his, his presence at her side a warm reassurance. Her smile became a bit more real. Porter kept staring at her, obviously waiting for more data.

"Earth is a low gravity planet," she said. "At least, for me. Biologically speaking. Are we done?"

"Not even nearly, but I'll leave you alone for now." Porter smirked at her, then turned and headed deeper into the crowded van.

Brock and Megan had joined the others inside the van's large space and were sitting on the bench built into one side to stay as out of the way as they could. Vaughn turned to see Dexter and Jonathan standing right behind her.

"Shall we?" Dexter said.

"Sure." Vaughn walked past him, grateful that Damien was keeping his grip on her hand.

They headed out, feet splashing in puddles from the rain. It had paused for the moment, the sky covered in a thick layer of steel gray clouds. The asphalt of the driveway gave way to grass as they headed around the barn to where she'd left the Black Shuck. Deep furrows of dark earth scarred the ground from the battle, leading up to a huge patch of grass that was pressed down from the weight of the beast. The beast that had been there a few minutes ago—but was now gone.

"No, no, no." Vaughn dropped Damien's hand and ran forward.

"What is it?" Dexter said.

"It was here," she said. "It was right here." She let the sample kit slide down her arm to the ground. Spinning in circles, she studied the treeline in the distance. There were no breaks in the branches, no tracks, no sign that it had wandered off. No way to know where it had gone.

"Come back," she yelled. "Please, come back!"

"Vaughn…" Damien's gentle voice communicated so much in that one word. Too much.

"This isn't happening." She ran her fingers through her hair, then pressed them to her mouth. "This can't be happening."

Damien reached for her, but she swatted him away, darting to the side.

"No," she said. "I am not— I do not need comforting. I am going to figure this out. I'm the IT gal. The alien clone-super scary to dwellers-figures out everything person that everyone depends on. And I—" Her voice hitched. "I depend on Marcus. And he depends on me. He is my best friend and he has never let me down. I'm not about to let him down now."

She looked up at the sky and shouted, "Do you hear me? I am not going to let down my best friend. I'm not going to leave him in stasis, poisoned and... *mangled.*"

She pinched her eyes shut and more fucking tears flowed out. How did she still have any left?

None of them knew what would happen when they took Marcus out of stasis. His only chance was if they had some treatment ready for the venom. Then maybe they could do surgery or something to repair his spine. The only reason he hadn't already died from the internal torsion was because of his dweller nature. His healing abilities had to be redlined, keeping him alive, and he had to be in absolute agony.

She had to do everything she could to help him. He was her best friend. She couldn't just leave him in stasis indefinitely. But if the Black Shuck didn't come back, that's what she was facing. She couldn't keep herself from calculating the odds of being able to track down an interphasic being that could go anywhere on the planet in multiple connected dimensions—especially if she didn't have as much sway over the beast as she thought she had.

God, is this what Damien has been feeling all along?

"How do you do it?" Vaughn said, turning to Damien. Zach had been in stasis for days. It didn't sound like that long, but Damien had *killed* Carey. It didn't matter that it was an accident. Damien felt responsible. Just like Vaughn felt responsible for Marcus. "How do you even function, carrying this… *weight?*" How could she have not really understood what he was dealing with before now?

"Don't do that," Damien said. "You can't take this on."

"How can I *not?*" she yelled. "Marcus was hurt helping *me.*"

"Then don't carry it alone." Damien stepped closer. "You want to know how I keep going? Because I don't let myself bear that weight on my own. I know I can't. No one could. You're helping me. Everyone here has been. I know I'm not alone in this—and neither is Carey. And that gives me hope. You have to hold onto that. See yourself on the other side of it."

"I can't." Her knees felt weak, her legs trembling. "All I see are probabilities. Without the Shuck… My god, there's nothing we can do. There's nothing *I* can do."

She let herself drop to the ground and buried her face in her hands. She couldn't even cry anymore. Finally, her tears had dried up. Or maybe it was that she'd lost her hope. Her chest felt empty, like it had been hollowed out. There was just… nothing.

"Vaughn." Damien nudged her shoulder gently. She couldn't bring herself to respond.

"Vaughn." His voice was insistent, a strange note to it that made her open her eyes as he nudged her again, harder. Only it wasn't Damien nudging her.

The Black Shuck stood in front of her. Except not

exactly the Black Shuck. It was one of the smaller versions. It must have split itself into several components again. It stared at her with two sets of unblinking, glowing green eyes, standing nose-to-nose with her. Vaughn made a strangled 'eep' sound and threw her arms around its neck, burying her face in the coarse black fur that ran down its spine and along its sides. The creature stiffened, but she couldn't help herself.

"Thank you," she said. "Thank you so much for coming back. I'm sorry about before. That isn't me, I swear. But I need your help. Please, please, will you help me?"

She leaned back so she could look at it. The lime green of its eyes swirled with energy, flickers of light appearing and disappearing like twinkling stars. How could she communicate with such an alien consciousness? Did it have a language she could decipher?

It wasn't running away or acting threatening in any way. That was a start. She reached over to the sample collection kit and pulled it closer. She didn't dare look away, afraid that if she took her eyes off of the Shuck, it might disappear. The clasp wouldn't open. She felt hands on hers, and then Damien was there, opening the box for her. He pulled out a test tube and tore the packet to get to it, then handed it to her.

"Thank you." She kept her gaze locked on the Shuck. "Both of you." Holding the test tube up, she said, "Can you open your mouth for me? Without biting?"

The creature didn't move. How could she make it understand?

Cautiously, she opened her own mouth, then moved the test tube toward it, mimicking what she hoped to accomplish. The Shuck angled its head toward the beaker. Its long, forked tongue darted in and out from its mouth.

"I just need some of your spit," Vaughn said. "Which, when I say it out loud, sounds so weird."

"Maybe this will help." Damien held his hand closer.

"This is my friend," she said carefully. "Please, do not hurt him."

The Shuck continued to placidly stare at her. Light glowed on Damien's hand. A small holoprojection of the Shuck appeared above it. The creature's eyes widened ever so slightly, its focus more intent on the image Damien was projecting. He added a tiny version of Vaughn holding out the test tube. The projection continued through her collecting the sample, then vanished.

"See?" Vaughn said. "We don't want to hurt you or experiment on you or anything. We just need a little of your venom so that we can help our friend. I know you didn't mean to hurt him. The Curator made you do it somehow." She swore its eyes narrowed and a soft hissing sound emanated from its throat. "I'm not going to force you to do anything. I'll never force you to do something. I'm asking you to please, please help me help my friend.

But in the end, it's up to you."

The Shuck straightened its legs, lifting its head higher. It curved its neck, then flicked out its tongue again, this time, right above the test tube. A thin line of viscous yellow-green fluid flowed down from it, dripping into the tube.

"Oh god, thank you," Vaughn said.

"Careful." Damien was a steady presence at her side.

"It's venom can't hurt me." Vaughn kept her focus on the test tube as she spoke. "I was coated in it before. Its saliva is acidic as well, at least when the being is in its combined form."

"So, that's what happened to your clothes," he said.

"I seem to be going through a lot of them lately." She half-smiled, hoping he would catch it without her having to turn to face him. The tube was filling up fast. "Do you think this is enough?"

"I'm sure Porter would say more is always better." Damien held up another readied test tube for her. "We don't want you to run out. Wait, how is this not vaporizing?"

"I'm not sure," she said. "We'll have to check on that. But I figured it wouldn't when I saw that it was staying in Marcus's system. I would guess that dwellers like this have to be able to produce something that doesn't vaporize for them to be able to poison their targets. We've never had someone survive being bitten or stung by a dweller with venom before. This is new territory."

She quickly sealed the one she was working on and handed it to him. "Now *you* be careful. Just in case any got on the outside of that."

"I'm always careful," he said.

She snorted, then took the fresh test tube and filled it the same way as the first. Damien handed her a third, but when she'd filled it, the Shuck pulled its tongue back into its mouth. It let out a long sigh that almost sounded as if it was bored. Vaughn couldn't help but let out a small laugh. The relief she felt had her giddy.

"Thank you so much," she said. "I really appreciate it." She dared to reach up and stroke the side of the creature's face. It leaned into her hand and closed the set of eyes on that side of its body. "Who's a good boy?" She used her most cloying voice.

"We're not keeping it." Dexter was still standing close, undoubtedly ready to defend them if necessary. It wouldn't be.

"You're forgetting whose name is on the deed to the property," Vaughn said. "If I want a lizard-doggie, I'll get a lizard-doggie." She scratched the top of its head and all four of its eyes closed. Its mouth even opened a little in what looked like a smile. "Porter is going to love you. Don't you worry. I'll make sure he plays nice."

Dexter let out an exasperated sound. "Could we wrap this up, please? I'm sure Porter would love to start testing that fluid and don't you need to check out the ranch?"

"Yeah," Vaughn said. "Yeah, I do."

The hollowness in her chest retreated, filled with a warmth that she'd been afraid was gone forever. Filled with hope. She handed the last test tube to Damien, who secured it with the others in the sample kit. He took her hand when he was done closing it up, walking at her side as they headed back to the barn. Dexter flanked them, with Jonathan trailing a bit behind.

Vaughn looked over her shoulder, curious what the component creature of the Black Shuck would do. It flicked its tongue over the nearby grass a few times, then lifted its belly off the ground and started after them. Dexter tensed, but Vaughn shushed him. They kept walking, the lizard-dog following a few paces behind.

"If we're keeping it, it needs a name," Damien said.

"How will Tessa and Marcus feel about keeping something around that almost killed him?" Dexter's voice was cool, but after that earlier outburst, Vaughn knew not to discount the emotions roiling underneath.

"It almost killed me, too." Damien shrugged. "You get over it."

Vaughn didn't like being reminded of that. But the Shuck had been under someone else's control. It was being so placid now, she had trouble believing it would ever attack if it wasn't threatened or controlled, and she was certain she was the one holding the reins now—not that she would use them. Thinking back over the fairy tales about the Black Shuck, it was seen as a harbinger of death, but never as a *deliverer* of death. If any of them wanted to be mad at someone, they should direct their ire at the Curator.

"I'm okay keeping Tessa around, and she tried to kill me a bunch of times while she was under someone else's control," Vaughn said. "I don't hold it against her. Hopefully, she'll be able to do the same for the Shuck."

"Chuck," Damien said.

"You're kidding, right?" Vaughn arched an eyebrow at him.

Damien shrugged. "Chuck the Shuck."

Jonathan made a little sound that was almost like a laugh. Everyone stopped and stared at him. He ignored them, continuing on into the barn. The Shuck—Chuck—followed him.

"Okay, that was super weird, right?" Damien said. "It's not just me?"

"Not weird." Vaughn smiled. "That was good. A really good sign. That was one of the most normal reactions I've ever seen from him."

"If you can call laughing at that lame joke 'normal.'" Dexter smirked as he walked past them.

"I thought it was funny." Vaughn started to walk again. "And Chuck is a fine name for him."

"Maybe we should come up with one of those multipurpose names for it—him? Like Bradley and Zach—" His voice cut off abruptly, his hand tightening around hers.

"We're going to get Carey back," Vaughn said. "And Marcus. We just have to be patient. We can't afford to make mistakes."

Damien nodded.

"And I think Chuck is a 'him,'" she continued. "At least, that's the sense I get."

"I wonder what the 'hers' are like with Black Shucks." Damien faked a shudder, then let go of Vaughn's hand so he could wrap his arm around her shoulder and pull her against his side.

"Maybe we'll find out one day," she said. "But peacefully, now that we have Chuck on our side."

"Let's hope."

They walked through the garage on the ground level. The back doors to the van were still open. Tessa was inside, along with Eli and Porter. Brock and Megan had moved to sit between the open doors, their legs dangling over the edge of the van's floor. Jonathan and Chuck had already walked down into the first sublevel, into the real garage. They must have passed the group, but Vaughn hadn't heard a peep from anyone.

"Hey," she said. "Everything still okay?"

"In that nothing has changed, yes." Porter kept staring at the readings, occasionally tapping one of the control panels. "I take it you were successful, based on Jonathan's new friend?"

"Um, yes." Vaughn couldn't believe how well everyone was taking it. Maybe they were all too worn out to react to anything else. If so, she didn't want anybody blowing up later. "If we can keep Chuck around, we have a continuous source of the venom to study."

"Chuck?" Brock arched an eyebrow.

"He looks like a 'Chuck,'" Vaughn said.

Brock shook his head.

"Jonathan liked it." Damien handed the sample kit to Brock.

"Well, that's something." Brock set the kit next to him. "We'll wait for your green light before we head into the sublevel. If we can get that quick, I think it'd be good for all of us."

"I'm on it." Vaughn stepped out from Damien's embrace and hurried down the ramp that led to the main garage. She didn't have to look to know that Damien was right behind her.

The lights and the bright white walls made her eyes water after the dim illumination from outside. She blinked several times as she adjusted to it. Jonathan and Dexter were waiting near the door to the corridor that led into the rest of the sublevel. Chuck was sitting at Jonathan's feet, his back actually resting against the replicant.

"You two are certainly getting on well," Vaughn said as she passed them.

She pulled out David and adjusted his settings so that she could start scanning the ranch's systems, searching for the virus. The scent of burnt wires stung her nose as they walked by her ops center, the mangled door still lying on the floor where Dexter had cut his way in.

It was hard to believe Jonathan had caused all that damage. But only after studying the monitor displaying the Black Shuck's movements. Had he figured something out by watching them? Something about himself? The Shucks could blink from one spot to another. Jonathan had seen that, and then used Brock to teleport to the location of the battle. The energy output had slagged everything—except her. Was that why Chuck was sticking close to Jonathan? She suspected the pair shared deeper similarities.

She added that mystery to the ever growing list of things she needed to figure out. Right now, the only answer she wanted was 'are the ranch and ship free from the virus?'

She placed her hand on the access panel for Porter's lab. The door slid open, revealing an empty room. Okay, it would also be nice to know where Scarecrow and her cronies were.

"Here goes nothing." Vaughn walked over to the main computer console and activated David. Scarecrow had added a pretty obvious new subroutine that would seek out the virus without making the tool vulnerable to it again.

Vaughn scanned the computer three times and didn't

find anything. She moved throughout the room with the same results returning from all of the equipment. That was a good start, but she had a lot of work to do.

"This room is clear." She smiled at the small group around her. "Let's head to the ship, and then we can work our way up, doing a more systematic sweep. I want to make sure Zach is okay before we check any of the other levels."

She caught Damien's gaze, his gratitude obvious. The others moved aside as she led the way to the elevator. She quickly scanned it for the virus, then smiled and gestured them forward when she found none. The elevator had always seemed spacious to her before, but with everyone accompanying her, it was downright packed.

"This is quite the entourage," Damien said.

"It's my magnetic personality." She cast a smile at him.

A few minutes later, they were crossing the cavern toward the ship. Stones skittered from the top of one of the nearby hills. Dexter froze, grabbing Vaughn's arm and shoving her behind him. The metal of the sheath holding his sword on his back rang as he drew the weapon. Chuck let out a low growl, but he was facing Dexter.

"Easy," Vaughn said, unsure who exactly she was aiming it at.

Spriggan popped up from the top of the hill. "They're over here!"

The dweller slid down the loose gravel, then ran up to

them. A spiky ball rolled over the hill, bumping and bouncing over the rocky terrain. It popped open several yards away, the goblin peering at them with his small black eyes.

"About time you got here," Johnny said. "I see you've added to your motley crew."

Spriggan let out a yelp, then jumped into Johnny's arms. The goblin's eyes widened in surprise.

"Johnny, you gotta save me," Spriggan yelled. "It's a dog and I'm a stick!"

Vaughn looked at Chuck. He wasn't paying Spriggan the slightest bit of attention. Still, she wanted to take its concerns seriously. They were hopefully building the foundation of a new relationship that could change the dynamic of the Blades for the better.

"Aren't you a stick that can turn into a giant tree?" Vaughn said.

"Oh yeah," Spriggan said. It grunted as Johnny dropped it on the ground.

"Except Chuck is also capable of becoming as big as the barn." Dexter sheathed his sword and started toward the ship again.

Spriggan let out another yelp and started climbing up onto Johnny's back. The goblin tried to swat it off, but Spriggan was tenacious. Even when Johnny tucked himself back into a ball and rolled around, all it did was embed Spriggan's twigs and branches between Johnny's spikes. The goblin finally gave up, popping back up so he could stand, with Spriggan stuck to his back.

"Scarecrow is waiting for us." Johnny seemed to be trying to muster as much dignity as he could when he spoke.

Vaughn pinched her lips together so she wouldn't laugh. She nodded, then hurried after Dexter.

"This place is great," Spriggan said. "Lotsa loose soil. I could make the biggest tree you ever seen here."

"It's too open," Johnny grumbled. "Things can come at you from all sides. Gimme a nice, damp tunnel any day."

"You're welcome to carve out some," Vaughn said. "I even have some machinery that can help you with that. Just make sure none of them connect to the surface. We don't want to make an easy access point for potentially hostile dwellers."

Johnny stared up at Vaughn as he waddled beside her. "And what makes you think I'm not a potentially hostile dweller?"

"Everybody can be hostile," Vaughn said. "But not everybody knows how to order groceries and have them delivered right to your door."

"What the heck does that have to do with anything?" he asked.

"You've never been in a store, have you?" Vaughn said. "Do you have any idea how much sugar a standard grocery store has? How many different types?" She smirked, then leaned a little closer. "Lots of them even have molasses."

"Great, now I'm hungry." Johnny was practically drooling. He wiped at his mouth, then narrowed his eyes at her. "I can still be hostile, even if you're promising me the sweet stuff."

"So can I." She winked at him, then straightened. She quickened her pace, but not before seeing the way Johnny recoiled, a hint of unease entering his features. Scarecrow seemed attached to these two, and if they stayed, maybe she would as well.

Vaughn put her mind back on her immediate task. The sooner they checked on Zach and made sure everything was okay in the ship, the sooner she could get Marcus on board. The ship had always felt like the safest place on the planet to Vaughn. She wanted that back. Whoever—whatever—the Curator was, she had no business messing around with *Vaughn's* ship. It was past time she learned that.

Chapter Twenty-One

Vaughn practically ran the last few feet to the door, slamming her palm against the control panel that gave them access to the ship. The door whooshed open, and she hurried inside. Damien looked over his shoulder at probably the weirdest team the Blades had ever assembled.

"Maybe you guys stay out here and start settling in, since it sounds like you'll be sticking around for a while." Damien wasn't sure what they'd find inside, and there were too many unknowns with these guys.

"Suit yourself," Johnny said. "It's not like we're itching to go into that thing." He tucked himself back into a ball and rolled away, Spriggan—still stuck to his back—making occasional, 'oof' sounds as he did. Jonathan and Chuck started after them at a leisurely pace.

"I'll keep an eye on everyone out here," Dexter said. "You need anything, just call for me."

"I will." Damien really hoped he wouldn't need to. They'd been through enough. Surely the universe could cut them a break.

The stasis chamber room was close to the hatch. Vaughn was standing just inside the door. Damien hurried to her side, looking into the room over her head. Scarecrow was standing in front of Zach's stasis chamber, her head angled as if studying it. Vaughn took Damien's hand as she walked into the room. Right, she would need him to translate.

'*You're up, guys,*' Damien thought. '*Anything Scarecrow—the 'fragment'—says, I need to understand.*'

Text appeared in his vision, suspended in a translucent display screen.

[STANDING BY]

'*I appreciate it.*'

"Hi, Scarecrow," Vaughn said.

The dweller didn't react to their presence. Vaughn moved deeper into the room, Damien right behind her. Vaughn dropped his hand, pulling out her favorite tool and starting to scan the room with it. Damien joined Scarecrow in front of the tank. Zach was still floating inside, his longish brown hair loose around his face from the zero-Gs. Damien knew what happened to Carey wasn't his fault, but it didn't stop the surge of guilt that flooded him, seeing Zach like this.

"That's Zach," Vaughn said, drawing close to them. "He's one of Brock's replicants. He lost his twin right before... A lot of stuff went down. We're hoping he'll split when we bring him out of stasis, and then we'll get Carey back."

Scarecrow turned to face them. Her eyes were sloped

downwards and she was frowning, as if she was sad. Damien tried not to read too much into the expression. He really tried. But his heartbeat picked up and his stomach felt like it was filled with shards of ice.

"I'm not detecting any trace of the virus," Vaughn said lightly. "How did it go with the rest of the ship and the ranch?"

Damien wasn't sure if she was so focused on the tech that she didn't notice Scarecrow's expression or if she was pushing any thoughts of that aside to try to stay hopeful. He wished he could do the same, but the worry was chewing at his gut.

Golden characters in that alien language appeared on the screen in Damien's vision. The characters spun as his nanites translated them, morphing into his language.

[VIRAL AGENT PURGED FROM ALL SYSTEMS]

"She says the virus has been purged from all systems," Damien said.

"All of them?" Vaughn asked. "Already?"

A small schematic of the ship appeared on Damien's viewscreen. Soft blue light emanated from the entire thing. The image zoomed out to show the cavern, including the elevator corridor that led up to the sublevels. It was all blue as well. The sublevels and the ranch appeared, also blue.

'Blue is good, right?' Damien thought. *'That's like your equivalent to our green light is good?'*

[AFFIRMATIVE]

"Everything's good," Damien said.

Vaughn let out a breath and laughed. She threw her arms around his neck, pulling him down for a long kiss. Some of the tightness in his chest loosened as he let himself sink into the soft warmth of her lips. He started to deepen the kiss, but she pulled back and cleared her throat.

Scarecrow was standing right next to them—like *right* next to them. Her eyes were shaped into hearts and her sparkling lights had made a huge smile on her face.

"I think we might have another romcom fan on our hands here," Damien said.

Vaughn laughed. "I'll want to check everything to confirm, but…" She turned to Scarecrow and smiled. "I trust our new friends."

"That seems kind of fast," Damien said. He looked at Scarecrow and added, "No offense."

"It's not fast. Johnny and Spriggan are with Scarecrow and she's part of this ship. *My* ship. And I know my ship. I may still be learning about it, but I know its core. I can feel it. It wants to help people be safe."

Damien hesitated for a moment, then said, "Johnny told us this is a prison ship."

"That doesn't mean it's malevolent." Lines of strain appeared at the edges of Vaughn's eyes. "From what I think I've figured out about the Curator, the people on the ship were doing good. And I know… *I know* she was doing terrible things. She needs to be stopped, Damien."

"We'll take care of it." He took her hands in his and squeezed them. "Together. But for now, we need to get Marcus settled down here and check out the rest of the base. You up for that?"

"As long as you're at my side, I think I'm up for anything." She rolled her eyes and smiled. "Did that sound as cheesy to you as it did to me?"

"No." He leaned in and kissed her again, a light kiss. "It sounded perfect. Just like you."

She looked down and smiled. "I'm starting to feel like we're in one of our romcom movies."

Damien furrowed his brow. "That would be a really weird, fucked up romcom."

They both laughed. He wrapped his arms around her and held her tight, but only for a moment. They had too much to do, though he would make sure they had time for their romcom moments later. The good parts, with the kissing.

"Since we know this room is clean, let's go ahead and get Marcus down here where it's safe," Damien said.

"Okay."

He draped an arm over her shoulders and headed for the door, but paused just before leaving the room. He looked back at Scarecrow and said, "You coming, or staying here?"

She turned back to the stasis chamber. Guess that was

the only answer he was going to get.

"Let's go," he said.

The next few hours were a blur of action. Porter and Vaughn set up Marcus's stasis chamber right next to Zach's. Damien tried not to think about how much room was left along the wall and the empty stasis chambers surrounding them—with limited success. How many Blades would end up there, waiting on Vaughn to find ways to save them?

He stuck with her as she scanned the rest of the systems, making sure the virus was truly gone. Every once in a while, Damien caught a flash of light just before Vaughn laughed and said something about Scarecrow haunting the ranch. He wished he could find it as cool that a wraith had taken up inhabiting the systems that ran their base.

Scarecrow seemed legit, but she had a hell of a lot of access and power. Vaughn was sure she'd use it to help keep them safe from the Curator. None of them were fool enough to think they'd stopped whoever that was. It was only a matter of time before she made a run at them again.

Vaughn insisted on modifying the interphasic disrupters to make an allowance for Chuck before bringing the defenses fully back online, which she managed to do in under an hour. She and Porter were already talking about tests to run on Jonathan to figure out how his teleportation worked. Developing an anti-venom to help Marcus was the highest priority for him, though. Vaughn was planning to focus on tracking down the Curator.

Damien stuck to her side the entire day, while they all worked to get the ranch back in order. It wasn't till that night, when they were setting up some spare beds down in the stasis chamber room for Tessa and the others to use so they could stay close to Marcus that they had a moment to themselves again.

"What's on your mind?" Vaughn asked, as they finished putting covers on the beds as a last touch.

"I was just thinking, we never did make it to a bed of our own." He grinned and even waggled his eyebrows.

Vaughn laughed, then walked around the bed so she could wrap her arms around his neck. He rested his hands on her hips and pulled her close.

"Do you have any plans for after dinner?" she said.

"I'm sure I can think of something." He leaned down and kissed her, deep and thorough. When he broke off the kiss, she let out a contented sigh. She took his hand in hers and started toward the door.

"Dexter is cooking, so this should be fun," she said. "He's actually halfway decent. Nothing close to my level of course, but then, so few have my skill in the kitchen."

Damien laughed as he followed her. He cast a glance over at Marcus and noticed glittering lights flowing over one of the control panels. Scarecrow was there, checking on the systems again. He was sure Tessa was on her way to be with Marcus. The pack would probably come down here to eat, needing some time to be together.

'Is Marcus safe enough for us to leave him alone for a moment?' Damien thought. *'Or at least alone with Scarecrow?'*

His nanites responded without hesitation. [AFFIRMATIVE]

Damien started toward the door again when text flashed in Scarecrow's golden font at the top of the translucent screen Damien's nanites were still projecting. She'd reached out to him directly a few times during the day, and he was almost getting used to it.

[DAMIEN...]

Holy shit. He didn't know she was aware of his name. He paused, waiting for the rest of her message to translate. The alien characters blinked several times before spinning around and turning into words he could read. Words that sent a shiver down his spine and made his blood feel like ice in his veins.

[NONE OF US ARE EVER SAFE]

"Did she say something?" Vaughn asked.

Damien shook his head and forced a smile. "Nothing important. Let's go."

Scarecrow was right. Blades were never really safe. It was part of the life they had all chosen. Putting themselves out there, trying to make the world a better place for dwellers and humans alike. But Damien had hope that they could make a better life for themselves as well as the people and beings they had sworn to protect. As long as the Blades stuck together. As long as they stayed a family.

"Let's find Brock before we eat," Damien said. "I think I'm ready to tell him my decision about whether or not I support the Blades."

—

Thank you so much for reading *Perihelion*, the third novel in *The Blades of Janus* series! Vaughn is one of my favorite characters. I even have a "Vaughn is my Copilot" shirt that I wear all the time. I'm thrilled to finally get to share her book with you and tell you more about what a curator is! It was about time she and Damien had their "Happily-ever-after." *Perihelion* surprised me in so many places and there is still so much to tell in the story of this group of found-family.

While you're waiting for more, check out the other adventures going on in my worlds. If you need a break from reality with some light-hearted, quick, quirky Science Fiction Romance novellas (with *lots* of 'adult' scenes), check out my *Department of Homeworld Security* series. Fun fact, The Homeworld universe is actually the same one as the Blades! But more on that later. If you want to keep exploring my darker works, you can look at some Paranormal Horror Romance with my *Summer Park*

Psychics series.

I'm guessing you're here for the werewolves, though, and I have more of that in my Paranormal Romance series, *Forbidden Knights*. Read on for an excerpt of the first *Forbidden Knights* novel, *Forbidden Instinct*.

—

Gasoline was spreading onto the street...

June 15 — 2:44 PM

In five minutes, Miranda's car would be a crumpled wreck. She checked her seatbelt with a shaking hand—again—to make sure it was fastened tight, then gripped the wheel hard enough to make her knuckles turn white.

A familiar silver minivan came into view ahead. She hadn't met the driver, but recognized the soccer-mom's short bobbed haircut. Miranda would never forget the woman's face—or the faces of the three children inside. Two of them were on the passenger's side. One of those was an infant.

The SUV is going to hit them from that side.

Her vision had been absolutely certain on that point.

She glanced at the clock, then stepped on the gas.

2:46 PM. She had three minutes to get in front of them and slow them down. Three minutes to beat them to the intersection and be the one in front of the SUV that was about to speed through a red light. If she did everything right, the accident would only take out her car.

Her heart pounded in her throat, making it hard to swallow. She couldn't let herself panic. She knew she would make it through this. She'd *seen* it.

How did mom do this, knowing she wouldn't *make it out?*

Miranda couldn't think about the past. If she started to cry, it would blur her vision, dull her reflexes, and facilitate a family reunion she wasn't ready for. The present—and the specific future she was trying to create— needed her full attention.

Her ancient car struggled to catch up as the minivan accelerated. She managed to get behind it, then swerved into the left lane, crossing the double lines. She jerked the wheel back to the right just in time to avoid a head-on collision with a blue pick-up truck.

"Beeeep! Beep-beep!" She sang along with the pick-up's horn, knowing precisely how it would sound. Other cars joined the chorus.

"Everybody's a critic," she muttered under her breath. "I'm trying to save lives here."

She slowed, herding the soccer-mom behind her. The

minivan's horn persisted.

"Yes, I know. I'm being an ass." She glanced into her rear-view mirror, taking in the angry expression of the woman behind her. "But I'm also saving yours."

Almost time...

She knew she had to steer away from the SUV right before it crashed into her. Maybe that act was going to offset the force of its impact or something. If she didn't time it right...

She *would* time it right.

A dark shape loomed in her peripheral vision and she jerked the wheel hard to the left. The first crash of metal hit her ears as she was hit. The second followed a split-second later—the minivan plowing into the back end of the SUV that had struck Miranda's car.

The world was set to tumble-dry as the street rolled around and around through the front windshield. Her car balanced on two tires for a last moment of teetering suspense before finishing its final roll and falling to the ground, upside-down. The roof crunched ominously, several inches closer to her head than it used to be—or maybe it was that she was hanging from the driver's seat, her seatbelt the only thing that kept her in place.

Probably both.

Tires screeched. People screamed. Horns kept blaring.

She laughed. It sounded hysterical, even to her. Tears ran over her temples and into her hair. Her eyes burned.

She wanted to unbuckle her seatbelt, but couldn't will herself to let go of the steering wheel. She felt oddly disconnected from her body.

Is this what shock feels like?

It didn't matter that she'd known she would walk away from the accident. She'd dreamt this version of the future over and over before waking. But the primal part of her brain had basically seen her chewed up and spit out by a saber-toothed tiger. It was still processing the events.

She hadn't bothered to count all the iterations of what could be. In the end, there was only one possibility that didn't end in death. Miranda had to be in that intersection at the exact moment of the accident. It had to be *her*.

Mom would be so proud...

Her tears came harder.

Why couldn't people believe? Miranda wished she could tell people about her visions and let them make their own decisions. She should be able to walk away. Maybe actually have a life of her own, find someone who could understand and support her.

Darren's face popped into her mind's eye.

If only...

Sweet, smart, gorgeous Darren—with his jet black hair and steel gray eyes—who laughed at her jokes, even if he didn't make many of his own.

Getting to know him had made her happy, which was terrifying. She never knew when her visions would call for a sacrifice, and he somehow seemed the type who would throw himself on a grenade for others. She didn't think she was strong enough to endure another vision that sent someone she cared about to their death.

She shouldn't let him get too close. But she couldn't stay away.

No one at the accident scene was having trouble staying away from her car. They probably thought she was dead, and no one wanted to be the one to find her gruesome remains. If she hadn't known to turn her wheel just before the moment of impact, they would have been right.

The surreal cast to her perception started to fade. Her skin tingled and her heart kept pounding in her throat. Each beat sent a spike of pain through her head. She needed to get out of her car.

All she could see through the cracked glass of the front windshield were people's feet as they hurried around the intersection. She noticed a pair heading straight toward her. Black dress shoes polished to a high sheen and nice slacks.

The man stopped just outside her door, probably bracing himself for the worst. She considered making a funny face to lighten the mood, and let out another semi-hysterical sounding laugh. She cut it short as he knelt next to her open window.

Oh, wow...

Steel gray eyes bored through her, surrounded by thick

dark lashes. The man's hair was raven-black, skin tanned to a deep bronze, jaw strong, features flawless. She had memorized his face weeks ago.

His eyes widened as he recognized her, too.

"Miranda?" he said.

"Hi, Darren. I'd offer to take your order, but I'm a little hung up right now."

She laughed, but her eyes had filled with tears again. He didn't laugh at her joke this time. She wished he would at least smile. Seeing his dimples always made her feel better. She wanted—needed—something that at least gave her the illusion of normalcy.

"You're going to be okay," he said.

She already knew that. Still, his seriousness brought home what she had risked. It made everything feel more real. She'd liked it better when her perception had that lingering sense of dreaming.

"Can you assess yourself?" he asked. "Do you know if you hit your head?"

"I didn't. I mean, my head hurts, but I think it's from the adrenaline."

He didn't look at all relieved. His eyes flicked to the ground, then back to hers.

"I need you to listen to me very carefully," he said. "We can't wait for the EMTs to arrive to check you out. We need to get you out of the car. Now."

Her visions tended to jump around, leaving large

swaths of time unseen. The universe didn't seem to want to spoil all of her surprises. Miranda took in the grim expression on Darren's face and figured this wasn't a good one. She took a deep breath to calm her nerves and finally registered what was making him look so worried.

Gasoline was spreading onto the street from underneath the roof of the car. Her heart started to pound again.

She had seen herself on the other side of this. Walking stiffly among the tables and booths at the diner, holding a carafe of coffee. She was *not* going to burn to death.

Please, don't let me burn to death...

"Stay calm," he said. "I'm right here with you. I won't leave."

She closed her eyes and took a shaky breath, then let it out. She believed him. It made her less afraid, but also brought home the sharp sting of her loneliness. She was usually better at keeping it at bay. It had been a long time since someone had helped her through the aftermath of a vision. A long time since she hadn't felt completely alone.

She opened her eyes as he stood. He tried the door handle a few times, but the metal frame was mangled. The world seemed to spin as fumes burned her lungs.

She wondered briefly why Darren didn't just rip the door off her car, then remembered he couldn't do that yet. No, that was wrong—people couldn't do things like that at all. Reality was warping—memory, dream, and vision bleeding together.

She heard fabric rustling, then Darren squatted next to her again. He'd taken off his jacket and wadded it into a ball that he placed under her head. Brown leather straps hugged his broad shoulders—and held a handgun in a holster. He'd never mentioned being a cop. All she knew about his job was that he kept late hours.

He squeezed as much of himself into the car as he could fit. He was kneeling in gasoline. "Let go of the steering wheel and put your hands on the roof of the car."

She *knew* that she would be okay and was still panicking. He had no assurances of safety and was trying to help her anyway. He was risking himself for her. Her eyes filled with tears again.

"It's okay." He placed his hand on hers. "I won't let anything happen to you."

She let him gently peel her fingers off of the wheel, grateful that the adrenaline flooding her system seemed to be blocking her ability to read futures through touch. His hands were warm, his skin smooth. He pressed her hands firmly on the roof of the car, then reached into his pocket and pulled out a knife.

"I can't reach the seatbelt release, so I'm going to cut it," he said. "When I do, you'll fall." He put one arm across her chest. "I'll slow your descent as best I can, but will need your help to make sure you don't get hurt, okay?"

She nodded, bracing herself. His knife cut the seatbelt

easily and gravity took over. She'd barely touched the floor before he was pulling her into his arms. She grabbed his jacket as she passed by, clinging to it. Darren tucked her against his chest and started running away from the car.

"There's gas over here," he shouted. "Everyone needs to stay clear."

A few bystanders glanced over, their jaws dropping open. The soccer-mom was among them, holding her baby while her other kids clung to her legs. Her gaze met Miranda's briefly, and the mix of horror and gratitude etched into her eyes was one Miranda didn't think she'd ever forget. Whatever happened next—whatever Miranda had to deal with after this—it had been worth it.

She turned into Darren's chest, letting it block out the rest of the world for a moment. Either the fumes, his proximity, or the adrenaline firing through her system was messing with her sense of reality again. Nestling in his arms, she felt like she was remembering something that hadn't happened yet.

A normal person could write it off as déjà vu. For her, it held more significance and a hope she shouldn't let herself feel.

He was going to hold her in his arms again.

—

I'd love to keep in touch. Join my newsletter at cassandra-chandler.com to hear about all the adventures happening in Cassland. And if you enjoyed this book, please consider leaving a review at your favorite book review site. I'd really appreciate it—reviews help readers and authors alike!

Thank you for reading *Perihelion!*

Cassandra Chandler

About the Author

USA Today Bestselling author Cassandra Chandler uses her vivid imagination to make the world more interesting, spawning the ideas she turns into her captivating Science Fiction Romances and enthralling Paranormal and Urban Fantasy Romances. Fast-paced and funny, lighthearted or filled with suspense, her stories will introduce you to characters you'll fall in love with and worlds you long to explore.

www.ingramcontent.com/pod-product-compliance
Lightning Source LLC
Chambersburg PA
CBHW072301020726
47501CB00002B/340